# A Road Trip to Remember

## Judith Keim

# BOOKS BY JUDITH KEIM

**THE HARTWELL WOMEN SERIES:**
The Talking Tree – 1
Sweet Talk – 2
Straight Talk – 3
Baby Talk – 4
The Hartwell Women – Boxed Set

**THE BEACH HOUSE HOTEL SERIES:**
Breakfast at The Beach House Hotel – 1
Lunch at The Beach House Hotel – 2
Dinner at The Beach House Hotel – 3
Christmas at The Beach House Hotel – 4
Margaritas at The Beach House Hotel – 5 (2021)
Dessert at The Beach House Hotel – 6 (2022)

**THE FAT FRIDAYS GROUP:**
Fat Fridays – 1
Sassy Saturdays – 2
Secret Sundays – 3

**SALTY KEY INN BOOKS:**
Finding Me – 1
Finding My Way – 2
Finding Love – 3
Finding Family – 4

**CHANDLER HILL INN BOOKS:**
Going Home – 1
Coming Home – 2
Home at Last – 3

For more information: **http://amzn.to/2jamIaF**

# PRAISE FOR JUDITH KEIM'S NOVELS

### THE BEACH HOUSE HOTEL SERIES

*"Love the characters in this series. This series was my first introduction to Judith Keim. She is now one of my favorites. Looking forward to reading more of her books."*

*BREAKFAST AT THE BEACH HOUSE HOTEL is an easy, delightful read that offers romance, family relationships, and strong women learning to be stronger. Real life situations filter through the pages. Enjoy!"*

*LUNCH AT THE BEACH HOUSE HOTEL – "This series is such a joy to read. You feel you are actually living with them. Can't wait to read the latest one."*

*DINNER AT THE BEACH HOUSE HOTEL – "A Terrific Read! As usual, Judith Keim did it again. Enjoyed immensely. Continue writing such pleasantly reading books for all of us readers."*

*CHRISTMAS AT THE BEACH HOUSE HOTEL – "Not Just Another Christmas Novel. This is book number four in the series and my introduction to Judith Keim's writing. I wasn't disappointed. The characters are dimensional and engaging. The plot is well crafted and advances at a pleasing pace. The Florida location is interesting and warming. It was a delight to read a romance novel with mature female protagonists. Ann and Rhoda have life experiences that enrich the story. It's a clever book about friends and extended family. Buy copies for your book group pals and enjoy this seasonal read."*

## THE HARTWELL WOMEN SERIES – Books 1 – 4

"This was an EXCELLENT series. When I discovered Judith Keim, I read all of her books back to back. I thoroughly enjoyed the women Keim has written about. They are believable and you want to just jump into their lives and be their friends! I can't wait for any upcoming books!"

"I fell into Judith Keim's Hartwell Women series and have read & enjoyed all of her books in every series. Each centers around a strong & interesting woman character and their family interaction. Good reads that leave you wanting more."

## THE FAT FRIDAYS GROUP – Books 1 – 3

"Excellent story line for each character, and an insightful representation of situations which deal with some of the contemporary issues women are faced with today."

"I love this author's books. Her characters and their lives are realistic. The power of women's friendships is a common and beautiful theme that is threaded throughout this story."

## THE SALTY KEY INN SERIES

FINDING ME – "I thoroughly enjoyed the first book in this series and cannot wait for the others! The characters are endearing with the same struggles we all encounter. The setting makes me feel like I am a guest at The Salty Key Inn...relaxed, happy & light-hearted! The men are yummy and the women strong. You can't get better than that! Happy Reading!"

FINDING MY WAY- "Loved the family dynamics as well as uncertain emotions of dating and falling in love.

Appreciated the morals and strength of parenting throughout. Just couldn't put this book down."

*FINDING LOVE* – "I waited for this book because the first two was such good reads. This one didn't disappoint.... Judith Keim always puts substance into her books. This book was no different, I learned about PTSD, accepting oneself, there is always going to be problems but stick it out and make it work. Just the way life is. In some ways a lot like my life. Judith is right, it needs another book and I will definitely be reading it. Hope you choose to read this series, you will get so much out of it."

*FINDING FAMILY* – "Completing this series is like eating the last chip. Love Judith's writing, and her female characters are always smart, strong, vulnerable to life and love experiences."

"This was a refreshing book. Bringing the heart and soul of the family to us."

## CHANDLER HILL INN SERIES

*GOING HOME* – "I absolutely could not put this book down. Started at night and read late into the middle of the night. As a child of the '60s, the Vietnam war was front and center so this resonated with me. All the characters in the book were so well developed that the reader felt like they were friends of the family."

"I was completely immersed in this book, with the beautiful descriptive writing, and the authors' way of bringing her characters to life. I felt like I was right inside her story."

*COMING HOME* – "Coming Home is a winner. The characters are well-developed, nuanced and likable. Enjoyed the vineyard setting, learning about wine growing and seeing the challenges Cami faces in running and growing a business. I look forward to the next book in this series!"

"Coming Home was such a wonderful story. The author has a gift for getting the reader right to the heart of things."

*HOME AT LAST* – "In this wonderful conclusion, to a heartfelt and emotional trilogy set in Oregon's stunning wine country, Judith Keim has tied up the Chandler Hill series with the perfect bow."

"Overall, this is truly a wonderful addition to the Chandler Hill Inn series. Judith Keim definitely knows how to perfectly weave together a beautiful and heartfelt story."

"The storyline has some beautiful scenes along with family drama. Judith Keim has created characters with interactions that are believable and some of the subjects the story deals with are poignant."

**SEASHELL COTTAGE BOOKS**

*A CHRISTMAS STAR* – "Love, laughter, sadness, great food, and hope for the future, all in one book. It doesn't get any better than this stunning read."

"A Christmas Star is a heartwarming Christmas story featuring endearing characters. So many Christmas books are set in snowbound places...it was a nice change to read a Christmas story that takes place on a warm sandy beach!" Susan Peterson

*CHANGE OF HEART* – *"CHANGE OF HEART is the summer read we've all been waiting for. Judith Keim is a master at creating fascinating characters that are simply irresistible. Her stories leave you with a big smile on your face and a heart bursting with love."*

~Kellie Coates Gilbert, author of the popular Sun Valley Series

*A SUMMER OF SURPRISES* – *"The story is filled with a roller coaster of emotions and self-discovery. Finding love again and rebuilding family relationships."*

*"Ms. Keim uses this book as an amazing platform to show that with hard emotional work, belief in yourself and love, the scars of abuse can be conquered. It in no way preaches, it's a lovely story with a happy ending."*

*"The character development was excellent. I felt I knew these people my whole life. The story development was very well thought out I was drawn [in] from the beginning."*

### DESERT SAGE INN BOOKS

*THE DESERT FLOWERS – ROSE* – *"The Desert Flowers - Rose, is the first book in the new series by Judith Keim. I always look forward to new books by Judith Keim, and this one is definitely a wonderful way to begin The Desert Sage Inn Series!"*

*"In this first of a series, we see each woman come into her own and view new beginnings even as they must take this tearful journey as they slowly lose a dear friend. This is a very well written book with well-developed and likable main characters. It was interesting and enlightening as the first*

*portion of this saga unfolded. I very much enjoyed this book and I do recommend it"*

*"Judith Keim is one of those authors that you can always depend on to give you a great story with fantastic characters. I'm excited to know that she is writing a new series and after reading book 1 in the series, I can't wait to read the rest of the books."!*

# A Road Trip to Remember

## A Seashell Cottage Book

## Judith Keim

Wild Quail Publishing

*A Road Trip to Remember* is a work of fiction. Names, characters, places, public or private institutions, corporations, towns, and incidents are the product of the author's imagination or are used fictitiously. Any resemblance to actual events, locales, or persons, living or dead, is coincidental.

No part of this book may be reproduced or transmitted in any form or by any electronic or mechanical means, including information storage and retrieval systems, without permission in writing from the author, except by a reviewer who may quote brief passages in a review. This book may not be resold or uploaded for distribution to others. For permissions contact the author directly via electronic mail:

**wildquail.pub@gmail.com**

**www.judithkeim.com,**

Published in the United States of America by:

Wild Quail Publishing
PO Box 171332
Boise, ID 83717-1332

ISBN# 978-1-7327494-7-4

# Dedication

In loving memory of my grandmother, Florence Williams,
and my great-aunt, Louise Williams:
women with spirit.

# CHAPTER ONE

## AGGIE

G ran! You can't be serious! I can't do that!"

"Yes, my darling, you can, and you will. I need your help." Agatha "Aggie" Robard put as much pleading into her voice as possible without breaking down and crying. She had a plan for a road trip, and by damn, she was going to do it! At seventy-two and just through recovering from pneumonia, she couldn't make the drive alone, and there was no way she was going to let down the man she'd promised to visit. He was, in some respects, the one who got away. Not that Arnold, God rest his soul, would mind. He'd always known she'd loved Donovan Bailey too.

"Just think about it," Aggie urged. "A road trip to remember."

It would be good for her granddaughter, Blythe, to get out of town, get over her boyfriend, and find a decent young man who'd adore her for being the loveable young woman she was. Two women on an adventure. That's what they'd be. Aggie grinned with anticipation. What could be better on this March morning when the rest of their family was about to leave for a fourteen-day vacation in Hawaii?

Aggie listened to Blythe go on about the need to stay in Ithaca to wrap up her college courses at Cornell before graduation. Aggie knew her beloved granddaughter had used that excuse to escape going home for Spring Break, gotten into an argument with her stepmother, Constance, about it, and was left out of the trip to Hawaii in the process.

"A Spring Break trip to Florida in early April will do you good," Aggie said, dangling this last piece of information in front of Blythe like a piece of her favorite toffee candy.

Blythe let out a breathy, "Oh? *That's* where you want me to take you?"

"Yes. I've rented a place on the Gulf Coast of Florida, the Seashell Cottage, for a week, starting at the end of March. That will give us time to get there, enjoy a week in the sun, and get back home again before anyone suspects a thing."

Suddenly, Blythe began to laugh. Her musical trills filled Aggie's ears and brought a smile to her face. "Gran! You're outrageous!" She paused. "Do you think we can pull off something like this? Constance will be furious if she ever finds out."

The smile disappeared from Aggie's face as if it had been ripped off with tape, leaving stinging skin behind. Constance Robard, her only child's second wife and Blythe's stepmother, was a pain in the behind, always trying to tell her what she could or could not do. Aggie fought to find the right words.

"Constance doesn't need to know everything little thing I'm doing. Just because she manipulated me into selling my house and moving into the New Life Assisted Living Community, it doesn't mean I can't have a life of my own. There's a dance or two in this old lady yet." No one was going to take away the power to live her life her way. Not even if it meant ruffling a few feathers.

"Gran, you're not that old," Blythe protested.

Aggie made her final plea. "So, will you do it?"

"You bet!" said Blythe, a new eagerness in her voice. "Florida sounds fantastic right now. I swear I haven't seen the sun in Ithaca for a week or more. I'll bring some work with me and do it there."

"Good," said Aggie. "Pick me up Tuesday morning at eight o'clock, and I'll take care of the rest. And pack suntan lotion. We'll take the convertible."

"I love you, Gran. Don't worry. I'll come home over the weekend and see you Tuesday morning. This road trip is going to be fun!"

"Don't I know it," Aggie said, feeling as if she was about to be handed a get-out-of-jail-free card.

Still smiling, Aggie clicked off the call. Blythe was a serious young woman in the final semester of her senior year at Cornell. She'd spent years doing what others had dictated and was just beginning to understand that life should be fun too. Aggie hoped if she left Blythe with anything to remember her by, it would be this.

Aggie's one suitcase sat beside the front entrance of the main building of the assisted-living complex she now called home. It wasn't a bad place to be. It had every convenience possible, good food, and lovely surroundings both in and outside the buildings. Best of all, she'd made some good friends here. Two of them, Edith Greenbaum and Rose Ragazzi, had suggested the Seashell Cottage as a place for her getaway. They'd once made that suggestion to Noelle North, the former head of the health program at New Life, and she'd ended up married to some hotel mogul. You never know what could happen. Aggie had sworn these friends to secrecy but felt it was only right for someone to know her true location should anything untoward happen. She owed that to her son, Brad, and daughter-in-law, Constance.

"So, you're going on vacation with your family," commented one of the staff. "How nice for you."

Aggie glanced at Edith and Rose, who'd come to say

goodbye, and nodded. She didn't like lying in any form and was relieved she actually was going on a family vacation, even if the only other family member was Blythe.

Her eye caught sight of something. She looked through the glass-paneled front door to see her white Mercedes convertible pull up to the front of the building with Blythe at the wheel. This car represented so much to Aggie. Her purchase of it had sent Constance into a rage, claiming Aggie was losing her mind to buy something like this at her age. It was the beginning of Constance's campaign to get her to move out of her big, old house in Dedham outside of Boston and into New Life.

Aggie had finally given in to Brad's pleas to put his mind at ease about her safety and had made the move. But she'd refused to get rid of the car. She kept the shiny new beauty in a storage facility nearby and gave Blythe the extra key fob to it. After she died, Blythe would have her car for her own use. For now, Aggie needed to know she had "wheels."

"Here's your ride," said Edith, hugging her. "Safe trip! And good luck with Donovan!"

Rose grinned at her and wrapped her arms around Aggie. "We'll be with you in spirit. Remember every little detail so you can tell us all about it."

Aggie held in a laugh. There was nothing Rose liked better than a good, romantic story.

Blythe hurried over to them and grabbed hold of Aggie's suitcase. "Hi, everyone." Green-eyed, black-haired Blythe reminded Aggie of a beautiful young woman who was just coming into her own. Long-legged, thin, and with a wild taste in clothes that drove her stepmother crazy, Blythe was the perfect person to take this trip with her. By the time they got back, Aggie hoped Blythe would have a better appreciation of herself.

After chatting politely, Blythe took hold of Aggie's arm. "C'mon, Gran. Time to hit the road."

Aggie marched to the car alongside Blythe, feeling like she was sprouting wings with each step, loving this new sense of freedom. After she buckled herself into the passenger seat, she turned to the small crowd gathered at the doorway and waved.

"Okay, pedal to the metal, girl," Aggie said, sitting back in her seat, eager to begin the journey ahead.

# CHAPTER TWO
## BLYTHE

Blythe laughed at her grandmother's words and did as she asked, making the engine of the car roar a little as she peeled out of the driveway. As long as she was going to end up in trouble, she might as well enjoy what she could of this adventure. Her stepmother thought Gran was losing it, but Blythe knew better. Gran was sometimes forgetful, but not in a serious way. Her mind was quick, as always.

As Blythe thought about how Constance always had to be right, had to have the last word even if no one agreed with what she said, a sigh escaped her. She had learned to fight back in different ways. The tie-dye T-shirt she was wearing and the tiny tattoo hidden beneath it were examples.

"I thought we'd make a few stops along the way," Gran announced. "Margaret Winters, one of my old college roommates, lives outside of New York City in Montclair, New Jersey. She's invited us to have lunch with her."

Blythe turned to her with surprise. "How long have you been planning this trip?"

"Since Margaret and another friend tried to put together a reunion of sorts for all the old gang a few months ago. There were twelve of us who hung around together at Cornell in the late '60s. That was a very unsettled time for all of us with the war and all the student demonstrations against it. Some armed students even took over the student union building for several days to protest."

"You mean Vietnam?"

"Yes," said Aggie. "Your grandfather was drafted right after graduation but was released because of a heart murmur he didn't know he had. He never got over the guilt of feeling relieved he didn't have to participate in a war he didn't support. His younger brother was killed in 'Nam."

"How awful for him," Blythe said. "As irritating as they can be, I wouldn't want anything bad to happen to my two little brothers."

"Having a stepparent and a new family can be difficult. How are things going? I dislike how Constance continues to put you down. And I know the troubles with your mother continue."

Blythe knew Gran wanted her to be okay with everything, but she couldn't lie. "Though it's irritating, I can deal with Constance. But my mother is, as she's always been, a mess. Last I heard, she's back in a mental institution. I tried reaching out to her, but it was painful. It is clear she wants nothing to do with me."

"I'm sorry, Blythe. It's such a difficult position for you. And so unfair. As much as I'd like to blame her, I understand she's mentally ill. It's not really about you, but about anyone from her past. Especially your father."

"Truthfully, it hurts. As far as Constance is concerned, I'm pleased for Dad that he's found a second chance and has had more children. But Constance and I will never get along. Her values and mine are too different."

Gran beamed at her. "That's my girl."

Blythe returned her smile. "You've never liked her."

"No, but I do what I can to make your father happy. Like you, I will never see eye to eye with Constance about many things. That's why this trip with you is so important."

Waiting for an explanation, Blythe glanced at her grandmother and turned back to the road. She'd taken the Mass Pike to I-84 and was now heading toward Hartford.

"Constance doesn't know I've retained majority ownership of The Robard Company, the corporation overseeing our hardware stores," continued Gran. "Your father and I agreed it would remain private information until we were ready to bring you on board. That time will come sooner rather than later."

Blythe's jaw dropped. "What do you mean?" Her heart was beating so loudly she almost didn't hear the roar of a truck behind her. She speeded up and pulled over into the lane on her right, allowing the truck to roar by them as she slowed down.

Gran placed a hand on her arm. "You know I'm not going to be around forever."

Blythe's fingers turned cold on the steering wheel. She glanced at Gran. "Oh, my God! Are you dying?"

"Not yet," said Gran, giving her a wink. "But I want these last years to be free from worry so I can have some fun. As long as I know you'll take over the business for me, it will put my mind at ease. And because I retain majority voting rights, Constance can do nothing about the decision I've made."

"She tells everyone that she and Dad own all the stores, you know," said Blythe, unable to hide her disgust. If her father were poor, she wondered if Constance would have married him.

"I know she does. She's proud of them, though, and that's good. She has some good qualities too, or else your father would never have married her. We need to keep telling ourselves that."

"Yeah, we do." Blythe knew how charming Constance could be, and she loved her father enough to force herself to get along with her stepmother.

"I'm not bringing up the subject of your running the stores out of the blue," said Gran. "We've talked about it many times before. But ever since your father and stepmother maneuvered me into New Life, I realize how easily things could get out of my control. I need to be watchful to make sure it's doesn't happen."

Blythe glanced at Gran. Petite, she was still in pretty good shape for her age. She wore her hair, dyed a soft blonde, in a short, curly style that suited the classic features of her face. Her blue eyes sparkled with life and intelligence. Not beautiful, she was striking because of the way she carried herself with authority. Blythe had thought of her as being bigger than she was. They'd always been close.

"I understand what you're saying, Gran. I've wanted to be part of the business since I was little, but I thought I'd have some time of my own before then." Becoming CEO of Robard's string of hardware stores was a big job. Was she ready to take it on? A part of her said "yes," while another part of her screamed "no."

"It's a big responsibility. But you need to learn more about what's going on behind the scenes. Now that you'll have more time, you might be freer to do so more quickly than you thought."

Blythe rolled her eyes. "You mean now that I'm rid of Chad and have no plans to marry?"

Gran caught her eye. "You'll see. It's all for the best. He was too controlling."

Blythe's stomach twisted. Gran was right. She'd escaped a bad relationship. It had started her sophomore year and lasted until the Christmas holidays this past year when she knew for sure she'd made a horrible mistake. Chad had demanded, not asked, that she invite him to Wellesley for the holidays so he could keep an eye on her. And the business! He'd always loved the idea that she would someday be CEO of The Robard Company.

Constance had thought he was perfect for her. But Gran had talked to her about him, asking questions that made her see Chad for who he was.

Blythe reached over and squeezed Gran's hand. She could always trust Gran to care enough to be honest with her.

# CHAPTER THREE
## *AGGIE*

Aggie stared out the car window, pleased with herself. She loved Blythe more than anyone but Brad, and she wanted Blythe to know her value. With a stepmother who undermined her and a mother who'd abandoned her, Blythe was unaware of how bright and stunning she was. Blythe, like herself, had a natural ability to understand retail business. At twenty-one and about to graduate from Cornell, Blythe was more than ready to learn the business.

Owning a chain of eleven hardware stores was hard work, especially in light of competition from the big chains like Home Depot and Lowe's. Still, Aggie knew that there was a place for smaller, friendlier, multi-purpose stores that offered high-quality, specialized hardware, seasonal lawn, garden, and home-maintenance equipment and products, and pet merchandise, along with gifts and interesting decorative objects for the home. It was this mix of goods that had made The Robard Company succeed.

Just after one, at Aggie's directions, Blythe exited the Garden State Parkway and began weaving through streets to reach Margaret's home, an impressive house on Eagle Rock Way in Montclair.

Aggie looked around with interest. Though they'd lost touch through the years, she knew from earlier correspondence that Margaret was the mother of two children. Divorced after ten years, Margaret still lived in the house her husband, Donald, had provided and had become a socialite in her own right. She was the one who'd been in touch with another friend to plan the reunion they'd hoped would take place in Naples, Florida. Sadly, Aggie was one of the few people still alive who was willing and able to make the trip. In the meantime, Margaret had received the news she was dying of cancer. Aggie wanted the chance to say goodbye and thank her once again for her friendship.

Even though they'd come from different worlds, she and Margaret had been close as freshman roommates at Cornell. Coming from Springfield, Massachusetts, Aggie was awed by Margaret's New York City beauty and sophistication. Looking back, Aggie realized how lucky she had been that Margaret considered her a project of sorts, exposing her to a world of money and power. It had given her a basis of knowledge that, in later years, helped grow the business Arnold had inherited. Aggie had always been grateful to Margaret for her friendship and wanted her to know it.

As she and Blythe walked up the flagstone pathway to the front of the house, Aggie drew a deep breath. Margaret had let her know she'd lost her hair from the chemotherapy treatments.

The woman who greeted them at the doorway was a shadow of the person Aggie remembered. At the smile that spread across Margaret's ravaged face, tears stung Aggie's eyes. She looked so frail.

"Hello, old friend!" Margaret said, her smile slicing her drawn face in half.

Aggie enveloped Margaret in her arms, careful not to hurt her. "It's been so long ... way too long ... since we've seen one another."

"I know. And this beautiful, young woman is Blythe? Why, I remember how happy you were when she was born."

Margaret held out her hand to Blythe. "I'm so glad you've come to lunch with your grandmother. My grandchildren live out on the west coast. How I've missed having them near as they grew up."

Blythe gently shook Margaret's hand. "I'm happy to be here. I know how excited Gran is to see you again."

"That's right," said Aggie. "I forgot that both John and Jake moved out west, true northwest people. It's been wonderful to have Blythe in the Boston area with me."

Margaret let out a soft sigh. "My boys still love it out in Seattle." She stepped back and indicated for them to come in. "But, no need to talk here. Let's go inside where we'll be more comfortable. Annie has prepared a wonderful lunch for us."

A young woman wearing a black skirt and a white blouse approached them.

Margaret smiled at her. "This is Annie McDougal. She owns a successful catering business and is a godsend to me when I entertain. Meet my dear old friend, Aggie Robard, and her granddaughter, Blythe."

They exchanged handshakes, and then Annie said, "Won't you come this way? I've set things up in the sunroom."

"You might want to freshen up first," Margaret said to Aggie. "If so, the powder room is on the way."

Margaret had always been so proper, thought Aggie. Even now, when she couldn't be feeling well, she was a gracious hostess. She took hold of Margaret's arm, aware of its thinness. "I'm glad you suggested a reunion of our old gang. It's too bad plans fell through, but it meant I could still see you and thank you for all you did for me." Again, tears blurred Aggie's vision.

Margaret patted her hand. "Yes. It's good that I can say goodbye to friends, old and new. We shared some wonderful times, didn't we?"

Aggie nodded, too emotional to speak. She hadn't realized this would be so difficult. But at her age, goodbyes were part of the reality of her life.

Feeling Margaret's shoulders shake, Aggie turned to see her laughing. "God! You were so outrageous! You wore all those crazy outfits, army boots and all. Remember all the marches we joined? The parties afterward?"

Aggie heard giggling behind her and joined in the laughter. "A certain someone recently told me I was outrageous. Guess I'll always be that way. But, Margaret, as I recall, you were right beside me. Maybe better dressed than I, but there."

Margaret's lips curved as she brushed at her black wool slacks, then fingered the pearls she wore with her beige sweater. "Ah, yes. Those were the days. I thought I was so free to be me."

"We all did," said Aggie, assisting Margaret into a chair at a glass-topped table set for three in the middle of a stunning room filled with plants and flowers. She took a seat opposite Margaret while Blythe sat between them.

"You haven't changed all that much," said Margaret. "I like the pink streak in your hair and the boots and leggings you're wearing."

Aggie laughed. "A little bit of rebellion."

"Gran's always been that way," said Blythe. "My stepmother doesn't like it."

"Constance, Brad's second wife, is a bit of a bore," said Aggie, fighting to keep from going overboard when talking about her.

"Yes, well, all families have someone like her, I suppose," Margaret said diplomatically. She waved Annie forward. "You may go ahead and serve."

Annie hurried away and returned carrying a large tray holding three salad plates filled with greens, sliced chicken, and an array of fresh fruits.

"This looks yummy," Blythe said.

"Annie does a lovely job," Margaret said. "You'll have to forgive me if I just pick at mine. That's the status of things these days."

"Please let us know if we're tiring you out," said Aggie.

"Thanks, but I want to spend every moment I can with you. I'm so happy to see you, Aggie."

"Me, too," Aggie said. She waited for Margaret to lift her fork, then she followed suit and took a bite of the salad. "Delicious," she murmured.

"Yes," said Blythe. "I love the dressing."

Margaret beamed at Annie standing nearby. "Another success. Thank you."

"You're welcome. Dessert is ready anytime you wish."

After Annie left the room, Margaret leaned forward. "Tell me, how do you like your new location? New Life, I believe it's called."

"Though I was opposed to the move, the assisted-living facility is wonderful with lots of activities, nice surroundings, and interesting people. It's not the same as living in my own house, but that place was getting to be way too much for me."

Margaret indicated the room with a sweep of her hand. "I should've moved long ago, and now it's too late. My sons will be left with a lot of work, sorting through and disposing of the accumulation of things my living here for over forty years has created. I've tried to do some of that already, but there's still a lot to do."

"Yes, it's a worry. When I sold the house, I was able to donate to several charities. Someday, Blythe will take over my position in the company. That's such a relief to me."

Margaret turned to Blythe. "So pretty and smart too. Aggie's lucky to have you. It was she who knew exactly what she wanted to do with the company." She faced Aggie. "Do you remember talking to Donald and me about it soon after you married Arnold?"

"Yes. I always had such big ideas. Arnold gave me free rein to do what I wanted with the merchandising. He had his faults, but he was generous in many ways."

"Still, it's satisfying to see how well you've succeeded. You're an inspiration for women."

"Not at all." Aggie felt heat rise to her cheeks. It hadn't been easy convincing bankers and purveyors that she, not Arnold, was in charge of certain aspects of the business. The '70s weren't that distinct from the '50s back then. The memory of how she'd been treated still irritated her.

Throughout the meal, Aggie and Margaret filled the air with small talk, trying to piece together one another's lives as best they could in the short time allotted them. As soon as Aggie and Blythe set their forks down after eating their salads, Annie placed individual lemon tarts before them.

"Would anyone like coffee? Tea? Anything else?" Annie asked.

Aggie looked to Blythe. "Do you need caffeine to help you keep driving?"

"I'm fine. Thanks. It's not that far to our stop in Virginia."

"How I envy the two of you, off on a secret girls' road trip," Margaret said, smiling at them.

Seeing how hard Margaret was struggling with fatigue, Aggie hurried through her dessert, folded her napkin, and placed it alongside her plate. "Thank you so much for a delicious lunch and the opportunity to spend some time together, Margaret. It's very gracious of you."

Margaret emitted a sigh. "Old friend, it's given me such pleasure."

Annie appeared.

"Will you show my guests to the door?" Margaret said. "And then you can help me to my room. The nurse will be here shortly."

Aggie went over to Margaret and hugged her close. "Thanks again for being as sweet as you are. I love you. Safe journey."

Margaret's eyes filled. "Love you too. Keep on being as outrageous as you can. It suits you."

Aggie gave her another hug and then stiff-backed, holding in tears, she followed Annie to the front door, Blythe at her side.

# CHAPTER FOUR
## BLYTHE

After they got settled in the car, Blythe followed Gran's directions to get back on the Garden State Parkway. From there, they'd pick up Interstate 95 and keep heading south.

"We'll stay just south of DC because there's another stop I want to make," Gran announced, checking over her notes.

"You've carefully planned everything," Blythe said with a smile of appreciation. "I was pretty impressed with what Margaret said about you. So, it was you, not Papa, who grew the company?"

"Well, let's say we worked together on it," Gran said, fidgeting in her seat. Shortly after they were married, when she discovered she was pregnant with Brad, Aggie realized that Arnold had a drinking problem. It took several difficult years before he became and remained sober.

Blythe gave Gran a knowing look. She knew The Robard Company wouldn't be the success it was without her grandmother's guidance. The woman had a knack for what people wanted and the sales talk to go along with it. She'd seen her in action before.

Though Gran was more than a competent salesperson, Blythe knew she would never sell anything she didn't believe in. Even the smallest, least expensive items had to be of good quality. That was one reason for customer loyalty.

"How are you going to train me if you're living at New

Life?" Blythe asked Gran.

"I may be at New Life, but, fortunately, I'm still able to function like always. I've already talked to your father and the staff about my need to be in my office. I'm hoping you'll come back to Boston after graduation, someplace near the office in Dedham. Then, you'd be able to pick me up in the morning and take me to the office. During nice weather, I'll be able to drive myself. I want to introduce you to staff members at various locations and our suppliers, along with my personal staff. You already know Suzie, my right-hand assistant. You know some of the other staff through working at the stores during summer breaks, but you must meet them on a different level—as their boss, not their co-worker."

"I guess it's a good thing I didn't marry Chad. He wanted to be a big part of this."

Gran clasped Blythe's hand. "When you meet the right man for you, we'll both know it."

"God! I was so stupid. Chad made it seem as if I owed it to him to do whatever he wanted. And Dad and Constance liked him."

"I love your father," said Gran, "but he didn't see Chad in action as I did. Funny, some people feel that as people age, they don't hear or see what's going on around them; they just fade into the background. It worked to your advantage for me to be able to see the side of him that he kept hidden from your parents."

"He was handsome, ambitious," she paused and let out a long sigh, "and a real loser."

Gran clucked her tongue. "I'm sorry, darling, but it's the truth."

"I just want to learn all I can about Robard's stores and do the best job I can for you and Dad."

###

By the time Blythe pulled into the hotel in Arlington, Virginia, she was ready for a break. Groaning with fatigue, she got out of the car and stretched. The car was comfortable, but traffic along the way had been a constant concern, causing stiffness in her shoulders.

She looked around. It seemed like a nice hotel with easy access off and onto the highway. Better yet, several restaurants were within easy walking distance. Gran had been particular about where they were staying but had refused to tell her why. "You'll see in the morning," was all she'd say.

Blythe pushed her questions aside and unloaded the suitcases from the car while Gran cleaned out toffee candy wrappers and empty water bottles from the front seat.

After they checked in, Gran said, "What do you want for dinner? It looks like we have many choices."

"How about something simple? The menu from the Hometown Cafeteria has a broad selection. Want to give it a try?"

"Sure. That will make it nice and easy. We need to get up by six tomorrow morning."

"We do?" Blythe asked, wondering what Gran had planned.

"Yes. That timing should be perfect."

"And you're still not telling me why?" said Blythe.

Gran shook her head. "Nope. It would spoil my surprise."

The next morning, after a fractured sleep, Blythe awoke to the sound of the alarm clock. Gran was already standing by her bed.

"Time to get up?" Blythe groaned.

"Yes. Hurry and get ready. I'll make coffee. We can take it with us." Gran peered out the window. "Looks like it's going to be a beautiful day."

Blythe heard the excitement in Gran's voice and climbed out of bed. After performing her morning routines, she gratefully took a sip of the coffee Gran handed her.

"Let's get on the road. We'll grab breakfast later," Gran said, zipping up her suitcase.

When they stepped outside into the cool air, a streak of light showed itself on the horizon in the brightening sky—a glimmer of the day to come.

"We're going into the District. At this early hour, I'm hoping to beat the worst of the traffic."

As Blythe followed Gran's directions, she soon realized their destination. After finding a parking spot, Blythe got out of the car and helped her grandmother walk up to the Abraham Lincoln Memorial.

"It's so big," whispered Blythe, staring at the impressive, white-marble building. Soft lighting backlit the massive columns in front, creating a breathtaking presence. But it was the huge figure sitting in the chair facing outward that kept her gaze. With the light shining on the white marble that formed him, the sculpture seemed almost heaven-sent against the brightening sky around the building.

In a daze, Blythe climbed the steps to reach the statue of the 16th president of the United States. With all the political in-fighting and constant bickering of present-day politics, she needed this reminder of the greatness of this country and its leaders through the years.

Blythe didn't know how long she'd been standing looking at the man and the words carved into stone above him when she felt a hand on her shoulder.

"So humbling," murmured Gran.

Blythe nodded, moved by what she saw. "I feel as if I'm in a church."

They stood together, staring at the words above the statue:

**"IN THIS TEMPLE, AS IN THE HEARTS OF THE PEOPLE FOR WHOM HE SAVED THE UNION THE MEMORY OF ABRAHAM LINCOLN IS ENSHRINED FOREVER."**

"Let's take a look at the Vietnam Veterans Memorial. I wanted to stop here for Arnold. He never would come to see the wall. He said it would be too difficult."

Blythe took Gran's elbow. They walked back down the steps and over to what, according to the brochure Gran handed her, was also called "The Wall that Heals." Blythe read that the two walls that made up the memorial contained more than 58,000 names listed in chronological order based on the date of casualty. Within each day, they were shown in alphabetical order.

Gran took hold of Blythe's hand. "Let's look for Arnold's brother, John. He died in September of 1969."

They'd been searching for a few minutes when Blythe heard a sob coming from Gran. "So many names," Gran whispered. She pulled a tissue from her coat pocket and dabbed at her eyes.

Blythe wrapped an arm around Gran, her own vision blurred by the impact of realizing how many soldiers had died. As Blythe looked over their names listed one after the other in row after row, sorrow created a knot inside her. No wonder Papa hadn't wanted to see his brother's name here. The guilt he'd always felt would have brought him to his knees.

Blythe fingered the names of men she'd never known, would never meet, and drew a shaky breath.

Eyes rimmed in red from the tears she'd shed, Gran turned to her. "I'm ready to leave. Thanks for coming here with me. I think Arnold would be pleased."

They checked out the Vietnam Women's Memorial and the Three Soldiers and then went to Gran's car, walking together silently.

As she slid behind the wheel of the car, Blythe knew her experiences this morning with her grandmother would always remain a part of her. The memorials themselves were touching, but being with Gran, doing something for her grandfather, made it even more special.

She glanced at Gran, trying to envision her as a college student wearing Doc Martens as she protested the war.

As if she knew what Blythe was thinking, Gran glanced over and gave her the peace sign.

Blythe laughed and squeezed her arm.

# CHAPTER FIVE
## AGGIE

Still shaken by the haunting images of what she and Blythe had seen today, Aggie struggled to settle her emotions. She sat quietly in the car as Blythe pulled out of the parking area. Following her directions, they headed back into Virginia. Blythe was quiet as well, which suited Aggie's mood. The visit to the memorial had brought back so many memories of Arnold and his struggle to be the best and do the best, not only for himself but for his brother.

After connecting to Interstate 95, Blythe broke into the silence. "I'm hungry. Let's stop for breakfast, and then you can tell me where we're going."

"Oh, yes. I'm sorry. You must be starving. Let's get off here in Springfield."

After taking the exit, they found a diner and pulled into the busy parking lot.

"I'm ready for another cup of coffee," Blythe confessed. "I can't stop thinking about what we saw this morning at the memorial. I wasn't even born when the war took place, yet it was so powerful to see that wall."

"Your father wasn't born either," said Aggie. "I hope people remember that war and what it cost. Some have forgotten World War II and all that happened during that awful time or have even denied some of the most horrifying events. We must keep these pieces of history alive so that our country continues to move forward with respect for all that happened.

Unless we learn from the past, history may repeat itself. We must remember."

Blythe turned to her and gazed into her eyes. "Is that why we're on this trip? A chance to remember that and other things?"

Acknowledging her granddaughter's question, Aggie nodded. Though she hadn't expressed it, she supposed it was true. Moving out of the house she and Arnold had lived in for so many years and into a lovely facility but would never be home had made her long for old friends, old memories. Plus, she had to speak to Donovan in person.

"Thank you for inviting me along for the trip," Blythe said. "I consider it an honor."

"My sweet girl, I love you so much!" Aggie said, clasping Blythe's face and kissing her. "I'm proud of the woman you've become." Aggie had been relieved when Blythe's relationship with her boyfriend ended. Blythe deserved someone who appreciated her for the caring person she was, not someone interested in her because she was beautiful and might inherit wealth someday.

They got out of the car and walked into the diner.

Inside, seated in a booth with red vinyl-covered benches, Aggie quickly decided on scrambled eggs and a biscuit and waited while Blythe perused the menu.

The waitress poured cups of coffee for them and took their orders. When she placed their meals in front of them, Aggie realized how hungry she was and eagerly dug in.

"Who are we going to visit in Durham, North Carolina?" Blythe asked between taking bites of her eggs.

Aggie felt her face soften and said, "Mack Townsend, an old friend who was part of the college gang. He was considered quite the catch—handsome, bright, and very kind. He became a professor at the University of North Carolina. I think he married, but there's no mention of a wife. He was a good friend to me."

"And where are we staying?" Blythe asked, an amused expression on her face. "This whole trip is a bit of a surprise."

Aggie couldn't hold back a chuckle. "Yes, it took quite some doing to make it all come together. Mack has invited us to stay at his place. He told me he has enough room to spare. He sounded excited by the idea."

Blythe gave her a sly look. "What are his intentions?"

Aggie laughed and waved away any sense of impropriety.

As Blythe slid behind the wheel of the car, she grinned. "Almost warm enough to put the top down." The sound of her cell caught her attention. She checked her screen and groaned.

"Chad is texting me. *Again*. I told him it was over between us, but he's suddenly decided the girl he's been with isn't right for him."

"I'll be glad to answer for you," Aggie said with a little more disgust than she'd planned.

Blythe laughed. "No need. I'm going to ignore it. Oh, it looks like I missed a text from Constance." She read it and turned to Aggie. "She says she misses me and hopes I'm doing well in Ithaca getting caught up on my work."

"Good thing she doesn't know about our road trip," Aggie commented. She'd hate for a family fight to break out because Blythe was helping her.

"I'm going to enjoy every moment of this trip," Blythe said with a sound of defiance in her voice Aggie liked.

She reached over and gave Blythe's shoulder a loving pat. Blythe wasn't perfect, but pretty close to it. "Durham should be an easy trip from here. I told Mack we'd arrive by mid-afternoon in time for dinner."

"Lean back and enjoy the ride," Blythe said with a fresh sparkle to her eye, making Aggie love her even more.

When they finally pulled into Mack's driveway, Aggie was ready to get out of the car for a long break. She climbed out of the passenger's seat, stretched her legs, and stared at Mack's house. A Colonial, the exterior was painted gray with crisp white trim, including the balustrade bordering a narrow front porch that stretched across most of the front of the house. A table sat between two rockers on one side of the front entry. The other side contained a hanging, bench-style swing with plenty of room to move back and forth. Charmed already, Aggie gazed at the handsome, gray-haired man emerging from the house.

"Hi, Aggie! It's so good to see you," he said, moving toward her with a smile that lit his blue eyes. She moved easily into his outspread arms. He hugged her and turned to Blythe. "And this must be your granddaughter, Blythe. Hi, I'm Mack Townsend. We're so glad you and your grandmother could spend some time here."

"Thanks," said Blythe.

"Yes, thank you for having us," said Aggie. She'd forgotten how good-looking, how charming Mack could be.

"No problem at all. My husband loves to entertain. He'll be joining us shortly. He's just changing out of his lawyering clothes, as we like to say." A noise behind Mack made him turn. "Ah, here he is now."

A heavy-set man with dark hair graying at the temples walked onto the porch and down the front steps, wearing a smile. "Is this Aggie and Blythe? Welcome. I'm Simon Perkins. Mack was very excited when you agreed to spend the night with us." He shook hands with each of them. "Any friend of Mack's is a friend of mine."

"The pleasure is ours. We appreciate the opportunity to meet you and for me to see Mack after too many years," said Aggie, hiding her surprise at the circumstances. In college, Mack had dated a lot of girls who were crazy about him.

Mack put his arm around Aggie. "Come on inside, old friend. I want to hear all about you and yours."

Aggie followed him inside, taking in as much as she could of the details of a library off to the left, the living room opposite it, and the powder room just beyond the living room before stepping into the beautiful, professional-looking kitchen and open family room that spread across the back of the house.

"Everything's beautiful," gushed Blythe. "I love all the touches you've given the space to make it so open, light, and airy."

"Yes," Aggie quickly agreed. The contemporary feel they'd given to the house worked beautifully with the space.

Mack smiled at Simon. "We had fun making it ours. Not your ordinary colonial."

"How long have you been together?" Blythe asked him.

"Thirty years, married for three," said Mack, beaming.

"I'm happy for you, Mack," said Aggie, realizing how right it was to see Simon and him together. Now, a lot of things clicked into place. Mack had dated many women but never got serious about any of them. He'd never provided any marriage information in the annual news posts, and he'd always been single at weddings or gatherings in the group following their college years.

He grinned at her. "Took me a while to come out, but I'm glad I did."

"Me, too," said Simon, and the four of them laughed together.

Seeing Mack this happy brought a sting of tears to Aggie's eyes. To Blythe, it might seem normal to see this happy couple, but back in the sixties when they were in college, being gay was something that many kept hidden.

After the men brought in their luggage and Aggie and Blythe had settled in their rooms, they met downstairs in the kitchen.

"If it's agreeable to you, I've chosen a nice pinot noir for us to drink while sampling appetizers," said Mack. "Simon is a terrific cook, but I know my wine."

"Wonderful." Aggie grinned. "I remember everyone in college thought you were so sophisticated when we went out to eat because you'd order wine instead of cheap beer."

"Is that so?" Simon said, winking at Mack. "He's always enjoyed good wine. That's one of the reasons we clicked from the beginning. Good food, too."

Mack poured wine and handed each of them a glass.

"Everyone can relax in the family room while I prep a few things for dinner," said Simon, lifting his glass of wine in a salute.

"If you don't mind, Simon, I'd like to watch," said Blythe.

"No problem." He winked at her. "I'll even let you make any suggestions."

Blythe laughed. "You don't want any from me. I'm just starting to get serious about cooking."

"Simon's a wonderful cook," said Mack. "C'mon, Aggie, let's sit in the family room. I want to hear all about your new place."

Aggie took a seat on the couch. Mack settled in at the other end of it and faced her.

"Here's to us," he said, lifting his glass.

"Yes, to us," Aggie said. "I'm pleased to be here. How did you and Simon meet?"

Mack's features softened into a smile. "I needed some legal advice for the course I was teaching, and there he was. As he said, we hit it off from the beginning. I'd recently come out and was still nervous about it. You may remember my parents were very conservative people." As he shook his head, he let out a snort of disgust. "I even got engaged to marry a woman once, just to please them. But I couldn't go through with it. I didn't want to hurt her."

"You've always been a very kind person," Aggie said. "I've loved that about you."

"Thanks. Tell me more about Blythe. She's Brad's daughter, right?"

Aggie filled with pride and nodded. "She's a treasure. Brad married her mother after she discovered she was pregnant. It was an honorable thing to do, but we all knew it was never going to last. She had many mental health issues. It wasn't long before she wanted out of the marriage. Blythe was five when her mother finally left for good."

"Such a shame," commented Mack.

"After being a single dad for six years, Brad remarried. They seem happy, but Constance, his wife, hasn't been very kind to Blythe. A bit of a jealousy issue, if you ask me. But Blythe is a strong woman and smart as a whip. I'm praying she'll find someone who adores her for the wonderful person she is."

Mack grinned. "Spoken like a true, doting grandmother."

"You bet! You know I always did speak my mind."

"Oh, yes!" Mack said, chuckling. "I remember all the arguments you and Donovan got into over politics. I always thought you two would end up together, but then you married Arnold."

"Donovan was my first real love, but Arnold was the love of my life," said Aggie, feeling a smile cross her face. "We had many wonderful years together. He's been gone three years now. Dropped dead right before me." Her vision blurred. "I'll never get over it."

Mack reached for her hand. "I'm sorry. Before I met Simon, I watched a partner of mine die, too. He was a wonderful man."

"Life is full of twists and turns, isn't it?" Aggie said. "I'm happy Margaret made sure we all got in touch with one another. Now, she's not able to participate. It doesn't seem fair."

Mack's expression was tinged with sadness. "Life isn't fair. But we take what we've been given and work with it. That's the best way I know of to succeed."

Aggie studied him. "Good advice. You're clearly happy."

"Yes. Life is good. I'm grateful for that."

"Me, too. I'm especially grateful that Blythe is going to come into the business, taking over for me. Brad works with me too, but I wanted to make sure she'd be part of the operation. Another female in the family and all that. And Brad's heart isn't really into it. He's stayed to help me, but he'd love to be able to leave."

"I get it. As I recall, you were the one who encouraged Arnold to grow the business. I remember hearing you talk about the plans you had for it."

"True. The Robard Company has always been a big part of my life. I was so angry when my daughter-in-law, Constance, tried to orchestrate my moving out of my house and into the assisted living facility where I reside. I think she thought I'd retire and hand the entire business over to Brad. But I couldn't. And as it's turned out, New Life is a nice place for me. Getting old is something we can't stop. Besides, the alternative isn't that great."

He laughed. "Aggie, you don't look or act your age. You've got a dance or two left in you yet."

Blythe approached. "I heard that! That's what Gran keeps saying." She sat on the arm of the couch next to Aggie and put an arm around her. "I want to be just like her when I grow up."

Aggie beamed at her. "You're already way ahead of me, honey."

"Anyone hungry?" asked Simon coming over to them. "I'm ready for you."

He ushered them to the dining area, where they each took a seat at the oval oak table.

Gazing at each of them, Aggie was pleased she'd planned this trip. Seeing Mack brought back many happy memories. It was fun to reminisce about earlier days and see old friends, part of the process of letting go.

# CHAPTER SIX
## BLYTHE

Blythe listened to the conversation around her, hiding her dismay at how many changes had taken place in their lives since Gran and Mack were in college. In the past fifty years, with the advent of, first, cellphones and then smartphones and all the other things that went with them, communication alone had exploded. It was hard to imagine a time when you couldn't easily be in touch with someone or spend many hours alone, content to play 3-D games. And those were only some of the changes that had evolved. She studied the three older people, observing their interplay, realizing how disconnected she felt from her friends. Texts and talk on the phone couldn't compare to real face-to-face conversation.

Mack turned to her. "Did you know your grandmother was quite the dancer in her time? She took the Hustle to a whole other level."

Gran's cheeks turned pink. "Hey, if you got rhythm, go with it!"

"You and Donovan were quite the pair," said Mack, chuckling.

"Whoa! Who's this Donovan?" Blythe said. "I thought you met Papa in college."

"I did. But not until I'd dated Donovan for a couple of years. He lives in Florida now. You're going to meet him."

"Another one of our scheduled stops?" Blythe asked,

raising an eyebrow.

Gran's lips curved. "Yep, all part of the plan."

Suspicion coiled inside Blythe. "What plan?"

"You'll see." Gran lifted her empty glass. "This wine was delicious."

"So glad you liked it. It's one of my favorites," said Simon. "Are you ready for more?"

"You bet," said Gran, winking at Blythe. "We don't have to worry about drinking and driving tonight."

"You shouldn't have to worry about driving anyway," said Mack. "Blythe is the driver."

"And Gran is the backseat driver," Blythe quickly interjected.

"See?" said Gran. "She's a step ahead of me."

Amid the laughter that followed, Blythe decided to let Gran take them wherever she wanted. So far, it had been interesting. She'd always known Gran had a lot of spunk, but she was catching glimpses of the young girl Gran had been, and she liked it.

After a scrumptious breakfast of Simon's orange French toast, crisp bacon, and strong coffee, Blythe was ready to hit the road again. Their destination was St. Augustine, where Gran's friends ran a bed and breakfast right on the coast.

Outside, the men loaded their luggage into the car, and then they all exchanged hugs and best wishes.

"Thank you, Mack, for your friendship," said Gran. "Seeing you again brings back many happy memories of being with you and the others in the gang."

"My pleasure. Too bad plans for the reunion fell apart, but I'm delighted we had the chance to be together. Those were good times. Stay well, Aggie, and keep in touch."

They hugged again.

While Mack helped Gran into her seat, Blythe settled behind the wheel. After spending the night in St. Augustine, they'd go directly to Seashell Cottage. Maybe then, she'd know what Gran had planned.

Later, when they stopped for gas, they not only got fuel but a full assortment of snacks. They were aiming for South Carolina barbeque for lunch.

As Blythe continued driving, her mind stayed on the two "college friend" visits she'd made with Gran already. "Who else was in your group you called the "Dirty Dozen?"

Gran gave her a smile that lit her eyes. "You've met Margaret and Mack, and you know that Donovan, Arnold, and I were part of it. Sandy and John Nickerson are two more. The rest, I'm sorry to say, are gone. Mike Masterson and Dick Haines both died in the Vietnam War. I tried to find their names on the wall but couldn't. Nancy Howell and Betsy White died of cancer, and Margaret couldn't locate Sally Thompson. She married several times, and people lost track of her."

"It's nice that you could see Margaret and Mack after so much time. They seem nice."

"Oh, yes. We were a diverse group, coming from very different backgrounds, but we all wanted to have fun as well as get a good education. In today's world, we'd be called nerds. But then, for most of us, education was the way to better ourselves and build a bright future."

"Even with all the politics?"

"Our world was much smaller then. We weren't overwhelmed by a constant barrage of bad news as you are now. It worries me that young people today don't have the optimism we did. Without it, Papa and I might not have been so bold building the business."

"I love hearing how you took one store and made it a series of stores that survive today, even with all the competition."

"It's a constant struggle, but well worth the challenge and the reward. I'm so glad you're going to be a part of it, Blythe. I trust you."

Blythe filled with pride and then thought of her stepmother. She'd never understood why Constance didn't like her. Constance said the right things, did little favors for her, but Blythe knew Constance's heart wasn't in the empty words or actions. Now, by Blythe coming into the business, Constance would find another reason to be critical of her. Blythe had tried talking to her father about it, but while he listened to her, he disagreed that tension between them was always due to Constance. Blythe didn't push it because she knew she sometimes baited Constance, and she didn't want to disrupt his happy marriage. Still, it rankled. Only Gran understood.

She glanced over at her grandmother. The soft sound of snoring came from Gran's open mouth. Seeing her like this reminded Blythe once again that though she didn't look or act her age, she was getting older. Sorrow at the thought of one day losing her made her draw in a deep breath. At dinner last night, Mack had talked about making every day count. She vowed to do better. That's the reason she was making this road trip with Gran—to forget her past with Chad and to gear up for graduation and her new job.

As she pulled up to the Sunny Shores Inn in St. Augustine, Blythe let out a sigh of relief. It had been another long day of driving. The big, white-clapboard house overlooking the shoreline seemed as welcoming as its name. She stepped out of the car and stretched her back, inhaling the salty tang of the warm air with a soft moan of pleasure.

A heavy-set woman followed a tall, thin man out of the house, waving to Gran as she hurried toward them. "Aggie Robard! What a sight for sore eyes! So glad you're here! We've got a lot of catching up to do."

Laughing, Gran hugged the woman. "I'm so happy to see you, Sandy. Where have all the years gone?" She turned to the man. "And John, I can't believe you finally retired from the restaurant business and are now doing this."

He grinned. "Couldn't quite stay away from the hospitality business altogether. But living here is a good way to spend these years."

"We've saved the downstairs suite for you and Blythe," said Sandy, smiling at Blythe. "You look just like Aggie did at your age. Two peas in a pod."

Blythe returned Sandy's smile, loving the compliment. She accepted a quick embrace from Sandy. "This place is gorgeous. Can't wait to see the inside."

"We've just finished redoing it," said John. "It's up to our standards now. I think you'll be pleased."

"And the food is good, too," said Sandy, smiling at her husband. "Once a chef, always a chef." She patted her stomach. "John is still a whiz in the kitchen. You'll see."

She led them to the front entrance of the inn.

From the moment Blythe walked inside, she was smitten. The interior, painted in warm shades of yellow and pale blue, welcomed her. Comfy couches and chairs spaced throughout the living area and den invited her to sit and relax. Best of all were the aromas wafting out of the kitchen. Her mouth watered with anticipation as she followed John to the back of the first floor to a large suite where a cozy sitting area sat between two bedrooms.

"Lovely," she said, trying not to think of how fluffy and soft the pillow looked, urging her to lie down.

"Even prettier than the pictures," said Gran. She turned to Sandy with a smile. "I feel at home already."

Looking pleased, Sandy said, "More than one guest has extended his or her stay. You'll find it very peaceful. But now, let's have some wine and sit and talk. Can't wait to hear about your new place."

"New Life is everything the brochures said it would be, but it's still not home to me yet," Gran said.

Listening to her, Blythe felt a pang of sympathy. If she'd had a real choice, Gran would probably still be living in the big house she'd called home for years. But practicality dictated otherwise. She'd fallen once and was lying on the floor for over an hour before she was able to reach a phone and call for help. As reticent as she was about telling her, Blythe was relieved to know Gran was well taken care of, even if it meant moving.

Before they headed outside to the wide front porch, Sandy wrapped a shawl around her shoulders. Blythe didn't bother putting something over her light-weight shirt. The salty air, so much warmer than back home, felt wonderful.

While Sandy and Gran settled beside one another on a double swing, Blythe took a seat in one of the several rocking chairs facing the shoreline. Sipping the wine John offered her, she gazed at the moving water, mesmerized by the motion.

Though Blythe and Gran had spent a lot of the time in the car listening to an audiobook, she'd had time to think about the future. Working with her father would be challenging. He was not tech savvy, and she knew if the family business were to continue to do well, they'd need to be competitive on social media and use it to their advantage.

"Blythe, darling, come sit by us," Gran urged. "Sandy said

other guests are staying in the house and will need to use their share of the porch."

"Okay." Blythe moved to the other end, where they sat. "No little secrets you don't want to share?" she teased.

Sandy gave her a sly smile. "Your grandmother tells me she's going to see her old beau, Donovan Bailey. Bet you didn't know they planned to marry before Donovan unexpectedly went abroad for the summer."

"Whaat? You came close to marrying him?" Blythe couldn't hold back her surprise. "You've always said Papa was the love of your life."

"As it turns out, he was." Gran refused to meet her eyes.

"We know that," said Sandy, turning as John approached with a plate of appetizers. "Arnie was a great guy. Always a gentleman."

"You talking about Arnie and Donovan?" John said, grinning as he set the plate down on the table.

"Yes. I remember how Aggie had them both starry-eyed," said Sandy.

"That she did," said John, winking at Blythe.

Blythe smiled, knowing there was a whole lot more to the story, a story she'd never heard before.

"Your grandmother was everyone's favorite," John said, sitting down beside Blythe.

"What was the name of the student teacher who helped you with Spanish? He was more than happy to tutor you." Sandy gave Gran a coy smile.

Gran's cheeks turned pink. "That was Paco." She let out a girlish giggle. "More than one girl in class suddenly decided she needed a tutor when they saw him helping me." Still chuckling, she said, "Those days were such fun."

"We thought we knew everything, including what our lives might be ahead of us," said Sandy.

"All part of youth," John said, smiling at Sandy. "We've had a good life with a few surprises."

"Me, too," Gran said. "Some good. Some bad. I would never have guessed I'd now be a widow. Arnie seemed so alive."

"It was that heart of his, right?" John said.

"Yes. It just gave out on him," Gran said, a note of sadness in her voice.

Blythe exchanged a sympathetic look with her. She'd loved her grandfather and had been devastated by his unexpected death.

# CHAPTER SEVEN
## AGGIE

Long after Aggie went to bed, she lay awake in the darkness revisiting her conversations with John and Sandy, Mack, and Margaret. The world they'd shared long ago was nothing like today. But, as John had pointed out, the ups, as well as the downs, had been part of their lives. Recently, she'd felt pressure to see her old friends and to thank them for being part of her younger years. Since moving into New Life where many people's lives ended, she was determined to move ahead, to enjoy her days with a new sense of abandon.

Naturally, her thoughts turned to Donovan. Their history was complicated. All of their college friends thought they'd get married. But no one, least of all Donovan, realized when he suddenly took off for Europe following graduation that life would play tricks on both of them—him, for not recognizing his selfish act would cost him, and her, for finding someone else who would bring her both the best and worst of life.

Aggie rolled over and clung to her pillow, remembering the two men she'd always loved. Donovan was a talented, strong-willed, wealthy young man full of ideas who sometimes forgot to think of others in his mad dash to claim his place in the world. Arnold was the opposite—kind, generous, and eager to please her. But he was troubled, too, by a childhood without love and an addiction to alcohol. She'd had to teach him to trust her. It had sometimes been exhausting. But his steadfast love was a blessing she still carried with her today.

Unable to sleep, Aggie rose and padded into the sitting area.

She gasped at the sight of Blythe sitting on the couch. "You can't sleep either?"

Blythe shook her head. "In my mind, I'm still seeing cars rolling along the highway."

Aggie immediately felt contrite. She sat beside Blythe and clasped her hand. "Oh, sweet girl, am I asking too much of you?"

"No, Gran. This road trip is a good idea. It's given me a chance to see my relationship with Chad for what it was—a chance to please my parents. The thing is, I want to be in a relationship with a good guy interested in me, not someone who was controlling and focused on the possibility of my someday owning The Robard Company. I get it. He was from a poor background and ambitious."

"And going forward?" Aggie asked.

"I'm not going to get serious with anyone until I've had a chance to get my arms around my new duties."

Aggie studied the grandchild she loved so much. "Running a business is a ton of work but rewarding for someone as smart and talented as you are. Finding a person to share your life with is important too. Don't leave that out of any long-term plans."

"You and Papa had a good life working together. I want that too. But, Gran, who is this Donovan everyone keeps talking about?"

"That, my dear, is a story for another time. I'm suddenly sleepy. It'll be a busy day tomorrow. We'll arrive at the Seashell Cottage and have plenty of time to talk there."

"Fair enough," said Blythe, kissing her on the cheek. "I'd better get some sleep too. For the next few days, I plan to nap on the beach in between working on a paper. Can't wait!"

"Good girl." Aggie got to her feet and headed into her room. Talk of Donovan would wait.


Rain had moved into the area and was still falling when Aggie got out of bed. The apprehension she'd kept at bay crept into her thoughts. Was she crazy for making a trip like this and pulling Blythe into this secret escapade? They both knew Constance would make a fuss about it. Worse, Donovan might ruin all she was trying to do by remaining aloof at best, bitter at worst. She studied the palm trees outside her window. Their fronds tossed about in the wind and reminded her of their resilience. She decided not to second-guess her actions. Time would tell if she'd been right to do this.

Quietly, so as not to disturb Blythe, Aggie stepped into the bathroom and took a shower. As the water sluiced over her body, she recalled how thrilled she'd been with Blythe's birth. The situation wasn't ideal, with Brad feeling forced to marry Blythe's mother as a matter of honor, but it had been a wonderful event anyway. And now, knowing Blythe's willingness to take over the business in due time, it seemed right for Aggie to step down. Blythe was smart and innovative, good attributes for a woman moving into the business world. She'd already proved it with summer internships.

By the time Aggie had dressed and was ready to begin the day, she was eager to move forward. When she stepped into the dining room, another couple greeted her with warm smiles. She sat down, curious to learn about them.

Sandy, the perfect hostess, offered them all coffee, tea, and juice, then announced the breakfast that morning was a cheese-and-veggie omelet, sausage casserole, and blueberry muffins.

Blythe and four other guests joined them in the dining room, dispelling any of the gloominess outside with cheerful talk.

After breakfast, Aggie went into the kitchen to say goodbye to John, who was cooking breakfast for the guests who kept arriving in the dining room.

"John, I want to thank you for being a friend all those years ago. This trip has brought back such happy memories of all of us being together."

"Good to see you, Aggie," John said, giving her a quick embrace. "Stay in better touch. And be sure to tell Donovan he should visit us."

"Will do," she responded before turning to Sandy, who'd joined them. "Thank you so much for a wonderful stay. I'll be telling all my friends back home that when they need a perfect escape, they should come and stay here. It's charming. And as I told John, thanks for your friendship. It meant and means so much to me."

"Thanks. I hope you come back for a longer stay. And as John says, Donovan needs to come for a visit. He's not that far." Sandy threw her arms around her. "Aggie, I hope everything works out between you and Donovan. I remember that day when he came to see you. He never should've done that. It wasn't fair."

Aggie gazed at her friend. "It's something I need to resolve. That is one reason I'm making this trip."

"And the other?" Sandy asked, grinning at her.

"To prove that I still have the power to live my own life as I see fit."

Sandy chuckled. "That's my friend, Aggie. I say go for it!"

Before Aggie returned to her room, she stepped out onto the front porch. The sun was peeking through dollops of white clouds even as a fine mist continued to fall. A vivid rainbow made a colorful arc over the water, sending a silent message that all would be well.

Smiling, Aggie turned away to see if Blythe was ready for this last leg of the trip.


On the road again, Aggie settled in the passenger's seat and stared out the window at the passing scenery.

"Gran? What is all this talk about Donovan? Who is he, and what is he to you?"

Aggie knew it was time for her to tell Blythe the real reason she'd chosen Florida for her escape.

"I thought I was going to marry Donovan. We'd dated steadily, lived together our senior year in college, and had talked about marriage. No serious plans, no official engagement, mind you, but the topic came up more than once. I'd made plans to bring him home to Springfield to meet my parents after graduation. At the last minute, he backed out, informing me that his grandmother had made arrangements for him to spend the summer with some of the family in Europe. I was crushed. There was no way I could afford to join them, even if I'd been asked. We argued about his going, but he didn't understand my feelings about the trip or his lack of concern about leaving me for so long."

Aggie clasped her hands. "My initial plan was to wait for his return, but when weeks went by, and I didn't hear from him, I realized he wasn't as serious about me as I'd thought. That summer was when Arnold was booted out of the army because of his heart condition. He came home to Springfield to help with the family business. We started dating, and I realized what a wonderful man he was, far better suited to me than Donovan."

"You'd known him growing up together in Springfield,

right?" Blythe said.

"Knew of him, but he was a year older and traveled in different circles from me," Aggie said. "In college, he was part of my crowd, but we were just friends who saw each other in group situations." She sighed at the memory. "Anyway, when we started dating seriously, things happened fast. Arnold's father had a heart attack and died, making it necessary for Arnold to take over the business. He asked me to help him, and we formed a great team who worked together and played together. Your grandfather was everything I wanted in a husband—kind, generous, loving, and a fierce proponent of my being part of the business. He made me come alive. Does that make sense?"

"Yes, it does. Papa's always been supportive that way with me, as well. I realize that's what I want too."

"As long as the passion is there." Aggie reached over and squeezed Blythe's hand. "Arnold and I always had that. It's important."

"That's another reason it didn't last with Chad. It may sound silly, but I want all those things you read about in books—the racing heartbeats, the smiles that knock you out, the chemistry between two people who are totally hot for one another."

Aggie gave her a look of approval. She and Arnold had been just like that. In the early years, before he'd become addicted to pain medication following a skiing accident. And following, when alcohol became his choice.

"You'll find someone like that someday, Blythe. I'm sure of it."


Five hours later, Blythe pulled into the driveway of the Seashell Cottage.

"Wow! It's beautiful and right on the beach!" Blythe exclaimed, turning to her with a wide smile. "I'll get the suitcases in a while. First, I want to walk out onto the beach, feel the sand between my toes."

"Go run ahead, my darling! I'll join you."

Aggie climbed out of the car and watched as Blythe flung her shoes in the air and sprinted toward the water. Her lungs, which had been troubled by pneumonia, filled with fresh salt air in a gulp of pleasure. Maybe, Aggie thought, it was time to start a routine of spending more time out of the cold of the northeast.

Blythe hurried back to her and took her arm. "C'mon, Gran! It's beautiful. Let's get our toes in the water." She rolled up her jeans. "This is as good as Hawaii any day."

Pleased by Blythe's excitement, Aggie grinned. The dig about Hawaii told her Constance's actions still hurt Blythe.

Aggie kicked off her shoes and walked with Blythe to the edge of the water. The cool, frothy water swirled at her feet, licking her toes and pulling away again in a rhythmic pattern.

At the cry of birds, Aggie lifted her face to the bright blue sky. Large puffy clouds raced across it, the tail-end of the storm system that had affected St. Augustine earlier. Gulls swirled above them, their white wings forming an ever-changing dance against the blue background.

Sandpipers and other small birds raced along the edge of the water, their tiny feet leaving footprints behind, a declaration of their existence. Aggie stood a moment, taking it all in.

"Nice, huh?" Blythe said. "I feel so at peace here. It's well worth the long drive."

"It'll be good for you to relax and rest up," said Aggie. "No need to drive anywhere else today. I paid extra to have someone come in and stock the place with groceries. Now, let's go see our home away from home."

Grinning, they walked arm in arm toward Seashell Cottage.

# CHAPTER EIGHT
## BLYTHE

B lythe followed her grandmother into the house and filled with pleasure. It may be called a cottage, but Seashell Cottage was a lovely, upscale home. Ahead of her, a comfortable living room with a fireplace opened into a modern kitchen with what looked like every convenience. Further exploration led to a bedroom suite to the left of the front entrance. The room's large windows offered a stunning view of the beach and rolling water. On the other side of the entry, a hallway led to two additional bedroom suites whose sliding glass doors opened to an outdoor patio and pool.

"Very comfortable," Gran announced, looking pleased with herself. "This will do quite nicely. There's plenty of room for guests."

Blythe's eyebrows shot up. "Are we expecting guests?"

"I'm not sure," Gran responded. "I suppose it depends upon how things go."

Blythe frowned at her with a steady gaze. "What haven't you told me?"

"I thought Donovan and I should meet in a neutral place. He lives in nearby St. Petersburg." With a wave of her arm indicating the space around them, Gran said, "The Seashell Cottage is the perfect place for us to talk."

"Neutral place? That sounds weird. What's going on, Gran?"

"Let's get our things inside, get settled, and then we can

either take a walk on the beach or sit on the porch while I tell you a little more about Donovan and me."

"That's total evasion, but I'll be patient." Blythe walked over to the refrigerator and opened it. "You're right, Gran. We've got enough food and supplies to get by. Thanks for ordering the white wine. I'm going to have a glass before dinner."

"Nice," said Gran, coming up behind Blythe. "They've bought everything I've asked them to, including the champagne I ordered." She wrapped an arm around Blythe. "Hopefully, we'll have something to celebrate."

"I have a deep suspicion Constance will be unhappy about whatever you've got planned."

"Would serve her right," grumped Gran.

"I'll get the suitcases," Blythe said. "I'll put yours in the single bedroom facing the beach."

"That would be lovely, dear," Gran said. "I'll grab the smaller items from the car."


A short while later, Blythe changed out of her jeans into a pair of shorts she'd brought and then walked out to the porch where Gran was sitting.

"I'm mesmerized by the water," Gran said. "It's forever changing. A rhythmic song to soothe the soul."

"I'm ready for a glass of wine and your side of whatever story is about to unfold. How about you?"

"Sounds delightful," Gran said, starting to rise. "I put out some cheese to soften on a plate and found some crackers to go with it."

Blythe waved her back into her chair. "Stay there. I'll get it."

"Thanks. I don't know what I would've done if you hadn't

agreed to come with me on this journey." Gran's eyes grew misty. "You and me. We've always been a pair. I was the first person you smiled at when you were only a couple of months old. Everyone blamed it on gas, but I knew better."

Blythe's eyes twinkled as she laughed. "Remember the time we both dressed up as witches for Halloween? We had so much fun!"

"I do remember. I was short enough that the adults thought I was just a kid myself."

Still smiling, Blythe said, "I'll help you with whatever you've got planned. If I'm in this deep, I might as well go the whole way."

"That's my girl. Now, let's try that wine, and I'll tell you the story."

Anxious to learn more about Gran and Donovan, Blythe hurried into the kitchen to open the bottle of wine and fix the plate of crackers and cheese.

Moments later, she carried the appetizers and a bottle of chardonnay to the front porch, set them on a table, and returned to the kitchen for two wine glasses. It would be a good way to unwind from the trip. She'd already discovered a chicken casserole in the refrigerator. That and a salad mix would take care of an easy dinner.

Feeling more at peace with herself than she had in a long time, Blythe stepped onto the porch, poured wine into the glasses, and sat down facing the water. As it was too soon for the sun to set, the sky held a late afternoon glow that promised another nice day ahead.

Gran lifted her glass. "Here's to a wonderful vacation!"

"Yes!" said Blythe, clicking her glass against Gran's. "May it be everything you wanted."

She took a sip of the cool wine, allowing it to slide down her throat in soothing silkiness. After sitting quietly staring out at the waves rolling onto shore and pulling away in a continual, waltz-like dance, Blythe turned to Gran. "Tell me more of the story between you and Donovan. I know you've left something out."

Gran took a sip of wine and set down her glass. "Everyone thought Donovan and I would get married. I thought so too until he suddenly changed summer plans and left for Europe. What I didn't know was his family didn't want him to marry me and offered this trip for him to cool the relationship. What he didn't realize was I never received a letter from him that he mailed just before he left, sending me tickets to fly to Europe to meet him. So, when I didn't hear from him, and he stayed longer in Europe than originally planned, I thought it was over between us and moved forward with Arnold. It seemed as if that was the way it should be."

Gran stared out at the water for a moment. When she faced Blythe, her expression was sad. "Timing, however, was against us, or some would say the timing was for us, all along. With Arnold taking over his family business after his father's death, we married quickly."

"What happened when Donovan found out you married Papa?" Blythe asked.

"Donovan heard about us before we got married. Another mix-up. In all the business of preparing for my wedding to Arnold, I missed a phone call that came to my parents' house, and no one mentioned it."

"Poor Gran," commented Blythe.

Gran waved away her concern. "Not necessarily. Remember, I'd fallen in love with Arnold and realized he was far more suitable for me. Especially when I knew how Donovan's family felt about me."

After taking a sip of wine, Gran faced her again. "The day before my wedding, Donovan came to my parents' house. He was distraught that I hadn't responded to his letter and his phone call, hadn't even tried to be in touch with him for the past several months."

"How unfair!" Blythe said.

"Needless to say, the scene that followed was full of misunderstandings. Even though Donovan begged me to cancel the wedding, I wouldn't. I couldn't, you see. I loved Arnold in a way Donovan and I had never shared. Marriage is a partnership where each person is willing to give more than the other to make the union a strong, loving one. More than that, it is a commitment to the other always to be there for them. With all Arnold was going through, there was no way I'd ever leave him. Then, and for all our married years."

"Wow! That's huge. Chad and I didn't have that kind of relationship."

"It isn't easy. Arnold and I went through some tough times with his drinking, but we got through them. Our last years together were wonderful."

"He adored you," Blythe said with feeling.

"And I adored him. But I need to settle things with Donovan. A few weeks after Arnold and I were married, the post office delivered a torn, shredded letter to me in an envelope with a printed message of apology explaining it had been caught in a machine and tossed into a lost-letter box. It was the letter Donovan claimed he'd sent me before he left for Europe."

"Oh, my God! That's awful! Talk about star-crossed lovers!"

"I tried to reach out to Donovan, but he didn't respond when I told him what happened with the letter. He tried marriage a couple of times, but nothing lasted. Between marriages, he learned that Arnold was struggling with his drinking problem and came to visit me when Arnold was in rehab. He told me I deserved better, that he didn't care what his family thought, that he wanted a life with me."

"I hope you told him to go to hell," Blythe said.

Gran surprised her with laughter. "I pretty much did. And he hasn't spoken to me since. But through this group reunion that Margaret tried to put together, I was able to get Donovan to agree to see me if we could meet in Florida. He's not been well lately. He has MS and sometimes needs to use a walker."

"And that's where I come in as your driver," said Blythe. "This is like some kind of novel."

"Pretty much," Gran agreed. "And like a novel of this sort, I want a happy ending."

"Me, too. When do we get to meet him?"

"Tomorrow," Gran said, giving her a worried look.

# CHAPTER NINE
## AGGIE

After a quick meal of the chicken casserole and salad, Aggie and Blythe strolled the beach. The sun was a glowing globe sinking beneath the horizon as they walked along the packed sand near the water's edge. The white lace of the waves seemed to glow in the fading light as the water pulled away from the wet sand. Overhead, birds circled, their raucous cries shattering the stillness. Aggie didn't mind. She was as much at ease with herself and her surroundings as she'd been in a long, long time.

"I've thought about what you told me concerning you and Donovan," Blythe said to her. "You were right to stay with Papa, of course, but I'm glad you have this chance to have closure with Donovan. I'm glad, too, that I'm part of it."

Aggie cupped Blythe's face in her hands and kissed her on the cheek. "You're a sweetheart. I hope you find someone as wonderful as Papa to spend your life with."


The next morning, it took Aggie a few minutes to remember where she was. As if in a dream, she climbed out of bed and stared out the window at the beach. Sleep escaped her in a rush of joy. She'd made it to Florida and would see Donovan today.

She pulled on a terry robe she had found in her guestroom. She needed a good cup of coffee to settle her nerves. When she stepped into the kitchen, she was surprised to see Blythe already there working on her college paper.

Blythe looked up at her and smiled. "Hi, Gran. I just started the coffee. It should be ready soon."

"Bless you, child. No matter how old I get, I want coffee in the morning. I don't give a hoot about what some nutritionists say. It's good for me. The stronger, the better."

"You can have it any way you like," said Blythe. "I'm a coffee girl, too. Come sit down. When it's ready, I'll get yours as well as mine."

Aggie sat across the table from her. "I have to admit I'm nervous about seeing Donovan again. Though he's agreed to meet me here, I have no idea if he'll still be angry or not."

"The fact that he's coming here this morning proves he at least wants to see you. If he loved you as much as you said he once did, then things will be fine."

"Yes, but we were young ... so young and untested. According to what my friends have told me, life hasn't been that good to him. He went through two marriages and, like me, has one son. A late-in-life child."

"Don't worry so." Blythe got up from the table and returned with two cups of steaming hot coffee. "Here. Take a sip, Gran, and try to relax. I have a feeling everything is going to be just fine. After I meet him, I'll give you a wink if I approve."

As Aggie picked up the cup, the steam from the hot coffee rose and kissed her face. She told herself Blythe was right. The best way to prepare for this meeting was to relax and remember some of the good times she'd had with Donovan.


Later, all the butterflies Aggie had quieted in her stomach took flight once again. Donovan had called to say he was on his way and almost there. He'd sounded as tense as she felt.

"Come with me," said Aggie.

Blythe took hold of her hand and walked outside with her to wait for Donovan's arrival.

"Gran! Your hands are cold! Just relax."

"I wish I could," Aggie replied, feeling a little sick to her stomach.

A white Lexus SUV pulled into the driveway.

Aggie's heart pounded as she waited to see more clearly the man sitting in the passenger seat peering out at her. Even from this distance, he looked so ... so ... old! But then they both were.

A young man, Curtis, Aggie thought, hopped out of the car and hurried around the back to open the door for Donovan. As Donovan twisted around in his seat, Curtis opened the back door, slid out a lightweight walker, and placed it in front of him.

Donovan's figure rose. He was as tall, as thick-haired, as handsome as he'd always been.

Aggie started forward and felt Blythe's hand on her elbow, firmly holding her in place.

"Give him a chance to meet you on his terms," Blythe whispered in her ear.

The young man waited until Donovan started walking up the sidewalk before slamming the car doors shut and following him at a distance. Aggie knew then that Blythe was right. Donovan was a proud man who wouldn't want anyone to think he was helpless.

Donovan lifted a hand to wave at her.

Aggie rushed forward, fighting tears at the memory of how active he'd always been.

He stopped walking and stood in front of her. He gazed at her for a moment before his lips curved. "Not quite how I expected to see you again, but I don't always need this thing."

He jostled the walker. "It's just not one of my better days."

"I'm so happy to see you again. We have a lot to talk about." Aggie stood uncertainly, wondering how to maneuver around the walker.

"Come here, Aggie. It's been too long." Donovan shoved the walker aside and held out his arms.

Feeling as if she was flying, Aggie moved into his embrace and held onto him. When she looked up into his face, she saw the moisture in his eyes and knew he was as moved as she. Only then did she allow her tears to overflow.

He pulled her closer.

Observing movement nearby, Aggie gazed over at the young man who'd accompanied Donovan and let out a puff of surprise. "You're not Curtis! I've seen pictures of him and thought he'd be here."

The tall, broad-shouldered man laughed. "No, I'm Logan Pierce, Curt's best friend, just helping him and Donovan out for a couple of weeks while he's on a book tour." He deftly picked up the walker and brought it over to them.

Donovan grabbed hold of it. "Thanks, Logan. Don't know how I'd manage without Curt or Logan to help once in a while."

"My pleasure," Logan said, smiling at him. He held out his hand to her, and Aggie shook it.

"This is my granddaughter, Blythe Robard," Aggie said, urging Blythe forward.

Logan took off his aviator sunglasses and held out his hand. "Hi, Blythe. Logan Pierce. Glad to meet you."

Aggie glanced at Blythe, not at all surprised to see the stunned look on her face. Logan's eyes were a shocking light-blue, reminding her of the days when she'd thought Paul Newman was adorable. With his sandy-colored hair, broad shoulders, and masculine physique, Logan was what she'd call a hunk, and Blythe would probably call a hottie.

Aggie waved them toward the house. "Let's go sit on the porch. It's a lovely day. We can talk there."

"You go ahead," said Blythe. "I'll fix a tray in the kitchen."

"I'll help Donovan and join you," said Logan. "That'll give these two old friends some privacy."

"Perfect," Blythe said with a bright smile that filled Aggie's heart.

"Beautiful young woman," Donovan said, watching Blythe hurry toward the house. He turned his gaze on her. "You're still beautiful, Aggie, even after all these years."

She felt her cheeks heat from the compliment and tried to divert his attention. "I'm so glad I was able to rent this place for a week. It's a lovely place for us to get reacquainted."

Logan took the walker away from Donovan and held out his arm.

Donovan took hold of it and slowly climbed the stairs to the front porch. "It takes me a while, but I can still get around. When I'm having a relapse, I use the walker so I won't trip and fall."

"At our age, none of us wants to take a fall. It's the beginning of all kinds of problems. I'm cautious myself."

Once Donovan was seated in one of the rockers, Logan said, "I'll go help Blythe."

"Please wait!" Aggie said and turned to Donovan. "Would you like anything to drink—coffee, iced tea, sodas, beer if it's not too early, and wine."

"Unsweetened ice tea sounds great," he said, smiling.

"I'll have the same," she said.

"I'll let Blythe know." Logan gave them a little salute and disappeared inside.

"Nice young man," commented Aggie.

Donovan watched him go. "Very nice. Very capable. When

he decides what he wants to do and where he wants to work, he's going to knock 'em dead. He's devoted to me, and I'd hire him in a minute, but I know he doesn't want to stay in Florida. He loves Boston and hopes to work there."

"You're still working?" Aggie asked, surprised.

"Not really. I'm the manager of my family's philanthropic foundation. It keeps me busy and interested in what's going on." He studied her. "How about you, Aggie? Still running the stores?"

"I'm about to let go of the reins and pass them over to Blythe. My son, Bradley, owns forty-nine percent of the business, but my secret hope is to have Blythe bring in a bunch of young people to help so Brad can go his own way. He's worked in the business as a dutiful son, but he's always wanted to teach at one of the colleges in the area. I'd love to give him that opportunity. He's always been protective of me but deserves his own career. We'll see."

"I have one child, a stepson whom I've always loved as my own. I even adopted him. You mentioned his name. Curtis. How did you know? Have you been checking up on me?" He cocked an eyebrow at her.

Embarrassed, she forced a laugh. "Not until the idea of a reunion came up. I'm sorry to say I haven't kept in touch with most of the group through the years—just a Christmas card or two."

"I followed your company's activities for a few years."

"You married shortly after I did," said Aggie. "I read about it in the New York papers. A big fancy, social wedding."

Donovan made a face. "Never should've done it. A failure from the start."

"I'm sorry. And the second marriage?" Aggie knew it might be rude, but she couldn't stop asking questions.

"That one was better, but then I guess you felt from way

back that I'm not good marriage material. Diana left me for her tennis instructor. That's how bad it was."

"Where does Curtis come in?"

"He was part of the second marriage package with Diana. That's the only good thing that came from that union. I love him like crazy. He was twelve when his mother split. He opted to stay with me. She was fine with that."

"I'm glad you had the opportunity to be his parent," said Aggie, automatically reaching out and patting his hand.

He clasped her fingers and squeezed them affectionately.

"You and Arnold had one child?"

"Yes, I couldn't have any other children. I've always treasured Brad. And when he gave me my granddaughter, my joy overflowed. She's my heart."

Donovan studied her, his eyes reflecting sadness. "What would have happened if I hadn't gone to Europe? Or if you had received the letter with the tickets? Or I'd come back early?"

Aggie held out her hands helplessly. "We'll never know. Arnold and I had a good life, and I'm thankful for it. There's no point in going over and over all those things."

Donovan leaned forward. "Have you thought of me through the years?"

Aggie drew a breath and let it out slowly. She couldn't lie. "I have."

His lips curved into a happy smile. "I've thought about you, too. Life is funny. Fate has a way of leading us on paths we never thought of taking. But the alternative of just standing still while life passes by is even scarier. I believe we ought to make every moment count."

"When were you diagnosed with MS?" Aggie asked.

"Just before Curtis's mother left. Scared her silly. But I've done very well with it. Every now and then, I have some bad days, but most of the time, I'm okay. I don't have the more severe form of the disease though I suppose, in time, it may affect how much longer I live. Let me put it this way; I don't intend to die for several more years."

Aggie grinned. "Neither do I. As I told Blythe, there's a dance or two left in this old lady."

Donovan laughed. "That's the girl I remember. Maybe we should enjoy the time we have left doing things we might never do otherwise. What do you say?"

"Like what?" Aggie asked, intrigued by the devilish smile that crossed his face.

He waved his hand in dismissal. "I don't know. Just have fun."

They looked at one another and grinned.

"Here's your iced tea," interrupted Blythe, carrying a small tray with two glasses of iced tea and a plate of cookies. She set it down on the table between the two rocking chairs. "Logan and I are going to take a walk on the beach. See you later."

Aggie laughed when Blythe made a point of giving her an exaggerated wink of approval.

# CHAPTER TEN
## BLYTHE

As they walked toward the sand and surf, Blythe cast glances at Logan out of the corner of her eye. He certainly was handsome and seemed to be a nice guy. She was impressed with how gentle and caring he was with Donovan.

Impulsively, Blythe took off her sandals and ran into the water. She couldn't help thinking of her family in Hawaii. She'd received another text message and photo from Constance. Dealing with her was like riding a roller coaster of emotions. Blythe pushed away thoughts of her family and gazed up at the sky, loving the feeling of the warm sun on her face. Peace wrapped around her.

"Guess Donovan and your grandmother had a real thing for one another back in the day," Logan said, breaking into the quiet around them.

Blythe opened her eyes and turned to him with a smile. "They almost got married. Waiting for you to arrive, Gran was as nervous as I've ever seen her."

They headed down the beach.

"Donovan is usually low key, but he was anything but that this morning," Logan said. "Guess they might still have feelings for one another."

Smiling at the thought, Blythe nodded. "It's sweet. Gran loved Papa, but she loved Donovan when they were in college together."

"What about you? Are you dating anyone? You said you're going to graduate soon."

"No. Messy breakup. I'm focusing on other things. I'll be taking over my family's business for Gran and will be moving to Boston right after school ends."

"Boston is nice. I'm a grad of the B School at Harvard."

"I'm just finishing up my major in business at Cornell. For obvious reasons. Where are you working?"

"Nowhere at the moment," Logan said, sounding disappointed. "I've been doing a lot of traveling and then have been staying with Donovan. I've had a couple of offers that I'm still mulling. Donovan offered a job to me, helping him with the family foundation, but I don't want to live in Florida."

"Nice to have choices," Blythe said. A wistfulness crept into her voice she couldn't hide. "I've always known I would go into the family business, have always wanted it. I just thought it might not happen so quickly. But I'd do anything for my grandmother. She means the world to me."

"Is that why you drove her to Florida to meet up with her old boyfriend?"

"Yeah, I guess that's exactly what I did," Blythe said, laughing softly. "My stepmother will be furious and my father worried. But I couldn't refuse her. And we'll have time to get back home without anyone knowing. The rest of my family is vacationing in Hawaii."

"The plot thickens," he said. He picked up a broken shell and threw it way out into the water.

"I guess you could say so," Blythe said, pleased by the thought. "Wonder what they're up to? When I walked out onto the porch, they both wore guilty looks."

"Yeah? Well, good for them. I haven't seen Donovan this happy in a long time."

"You really like him, don't you?"

A serious expression replaced the smile on Logan's face. "Donovan saved my life back in Junior High when I was about to take a wrong turn into drugs and trouble. My mother is a single mom who couldn't handle me or a lot of other things. Donovan stepped in. Curt and I were best friends and have remained that way. Like you and your grandmother, I'd do anything for them."

"Nice." Blythe liked that Logan wasn't afraid to show his affection.

"I'll walk you down to the pier, and then we'd better head back," Logan said. "I promised Curt I'd keep an eye on his father."

"Okay. Let's run."

Logan easily kept pace with her as Blythe trotted to the pier. She liked the rhythm of their feet hitting the packed sand along the water's edge in tandem. It had been a long time since she was so comfortable with a man. Chad had made her feel unworthy of him.

She took a seat on one of the wooden benches lining the pier and worked to catch her breath.

Logan sat beside her. "Feels good to get some exercise."

"Looks like you get a lot of it," Blythe blurted before she could stop herself. He was a good-looking guy.

"That's one of the things Donovan taught me—to keep physically active so I'd stay out of trouble." He gazed out at the ceaseless movement of the water. "Poor guy. He gets around pretty well, but it's been very depressing for him to know he's never going to run and do all the things he used to do." He turned back to Blythe. "He's had to acclimate to a lot of changes."

"Gran has recently agreed to move into an assisted-living place. It's a wonderful facility with every convenience and a lot of great people, but she's still not used to it."

"All part of the aging process, I guess."

Blythe clasped her hands, sick at the thought of losing Gran. "I'm not ready for anything bad to happen to Gran. I want her to be around for a long time."

Logan gave her a sympathetic look. "I never had a grandmother I was close to, but I can tell how important she is to you."

"Let's head back," said Blythe getting to her feet. "I have a feeling the two of them might need us."

Blythe and Logan chatted about Boston as they walked back to the house. Blythe discovered they both loved clam chowder, the Red Sox, and Italian food from the North End.

As they approached the house, Blythe noticed the front porch empty of people. She hurried forward.

The plate of cookies and glasses of iced tea were untouched.

"Gran? Where are you?" Blythe called out, rushing into the house.

All was quiet.

Blythe turned to Logan, trying not to cry. "Where are they?"

"I'll be right back." He dashed outside and returned moments later. "Donovan's car is gone!"

Blythe's legs turned to butter. She sank onto a kitchen chair and grabbed onto the edge of the table to keep the room from spinning.

"Look! A note," said Logan, handing it to her.

**"Blythe, darling, Donovan and I decided we needed some time to ourselves. Don't worry. All is good. We'll return in time for dinner for the four of us. Have a nice afternoon. Love, Gran."**

With shaking hands, Blythe showed the note to Logan.

He let out a deep sigh. "Okay, then. We might as well do as she said and enjoy the afternoon. I saw a swimming pool. Shall we relax there?"

Blythe huffed out a breath. "We might as well. I'm certainly not going to call the cops on them. They're old enough to make their own decisions. But first, I need to go to the grocery store. Gran mentioned dinner, and I want to pick up a few things."

"I'm happy to help. I do a great job of grilling," said Logan.

"Great! Let me make a list. We're only here for six more days before we have to head back home."

After checking everything in the refrigerator and looking through the cupboards, Blythe had the list she needed.

They headed out to the Publix she'd seen nearby.

As they moved through the grocery store, picking out veggies and perusing the meat section, it seemed natural to Blythe to be with Logan. She quickly banished that thought from her mind. This was not the time, the place, or the man for her future love.


Blythe was lying on a lounge chair by the pool when she heard a car pull into the driveway. She put on a cover-up over her bathing suit and hurried to the driveway. Logan was right behind her.

Donovan's SUV sat in the driveway with Gran at the wheel. She waved gaily to Blythe and got out of the car.

"Gran! I was so worried about you! Where have you been?" Blythe said, wrapping her arms around her.

Gran giggled. "Sorry to cause you any worry. Donovan and I had lunch down the beach, and then he showed me his house. We had a lovely time."

Blythe followed her grandmother around to the back of the

car. Gran pushed a button and the hatch door opened with a soft sound.

"What are you doing?" Blythe asked.

"Getting Donovan's suitcase. He's staying with me this week."

Blythe's pulse raced. "With you? Do you mean with us?"

"He's staying with us in the house and with me in my bedroom," said Gran. A pink blush crept up her cheeks. "We've decided to spend as much time with one another while we can. Life is too short to let an opportunity like this pass us by."

Too surprised to speak, Blythe blinked rapidly as she studied the woman she thought she knew. Gran was not a promiscuous person, and she had never been. In fact, Gran's morals had helped shape her own.

"Now, now," Gran said quietly. "Shacking up at our age is quite harmless. I've simply missed being with a man I love."

"Gran, that's outrageous! You're talking about love already?" Blythe whispered, studying her grandmother with amazement.

"It's complicated," Gran whispered back, "but I do love Donovan. Not in the same way I loved Arnold, but with a sweetness of memory that means everything. We've decided to live life well in what time we have left."

"Is he dying?" asked Blythe, unwilling to believe this unexpected arrangement would go on for any length of time.

Gran actually laughed. "Good heavens, no. He's fine. Just dealing with a few issues, as he says. That's all."

Logan approached. "I've helped Donovan inside. How can I help you two ladies?"

"Would you take this?" said Gran, indicating the suitcase. "And please put it in my bedroom to the left of the hallway. You can put the suitcase on the bed to the left."

Logan's look of surprise was telling, but he did as he was asked and lifted the suitcase.

"We'll be right along," Gran said to him and turned to her. "I know what you're thinking. No need to worry. I'll handle your father and Constance. I *am* a grown woman, after all."

"Ok-a-a-a-ay," said Blythe. "I'll try not to ruin your getaway. But, Gran, remember, we only have six days before we head back north. We have to beat the rest of the family home, or we'll be in a lot more trouble than you're willing to admit to."

Gran squeezed her hand. "You have no idea how happy this time with Donovan is for me. It makes everything seem right— my marriage to Arnold, his marriages to other women. Love doesn't always have a beginning, a middle, and an end, like some people might think. Love is an ever- encompassing feeling, even when it comes by surprise or by repetition."

"Let's go," said Blythe. "We can't keep the guys waiting." She had a lot to work through in her mind. Later, when she was alone, she might be able to sort out her feelings. She was glad Logan was staying for dinner. It might make things less awkward.

When she entered the house, she didn't know what to expect from Donovan.

He looked up from the couch where he was sitting and patted the space next to him. "Blythe? Would you please sit with me for a moment?"

Blythe glanced at her grandmother, and at her encouraging smile, moved forward.

Logan and Gran left them to go into the kitchen.

Holding her breath, Blythe lowered herself onto the couch. "Yes?"

"I want you to know I won't ever hurt Aggie, and I have no intention of making things difficult for you. Aggie and I have a long history and now have this rare opportunity to spend as much time together as possible. If at any moment you're too uncomfortable with the situation, let me know, and I'll leave. It's as simple as that."

"But it isn't simple," Blythe said. "I love Gran and want her happy, but my father will be appalled by her behavior. My stepmother already thinks Gran is losing her mind. This will be used against her."

"Your grandmother is of sound mind. Anyone can see that. Don't worry. When the time comes, we'll protect her." He gazed at Gran in the distance.

Blythe observed the determination on Donovan's handsome face and let out a long sigh. Things might seem a mess, but they were simpler than she'd thought. Growing old didn't mean you couldn't live life. Was Constance so eager to have Gran out of the business so her husband could take over? Was that why Gran was making sure Blythe would come to Boston right after graduation? Only time would tell. But one thing was for sure. She wasn't Aggie Robard's granddaughter for nothing. She'd do right by Gran.

# CHAPTER ELEVEN
## AGGIE

Aggie sat next to Donovan on the couch, pleased with herself. She knew her decision to have Donovan stay with her was a surprise to Blythe, but maybe it was time for Blythe to learn it was okay to take chances in life. She gazed down at her shoes, recalling the Doc Martens she wore in college. There was a lot of love in this new decision of hers, but there was defiance too. How dare Constance make it seem as if she was unable to be on her own! It was time she showed everyone what she was made of. She'd stay at New Life, but only on her terms. And if she asked Blythe to drive her to Florida, that was okay too.

"You all right?" Donovan said, squeezing her hand.

Aggie lifted his hand and kissed it. "Happy that we can do what we want for a change. Your family certainly would disapprove of me now. Not that they ever had."

"I wish they could know how successful you've been. It would be a good moment for me."

"And me," Aggie added. She looked up as Logan carried in a tray of tall, frosty drinks. They'd opted for iced tea for the moment, but she'd already approved the bottle of cabernet for dinner.

As Logan left the room, Donovan said, "Don't know what I'd do without him. I'll be sorry to see him finally settle on a job."

"Why don't we ask him to stay here too? He'd have his own

room and would be available to help you with anything you might need."

"I know you, Aggie," teased Donovan. "You've got something up your sleeve. Trying to play matchmaker, are we?"

She laughed with him. "Ss-h-h-h! I don't want Blythe to suspect a thing. I keep thinking if he's as smart as you say and the two of them get along, I'd like to entertain the idea of bringing him into the business so Brad could move to a less time-consuming position, have more time to do what he wants."

"Why am I thinking of spiders and webs?" Donovan said.

"Sir Walter Scott's '*Oh, what a tangled web we weave, when first we practice to deceive!*'"

"That's the one. Be careful, Aggie. Logan has sworn off women for a while."

"Let's see how it all plays out, shall we?" She couldn't stop a smile from spreading across her face.

"Ah, sweet girl. I love your optimism."

From the couch where she and Donovan were sitting, Aggie could see Blythe and Logan working together to make the meal. Logan was going to grill steak. Blythe was putting together a tossed green salad and instructing Logan on how she wanted her diced potatoes stirred. A simple meal that would be the best she'd had in a long time.

Watching the two young people in the kitchen, Aggie recalled how well she and Arnold had worked together. That was part of the fabric of their marriage. Except for the time he was drinking, they could almost start or end each other's sentences. She pushed away those memories and turned to Donovan.

"Tell me about the trips you've taken. You've mentioned you've traveled the world."

He sat back in his chair. "For a few years, I kept a flat in London. From there, it was an easy trip to France and the continent. That's where I developed my love of food. Once you've dined in other countries, you learn what their good, fresh food tastes like. And of course, the wines, cheeses, and bread all seem to taste different there."

"Did your family travel with you?" Aggie realized how provincial she would seem. She'd never had time to do a lot of traveling.

Donovan shook his head. "No, this all happened before I married Diana and Curtis came into my life. After Diana left us, I took Curtis abroad several times, but it wasn't the same traveling with a child."

"I'd love to meet him sometime," Aggie said, meaning it. They might not be related by blood, but it was very apparent Donovan considered Curtis his son.

Blythe came into the room. "Why don't you two come into the kitchen? Logan is almost done cooking the steak, and everything else is ready."

Aggie moved the walker in front of Donovan and held onto it while he pulled himself up from the couch.

"Thanks," Donovan said and moved at a steady but slow pace across the room.

As Aggie watched him, her heart hurt. She didn't say or do anything to bring attention to him. He'd informed her he wouldn't tolerate that.

After being seated at the table, Aggie gave an approving nod to Blythe. "Everything looks wonderful, darling. Thank you."

"It's pretty basic, but I like to putter in the kitchen. Logan does too."

"Logan does too ... what?" Logan said, entering the kitchen with a platter loaded with the grilled steak.

"Cook," said Blythe, smiling at him.

"Let's just say my mother wasn't the best ... at anything," he said humbly. "It was me cooking or go hungry."

In the silence that followed, Donovan spoke up. "I seem to remember two boys, not one, at my dinner table."

Logan laughed. "Once I found out you could cook, there was no question of it." He and Donovan grinned at one another.

"Will you pour the wine, Logan?" Aggie asked.

He got to his feet, poured a little bit in Donovan's glass, and stood aside. "Will you do us the honor?"

Donovan's face brightened. "Of course." He held the glass up, swirled the wine gently, and took a sip. "Very good. I don't know who chose it, but it's very nice, with a long, smooth finish."

"Logan picked it out," said Blythe.

After all the wine had been poured, the four of them lifted their glasses.

"Here to us!" said Aggie. "All of us."

"To us!" came the response.

Aggie took another small sip of wine, enjoying the taste, and set down the glass.

"Logan, Donovan, and I were talking earlier about the possibility of your staying here at Seashell Cottage with us for the time we're here. It would make Donovan more comfortable to have you help him with certain things. We have a separate suite for you, so you needn't worry about your privacy."

Logan glanced at Blythe. "Would that be okay with you? I don't want to intrude on your vacation with your grandmother."

"My grandmother and Donovan," Blythe quickly corrected him.

"Right," he said, glancing at Aggie and Donovan.

"It would be helpful," Donovan said, giving Aggie a private smile.

"Okay. Sure. After dinner, I'll pick up my things and bring them here."

"Wonderful," said Aggie, pretending not to notice the frown on Blythe's face.

With the dinner over, Logan on his way to Donovan's house, and Donovan sitting on the porch, Aggie worked with Blythe to clear the table.

"Gran, you aren't purposely making trouble for me by asking Logan to stay here, are you? We've got our own stuff to figure out, and with all that's happening, I don't see a lot of time for personal issues. Not if I'm to get ready to take over a portion of your tasks as quickly as you'd like."

"The reason I asked him to stay was because of Donovan. We might want to be together, but neither of us is comfortable with the idea of my helping him with some of the more personal issues. That's why he has Logan help him."

"Okay. But I'm not going to entertain him," said Blythe. "He'll have to be on his own. It looks like this will be the only vacation I'll have for some time."

"Not a problem," Aggie said, pretty sure she knew how that would play out.

They finished the dishes and went out to the porch to join Donovan.

"How are you doing out here?" Aggie asked him. "It's a little chilly but otherwise a lovely evening."

"It's great," he said. "Remember those winters in Ithaca, New York? Talk about cold."

"And gray," Aggie added. "But we didn't care. Oh, to be

young again. That's why I'm glad you're here. It's as close to being young again as we're ever going to get."

Blythe turned to them. "While there's still some light in the sky, I'm going to walk on the beach. There's a beautiful sunset going on."

"Sunsets on the Gulf Coast are spectacular. Be sure to look for the green flash," said Donovan.

"Green flash? What's that?"

"They say if weather conditions are right that, at the exact moment the sun slips below the horizon, you can see a green flash of light. I've looked for it but never have seen it. Maybe you'll be lucky."

"Thanks. I'll look for it." Blythe thought she just might need a little luck.

# CHAPTER TWELVE
## BLYTHE

**B**lythe went inside and noticed Logan pulling up into the driveway. Needing to be alone, she grabbed her sweater and hurried out to the beach.

Walking slowly along the edge of the water, she allowed the lapping of the waves onto the sand to soothe her. This had already been a road trip to remember, and it wasn't half over. Gran had been one surprise after another. Constance might think Gran was becoming senile, but Blythe knew better. "I can't even think of such a thing," Blythe said aloud and kicked the sand with her toe.

"Really?" came a voice behind her.

Blythe whipped around to see Logan. "I didn't know you were there," she gasped, holding a hand to her chest.

Logan grinned at her. "It's okay. I won't tell anyone what you can't think about."

"It's this whole crazy trip. I can't believe it's happening quite this way."

"Yeah, me neither. But I see how happy Donovan and your grandmother are, and it feels good, you know?"

She studied him. No matter how much she might worry about repercussions, she was glad she'd agreed to drive Gran to Florida. She hoped she'd grow to be just like her—smart, fun, and a whole lot more daring than she'd thought. No wonder both Papa and Donovan had been crazy about her. Donovan still was. Someday she hoped a man would look at her like Donovan gazed at Gran.

"I hope I'm not intruding," said Logan, "but I had to get out of the house and stretch my legs a bit."

"I understand. You can help me look for the green flash."

"I've seen it just once," said Logan, "but I never tire of looking for it. C'mon, let's move so we can face the sunset straight on."

They walked farther down the beach and stopped. People in groups or standing alone had gathered on the sand up and down the beach.

The sun was a bright-orange orb hovering at the horizon.

"Look carefully," said Logan, standing behind her. "When the sun gets this close to sinking, it can happen quickly," he said, murmuring into her ear.

Blythe shivered as Logan's warm breath reached her, but she kept her eyes straight ahead. The sun lowered, slipping steadily below the horizon. And then it was gone.

"Did you see it?" Logan asked, grinning at her.

"Not this time. Guess I'd better get back to the house and check on Gran."

"Yeah, I'll help Donovan get settled for the night."

"It's odd, isn't it? It seems as if our roles are reversed," said Blythe. "I'm used to Gran looking out for me, not the other way around."

Logan laughed. "I have a feeling there's a lot more excitement to come. Donovan is a pretty interesting guy."

They walked back to the house together, not needing to talk. Blythe liked that about him. And now that they both had made it clear they had no interest in any relationship, Blythe felt relaxed enough with Logan to let the quiet between them continue.

When they reached the house, it was silent.

Blythe tapped on the door of Gran's bedroom. "Gran? Are

you all set? Do you need help with anything?"

Gran opened the door in her nightgown and robe. "Donovan would like Logan to help him prepare for bed. I'll wait out here with you."

Logan went into the bedroom, and Gran and Blythe sat together in the living room.

"I hope I'm not making it too difficult for you, Blythe. I understand how awkward this may seem, but it's what I want. With our ages and these circumstances, it's not about lust."

"I get it. I really do. Especially seeing you and Donovan together. This isn't hurting anyone. It will be a secret between you and me." Blythe leaned over and gave Gran a kiss. "I want you to be happy."

"You're such a dear girl," Gran told her, her eyes welling with tears. "I know I'm doing the right thing by stepping away from the business and leaving it in your hands. I've planned it for a long time."

"All those years of summer internships and training sessions are coming to fruition," said Blythe. "I've always known you and Papa wanted me to do this."

"Okay, Donovan's ready," said Logan joining them in the living room. "Good night, Mrs. Robard."

"Please call me Aggie. That sounds so much better." Gran got to her feet. "Good night, young ones. See you in the morning."

Blythe watched her grandmother head for her bedroom and then turned to Logan. "Are you all set in your room?"

When he nodded, Blythe took that moment to say, "I'm going to turn in too."

Logan gave her a little salute. "I'll turn off all the lights before I settle down for the night."

###

Inside her bedroom, Blythe brushed her teeth, performed her nightly routine of skincare, changed into a nightshirt, and climbed into bed. She'd ignored text messages from her father but couldn't hide from him any longer.

She quickly texted:

> **Good to hear from you. Glad you're having a good time in Hawaii. All's well with me. Gran is fine. With the rest of the family gone, we're spending quality time together for a few days.**

A twinge of guilt struck her at the information she'd left out, but when she remembered how Constance had arranged for the rest of the family to leave Gran and her behind, she didn't feel so bad. Besides, what harm could come from a road trip like this? Gran was delighted with the opportunity to make things right with Donovan.

Blythe turned out the light and lay back against her pillow. In the dark, she let her mind wander. There was so much to consider. She already knew she wouldn't live at home after graduation. Instead, she'd find a place to rent or even buy in the Boston area. Hopefully convenient to work. She had no illusions about the time commitment she'd have to make to the family business.

She'd been surprised to learn her father had no objection to her assuming more and more of Gran's end of the business. Not that he'd ever be pushed out. But still, he was aware that Blythe wanted to do a lot more with social media than he was comfortable doing. So, working together wouldn't always be easy.

Her thoughts turned to her present circumstances. How odd the trip had taken such a strange turn. Logan had been as surprised as she when Gran and Donovan decided he'd move in for the week. She thought of him. Logan was an all-around nice guy. If circumstances were different, she might allow herself romantic thoughts about him. At the moment, it was just another complication she had no interest in pursuing.

Blythe awoke to gray stillness. She got out of bed and padded over to the window. Outside, the sky to the east displayed pretty, light-pink streaks in the sky, welcoming her with the promise of a nice day ahead.

Quietly, so as not to disturb anyone, she dressed and tiptoed into the kitchen for a cup of coffee. She stopped in surprise when she saw Logan sitting at the table in a pair of jeans and nothing else. God, the man was ... delicious.

"Good morning," he said, looking up at her with those intriguing blue eyes of his. "Looks like it's going to be another nice day for your visit."

"Mmm," she said, heading for the coffee pot. She poured herself a cup of the warm, dark liquid, carried it to the table, and sat opposite Logan. She took a sip of coffee and closed her eyes with pleasure. "Ahhh, that first cup of coffee always tastes so good."

"How would you like to go to breakfast with me? I'm starving, and by going out, we won't disturb the two lovebirds. Donovan usually sleeps in."

"A good idea," said Blythe. "It must be all this sea air, but I'm hungry too. Give me a chance to write a note to Gran, and I'll be ready to go."

Blythe searched for something to write a note on, grabbed a pen and notepad out of one of the kitchen drawers, and hastily wrote a message. She was pleased to get out of the house and start the day with a good breakfast. Of all the daily meals, breakfast was her favorite. No matter how bad things got at home when she was a child, her dad always saw that she had a good, hot breakfast.

Blythe grabbed her purse and followed Logan out the door.

Outside, she breathed in the tangy, salty air with a sigh of appreciation for its warmth. Even in the warmest days of summer, the sea air around Boston held a hint of cold because the water in Massachusetts Bay never warmed above the low 60s.

"We can take Gran's car if you want," she said to Logan.

"No worries. I know where we're going, and Donovan has given me the keys to his SUV." Logan held the passenger's door for her.

"Thank you," said Blythe, sliding onto the seat. She waited until Logan was settled behind the wheel and asked, "Where are we going?"

"Gracie's. It's the best and right down the road at the Salty Key Inn. They also have a killer restaurant called Gavin's that is terrific. A buddy of mine just had his wedding reception there."

"I've always thought a beach wedding would be nice," Blythe said. "Someday, maybe."

"There's an interesting story behind the hotel. Three sisters inherited it from an uncle and now own it after turning it from a dump into an outstanding hotel."

"Oh, I love stories like that." Blythe's stomach growled loud enough for Logan to hear. "Hope the food is as good as you say."

He laughed. "It is. You'll see."

They pulled into the parking lot outside Gracie's. Even at this early hour, the lot was filling up fast.

Again, Logan proved to be a gentleman, standing by the passenger door as she climbed out of the car.

They hurried inside and were seated at a table for two in a

corner of the room. Waiting for a waitress, Blythe took the opportunity to look around. Light-blue-painted wainscoting on the walls displayed several seaside items—fishnets, shells, even a stuffed fish here and there. But it was the sweet cinnamon aroma that caught Blythe's attention.

"Something smells absolutely delicious," she murmured as a waitress headed their way carrying a pitcher of water and a coffee pot. Menus were tucked under her arm.

"Good morning. My name is Sally. What can I get you?" she asked, pouring water into the glasses on the table.

"Coffee," Blythe and Logan answered together, bringing a smile to Sally's lips.

"Right here. Cream and sugar are on the table." She handed them menus. "You'll find everything delicious here. Bertha's cinnamon rolls are still hot from the oven, and the bacon is maple-glazed. Take your time looking over the menu. I'll be back to get your order."

Blythe glanced at Logan. He looked as pleased as she was to find a place like this.

After much indecision, Blythe decided on scrambled eggs, bacon, and a cinnamon roll.

Logan placed his order for grapefruit juice, a short stack of blueberry pancakes, a fried egg, and breakfast sausage and turned to her. "It's refreshing to be with someone who isn't afraid to eat."

"Thanks. Good food is one of the joys of living. My father taught me that."

"Very sensible," Logan said. "Are you always sensible?"

"You're asking me that after knowing I'm on this road trip with my outrageous grandmother?" she said.

Grinning, he studied her. "I like you, Blythe. If I decide to take the job offer I have in Boston, I hope we can meet up once in a while."

"Sure. That would be fun."

They ate slowly, taking their time to enjoy the food and to keep the light conversation going. Blythe soon realized that, without Donovan's influence on him as a young boy, Logan might not have made it. He'd told her about a few encounters with drug-related issues and assured her that though drugs were no longer a problem, he was careful about drinking and chose his friends carefully.

"Most of all," he said, "I want to repay Donovan in any way I can for what he's done for me. That's more important than anything. How about you? Did you have a lot of friends growing up?

"Not really," said Blythe. "As a little girl, I had a problem making friends, mostly because I didn't want them to meet my mother, who could be verbally abusive. My father finally got full custody shortly after I was six, and school officials figured out what was going on."

"How's it going to be working with him and your grandmother?" Logan asked.

Blythe took a moment. "I'm not sure. Gran is as sweet a woman as you can find, but when it comes to business, she demands the best of you. My father tends to want to stick to routines. I've already told Gran if I'm to take over for her, I intend to make the stores more competitive against the big guys. She loved that, of course, but it will be a struggle to get everyone on board with the changes that will need to come. Changes concerning creating an updated presence on the internet and using social media to our greatest advantage."

"Makes sense to me. Business has changed a great deal, even from, say, ten years ago. The world is a marketplace for everyone. No longer can you deal with just a small trade area."

"Yes, but in our business, dealing with the people in town in a very personal way is what has made us successful. That personal service."

"Yes, of course," Logan quickly conceded. "But there's no reason a group of local stores can't be a world marketplace too."

Blythe gave him a thoughtful look. "You're right. Are you sure you don't want to come to work for Robard's?"

He laughed. "Someday maybe, after you have control. Now, I have to consider the options I already have. But thanks for the confidence."

They smiled at one another, and Blythe realized they were already becoming friends.

# CHAPTER THIRTEEN

## AGGIE

Aggie stirred and sleepily opened her eyes and blinked to get a sense of her bearings. Where was she?

"Aggie, can you help me get out of bed?"

Startled, she turned to see Donovan struggling to get to his feet. She jumped up and hurried over to his bed.

"I'm not usually this bad, but this damn flareup is taking forever to go away," he muttered, and Aggie knew how embarrassing he found his situation.

Aggie gripped his hands and pulled him to his feet. "There."

"Thanks. I'll be all right with the walker now that I'm upright. I hate this damn disease. I'm afraid of taking a tumble."

"No one our age wants to fall," she said, trying to give him some confidence. "I'll be right here beside you."

"I'll be fine. Just need to go to the bathroom, and then I'm coming over to your bed."

"I'll make room for you," she said with an eagerness she couldn't hide. After they'd gone to bed last night, they'd lain apart, talking for a while. Then, at his suggestion, she'd risen and climbed into his bed beside him. The years melted away as she'd cuddled up against him and accepted his warm kisses. Even now, the memory of his lips on hers sent frissons of electricity through her. They'd always had great chemistry.

As she lay in bed waiting for Donovan to come to her, Aggie thought of her family. She hoped they'd understand that love didn't die with age. Sexual drive might change, but that didn't stop someone from wanting to touch or feel caresses.

Donovan made his way toward her, a smile on his face. "What damsel is this?" he said, standing beside her.

She laughed. "Climb in, old man, and give me some more of your kisses."

"Old man? Once the medicine kicks in, I'll be back to my old self. Then, you'd better watch out."

Playing along, Aggie opened up her blanket and patted the spot beside her.

He plopped onto the bed and, with effort, swung his legs under the covers. Leaning back against the pillow, he let out a long sigh before turning to her. "Can't believe this is happening. You beside me. We should've been married all along."

"No, Donovan. It wouldn't have worked out back then, and I couldn't leave Arnold."

"You're right." He turned to her. "But, Aggie, will you marry me now?"

Aggie cupped his face in her hands, observing the sincerity in his handsome face, the way his dark eyes had softened with love.

"No, I won't marry you, but I'll be with you as much as I can. Marrying at this point would prove to be a legal nightmare. Let's just promise to spend time together. Later, after Blythe takes over the business, we can talk about it then."

He stiffened. "Maybe by then I won't want to marry you."

"Maybe not," she said amicably. Having lived alone for three years, she wasn't about to give up her freedom, something her family didn't understand. Everyone but Blythe that is. She, Aggie hoped, would come to appreciate this trip in a way she might not have done not so long ago.

"What I said isn't true. I'll always want to be with you,"

Donovan whispered in her ear, pulling her closer.

She relaxed in his arms, loving the feel of them around her. She might appear wanton to some, but she didn't give a damn. It was her life, and she was taking it back. She'd worked hard for her family, and now she was going to enjoy each day as it came, each opportunity for discovery as it came along.

Later, the sound of a car pulling into the driveway awakened her. She moved out of bed and slipped on the terry robe she had found in her room.

"Where are you going?" Donovan said, propping himself up on an elbow.

"Someone's here," she replied. "Probably the kids. I'll check. It's after eight-thirty. I never sleep this late."

"Maybe because you don't have me around," he teased, sitting up. "If it's the kids, can you please ask Logan to help me into the shower?"

"Sure." Aggie left him and walked into the living room as Blythe and Logan entered it. She gave Logan the message, and as he left, she said to Blythe, "Up and about, I see."

Blythe returned her smile. "We had the most delicious breakfast at Gracie's. It's a cute little restaurant just down the road at the Salty Key Inn. Then we walked around for a while. I really like this area. A perfect place for a wedding."

"A wedding? Are you and Logan talking about getting married?" Aggie's heart raced.

"What? No! For heaven's sake, Gran. Logan and I are just becoming friends! But someday, a beach wedding at a place like this would be beautiful."

"I agree. Come sit with me." Aggie headed into the kitchen and poured herself a cup of coffee. Blythe sat at the kitchen table, and Aggie joined her. "Donovan asked me to marry him."

"Whoa! Aren't things moving a little fast?" Blythe's face

drained of color.

"Not to worry," Aggie said, waving away her granddaughter's distress. "I have no plans to marry anybody. I want to keep my freedom. I'm telling you this because I want you to understand the importance of not only love but freedom. Chad was never going to allow you to grow and become the person I know you can be. At the same time, I hope you understand that I also have no intention of becoming promiscuous. Going from man to man at any age is reprehensible to me, and I hope to you."

Blythe studied her wide-eyed. "Even if you're not marrying Donovan, are you moving to Florida?"

"No, my darling. I must stay in Boston to train you, but I might schedule a lot of breaks to visit my dearest friend." A smile crossed Aggie's face, brightening it. "At my age, it's lovely to find an old friend, even more, a romantic one."

"So that is what this trip was all about? Reconnecting with friends and an old beau?"

"In part," Aggie said. "In this case, making amends following a series of mistakes in timing that should never have happened. Even if it all turned out well for me in the end."

"Dad and Constance won't be happy about this," Blythe said. "But I get it. I really do."

Logan walked into the room. "Am I interrupting?"

Aggie smiled up at him. "Not at all. I heard you had a nice breakfast."

Logan patted his stomach. "Gracie's is the best. I thought you and Donovan might enjoy going there sometime."

"And Gavin's looked spectacular for dinner," said Blythe.

"Wonderful. Why don't we make reservations for the four of us for tonight?" Aggie said. "I'm sure it will be fine with Donovan."

"What will be fine with me?" Donovan said, making his way

into the kitchen.

"Dinner at Gavin's tonight," Aggie said.

"Good place," said Donovan. "Okay by me."

Aggie got to her feet. "The kids have already had breakfast. How about my fixing you something? A bowl of cereal with fresh strawberries?"

"Sounds good." Donovan sat down at the table.

Aggie noticed Blythe studying him and felt her lips curve. She did not doubt that Donovan would end up charming her. He was such an interesting man.

That night, as Aggie walked into Gavin's with Donovan, she was amazed at the number of people who called out greetings to him.

"Didn't know you were so popular," Aggie said to him.

"It's all the community work I'm involved in," he said. "I try to do as much as I can for charities in the area. Many people are reaching out to faraway places to provide charity and are forgetting their own neighborhoods. I make sure the foundation takes care of those close to home."

A hostess greeted them. "We have the table you requested all ready for you, Mr. Bailey."

"Thanks," he said. "Are any of the owners here tonight?"

"Sheena was here earlier. She told me to say hello to you. She'll be back sometime later."

"Sorry to miss her," Donovan said. "I wanted to introduce her to my friend, Aggie."

The hostess beamed at him. "I'll let her know. Here's the maître d. He'll lead you to your table."

Aggie absorbed the sights and aromas around her as she followed the man to a table in a small alcove at the side of the room. After being helped into her chair, she waited for the others to be seated.

"This is lovely," she said to Donovan. The dark paneling of the main room glistened with light from sparkling crystal chandeliers and sconces mounted on the walls. Looking through the alcove's window at her side, she admired the twinkling white lights that winked at her from the green foliage and colorful flowers of the landscaping.

"It smells delicious," said Blythe. "I already know what I'm going to order."

"You do?" said Logan.

She gave him a bright smile. "I looked up the menu online. I want the sea bass."

Aggie patted Blythe's hand affectionately. "She's always known what she wanted."

The waiter arrived with menus, and while they perused them, a wine steward approached.

"How does everyone feel about a little sparkly champagne?" Donovan asked. Hearing their assents, he turned to the wine steward. "A bottle of Dom Pérignon, please. This is a celebration."

The wine steward bobbed his head. "Fine choice, sir. I'll bring it right out."

"How nice," Aggie said to him.

"It's not every day we can be together," he said, smiling at her. "Let's enjoy it."

Moments later, the champagne arrived in a silver bucket filled with ice, along with four tulip glasses.

As Aggie waited with the others for the waiter to uncork the bottle, she was unable to remember when she'd had an occasion to celebrate like this. With Arnold maintaining his sobriety, their celebrations had consisted of food, not alcohol.

After Donovan had approved the wine, Aggie watched while the wine steward poured a small amount of bubbly white wine into her glass.

Donovan lifted his glass. "Here's to life!"

"Hear! Hear!" Aggie said along with Blythe and Logan, feeling as if her life was beginning anew.

The dinner that followed was every bit as good as the waiter assured them it would be. Blythe loved her soy-and-honey-glazed sea bass served with a ginger-butter-and-cream sauce. The men ate every bit of their steak, and she, herself, knew that she'd always remember the snapper almondine she had chosen.

When it came time for dessert, they all demurred.

Later, as they prepared to leave the restaurant, a dark-haired woman approached the table. "Hello, I'm Regan. My sister Sheena asked to be remembered to you, Mr. Bailey. I hope your meal was excellent."

Donovan beamed at her and patted his stomach. "Superb as usual. Thank you."

"Wonderful! We're so glad you enjoyed it. We hope to see you again soon," Regan said before turning away to greet others.

"I'll always remember this evening," said Aggie. "Thank you."

"The first of many, I hope," he responded, winking at her.

Aggie returned his smile, feeling warm inside.

# CHAPTER FOURTEEN
## BLYTHE

When she got back to Seashell Cottage, Blythe went into her room, took off her dress and heels, and put on jeans and a sweatshirt. After a wonderful meal, she intended to take a walk on the beach.

"Where are you going, dear?" Gran asked when she joined the others in the living room.

"For a walk on the beach. I need to work off my dinner."

"Mind if I join you?" Logan asked.

Blythe hesitated. "Not at all." She waited on the porch while Logan changed his clothes. The moon, round and full, shone down on her surroundings, lending a silver glow to the landscaped area and beyond it to the sandy shore.

"Thanks for waiting," Logan said, joining her. "It's a great night. Like you, I need this walk."

They headed out.

Blythe stepped onto the sand and lifted her arms to the sky, wanting to embrace the shining globe in the sky. She felt so relaxed from the wine, the food, the company. She realized how regimented she'd become at school, wanting to be her best, anxious to please others. Chad had once called her too focused. Maybe he was right, she thought, staring at the water.

Moonlight crowned the tops of the waves that rolled into shore and kissed the sand before pulling away again. The ceaseless movement filled her with peace. How many years had this same water moved like this, she wondered. She gazed up at the stars twinkling above her. Had they always been here, or had they appeared one by one over time until they filled the sky? So many questions ...

Logan came up behind her and put a hand on her shoulder. "Beautiful night, huh?"

Desire threaded through her, weaving a magic she'd never felt. She turned and stared up at him.

His gaze met hers. He bent down and kissed her, tentatively at first and then with a sweet assurance she liked. Her arms came up around his neck, and she closed her eyes, allowing herself a moment to enjoy what she'd wanted all along.

After a moment, Logan stepped away. "I'm sorry. I shouldn't have done that." He paused, waiting for her to say something.

Surprised by his reaction, she swallowed hard and willed her heartbeat to slow. "We've both said we aren't ready for any relationships at this point in our lives."

"That's what I thought you'd say. I like you, Blythe. I really do."

The word *but* hung in the air, ready to sting her. She hurried away from him. She'd been hurt once and didn't want that to happen again.

He caught up to her. "Stop, Blythe. This went all wrong. I'm just trying not to rush you." He drew her to him. "Could we try again?"

She thought about all Gran had told her about freedom and pulled away. "I think you're right. We should stop this. But I'd like to be friends."

In the dark, his light eyes caught the glow of moonlight, allowing her to see the disappointment in them.

"I'm sorry, because I really like you too, Logan."

He let out a long breath. "Okay, then. Friends."

They didn't speak as they walked along the water's edge. It was just as well, Blythe thought. Life was complicated enough.


The next few days passed in a blur as Blythe relaxed in a way she hadn't allowed herself before. She had a better idea of what work lay ahead, finished her college paper, and with the drive home and final exams waiting for her, she decided to push all worries aside.

She and Logan continued to spend time together, walking the beach and talking. One morning Logan surprised her on the beach with a kite. "Thought we'd have some fun with this."

Blythe clapped her hands with delight. "What fun! I haven't flown a kite for a long time."

They opened up the colorful package and put together the kite, which had a long, rainbow-colored tail.

"It's beautiful!" Blythe exclaimed.

After the string on a special spool was attached, Logan grinned at her. "Okay, let's go!"

Side by side, they ran along the beach until the onshore breeze caught hold of the kite and lifted it into the sky. The string unrolled in a blur, and soon the kite was riding high in the sky. They took turns holding the kite string as the wind made the tail flap like a bird's wings.

A little boy Blythe guessed was about six came running over to them with a big smile on his face. "Can I fly it too?"

Blythe waited to see what Logan would say.

"Sure. What's your name? We'll hold onto the string together because it's pulling hard in the wind," he said.

"I'm Jonathan O'Keefe," the little boy said proudly. The boy gazed up at Logan with a look of delight.

"Okay, you can help too," Logan said, ruffling the boy's red hair.

Together Logan, Blythe, and the boy stood and watched the kite wave back and forth in the breeze. Blythe thought what a wonderful father Logan would make someday and felt her resolve about being just friends weaken until she reminded herself of the work ahead of her.

When the boy's mother called to him, Jonathan said, "Thanks!" to both of them, gave them a little wave, and ran over to her.

"I'm ready for a break," said Logan. "Why don't we tie this to a tree and let it continue to fly while we take a swim in the pool."

"That sounds wonderful. The sun is hot."

On the way back to the cottage, tugging the kite behind him, Logan found a suitable small palm tree and tied the string around its trunk. "Hope this works."

"Unless it's meant to fly free," teased Blythe.

"We'll see." He winked at her.

They walked back to the cottage, empty with Gran and Donovan gone, and went out to the pool.

Logan dived into the pool and emerged from the water with a grin on his face. "Refreshing. C'mon in!"

"I am." She stepped cautiously down one step after another.

"Baby! Just jump in!" chided Logan, swimming over to her and tugging on one of her legs.

"Help!" she cried, falling into his arms.

He held her up, and suddenly aware of skin touching skin, she went to move away. But Logan held tight, and when she gazed at him, their surroundings seemed to grow silent, and then his lips were on hers.

She didn't think, simply reacted, her body filling with need.

When they pulled apart, Logan's blue eyes pierced hers. "Wow."

"Yeah, well, we'd better cool it." She'd never been kissed like that, and it scared her. Before she could change her mind like she wanted, she swam away from him.

This time he let her go.


The next day, Blythe did her best not to act interested in Logan but played the role of a friend as they drove to Clearwater Beach for lunch as Gran and Donovan suggested. Thinking they wanted to be alone, she and Logan obliged them.

They found a fun Mexican restaurant and sat with other guests on a patio overlooking the beach, sipping cold beer.

"When do you think you'll decide on a job?" Blythe asked him, trying to keep the conversation going.

"Soon. I've decided to follow Donovan's suggestion and take a job in the location I want. That's Boston. Being there was good for me. Lots to do and see. Close to skiing and water sports like sailing. I like the four seasons."

"It's a great place to live. Lots going on," commented Blythe.

"An old roommate of mine lives there. I can bunk in with him for a while if I get the job I want."

"Sounds good. I hope you get it."

Their food came. Blythe was happy to devote attention to it because the thought of Logan living in Boston was rattling her.


When the last day at the cottage arrived, Blythe decided to make the most of it and headed up the beach alone. Breakfast at Gracie's would be her last treat before getting things organized for the trip home. With luck, if she pushed herself, they could easily make it back to Boston with plenty of time for her to fly back to Ithaca without her family knowing.

That afternoon, she watched Donovan and Gran head to the beach. The medicine Donovan had talked about had settled a flareup of his MS, and, feeling and moving better, he wanted to exercise his legs.

"Guess after tonight I might not see you," said Logan taking a seat on the porch in a chair beside her. "I have something for you. A trinket, really. But it's my way of saying thanks for being understanding about the time in the pool."

She turned to him with a smile. "Thanks. It's nice to have a guy friend. I appreciate all the times you listened to my ideas about the business while we walked on the beach. That means a lot to me."

"You're going to be great." He handed her a small, white cardboard box. "Here. As I said, it's something small. I noticed it in one of the tourist shops we've visited. Hope you like it."

Blythe took the lid off and studied the sterling silver necklace mounted on a card and the jagged piece of green stone that hung from it. "What is it?"

"Turn the card over."

Blythe read the message on the back:

*A reminder of Florida sunsets and the green flash that comes with them to bring you luck.*

"Oh, how sweet! I love it!" she exclaimed. "Here. Help me put it on."

They unhooked the necklace from the card, and then Logan looped it around her neck. He studied it and then looked into her face. "It brings out the green in your eyes."

"I'm going to wear this for a long time to remember ... everything."

"Good. Overall, it's been a great week. After you leave, I'll have to make up my mind about job offers."

"Think about Boston," Blythe said. Though the thought unsettled her, she wanted him there.

"Will do. Thanks."

As they stood facing one another, the sound of sirens caught their attention.

"Wonder what's up," Blythe said. As the sound grew louder, she reached for Logan's hand. "Sounds like it's getting closer."

An emergency vehicle, followed by a fire truck, pulled into the driveway.

Logan dropped Blythe's hand and jogged over to the man climbing out of the emergency vehicle.

Blythe followed at his heels.

"Hey! What's going on?" Logan asked.

"We got a call about a woman falling," the EMT said. "Where is she? Inside?"

"What? No, there's no one inside. You must have the wrong place," said Logan.

"Is this Seashell Cottage? Does a man named Donovan Bailey live here?"

Blythe felt the blood drain from her face. "Oh my God! It must be Gran!" She turned to the EMT and the woman accompanying him. "My grandmother and Donovan took a walk on the beach. That must be where it happened. Donovan must have called you from his cell. Come this way!"

Blythe's pulse sprinted through her, leaving her fighting for breath as she trotted toward the beach, Logan at her side. Worries swirled in her head. *Had Gran tripped? Or collapsed on the beach from a heart attack?* The thought of Gran dying brought tears to her eyes. She tripped.

Logan grabbed her arm. "Hold on!"

As soon as they stepped onto the sand, they saw a crowd

gathered a distance away.

Blythe picked up speed.

Logan kept pace at her side, looking as worried as she felt.

The EMTs arrived ahead of them and began moving the crowd back, clearing Blythe's view. Gran was lying on the ground. Donovan knelt beside her, holding her hand.

Bile rose in Blythe's throat. She speeded up and raced to her side. "Gran! Gran! Are you all right?"

Gran looked up at her and grimaced. "I think I broke something. It really hurts."

Blythe gazed down at her grandmother. "What happened?"

Gran glanced at Donovan.

"She was dancing on the beach and fell," Donovan said. "A pure accident."

"Dancing? Gran, that's outrageous!"

"The good thing is you fell on the sand," said the EMT, checking Gran's vitals. "The bad thing is I think you might have landed on this large shell nearby. It looks like you hurt your hip. We're going to get you to the hospital and have you checked there. Your vitals are showing signs of stress but are otherwise fine. Still, we'll want to monitor you. We'll give you something now for the pain and get you onto our stretcher."

"No sirens, please," Gran said. Her lips trembled. She gazed up at Blythe with a pleading look. "Darling, I'm so, so sorry this happened. It makes a mess of our plans."

Blythe took hold of her grandmother's hand. "I'll have to call Dad. He deserves to know what happened. He'll want to be here."

"Let's wait until I'm given a diagnosis. Then we'll both call him." Her eyes began to droop from the medication. "Promise me, Blythe."

Blythe patted Gran's hand. "Okay. That's what we'll do." The thought of talking to her father made Blythe's stomach churn. What had started as a lark had turned into a disaster.

After helping Donovan to his feet, Logan came over to her. "I'll drive you to the hospital. Donovan is riding in the ambulance with your grandmother."

"Thanks," Blythe said, trying to hold back her tears.


The thirty-five-minute drive to Tampa General Hospital, where Donovan insisted Gran be taken, seemed to go on forever. But according to Donovan and the EMTs, the Joint Center there was one of the best in the country. Blythe agreed to seek the best care possible for Gran. Besides, her father would undoubtedly fly into Tampa, and the hospital on Davis Island was not too far from the airport.

Gran was taken to the Emergency Area, and an MRI showed a fracture of the femur. As the surgeon explained to her, total hip replacement wouldn't be required, but surgery to reduce the fracture would be in order.

Blythe listened to the doctor talk about their facility and the 30-bed unit for rehabilitation therapy. It all sounded so professional, and yet the idea of Gran going through all this made a sick feeling race through her. She clutched her head in her hands.

Logan patted her shoulder. "It's going to be all right."

"I want to see Gran before they take her into surgery," Blythe said.

The surgeon bobbed his head. "Come with me. They're prepping her now, but she might still be awake."

Blythe stepped into a curtained area and stared at her grandmother lying in bed. Needles had been inserted into her hand and taped in place. Liquid from a plastic bag full hanging from a pole next to her bed slowly dripped through tubing into her. Wires were stuck to her body in various areas, leading to a heart monitor, and other monitors recorded vital signs.

A dreamy smile crossed Gran's face when she noticed Blythe. "So sorry about this, darling. I was doing so well dancing on the beach."

Sighing, Blythe patted Gran's free hand, wondering if Constance was right and Gran was losing her mind. "I'll call Dad and tell him what happened. I'm sure he'll come right away."

"No! I don't want to ruin his vacation. I'll be here in Florida for a while."

"He needs to know," Blythe said simply. "Don't worry. It'll all work out." Blythe knew she was being optimistic. Her normally easy-going father would be pissed at Gran for not telling him the truth about where they were and for her antics on the beach.

"How's Donovan?" Gran asked, her voice fading as she closed her eyes.

A nurse came inside the curtained area and checked the monitors that tracked Gran's vital signs. "Looks like she's ready. Someone is coming from the OR to get her at any moment. I suggest you say goodbye to her now."

The nurse left. Blythe took a moment to study the woman she loved like no other. Gran seemed so small, so fragile, so old without her usual smile lighting her face. Tears filled Blythe's eyes. She leaned over and kissed Gran's cheek. "Please keep her safe," Blythe whispered, and she left to find Logan and Donovan.

Donovan was sitting in a chair in the surgical waiting area, holding his head in his hands. Logan was sitting next to him, checking his phone. When he noticed her, Logan jumped to his feet. "How is she?"

Donovan rose and gave her a worried look. "How is Aggie doing?"

"She's about to be taken into the operating room." Blythe glanced at Donovan. "She was wondering how you were."

Donovan swiped at his eyes with the back of his hand. "All my fault. I should have made her stop. But she was having so much fun."

"It's no one's fault," Blythe said.

"Accidents happen," added Logan, patting Donovan on the back.

"Logan's right. Gran wouldn't want you to blame yourself," Blythe said, trying to reassure him.

Donovan sat back down. "I'll make it up to her. I promise."

"How about fresh coffee? Or water?" Logan said. "I'll go find some."

"Water," said Blythe. "Thanks."

"Me, too," said Donovan.

Logan gave them a salute and left the room.

Donovan turned to her. "Blythe, I want you to know how much your grandmother loves you, admires you, and believes in you. You're an exceptional young woman, much like she was at your age. I know your time at the Seashell Cottage has turned out to be much different from what you might've thought, but I want you to know how much I appreciate your willingness to give Aggie and me special time together. If your family gives you any trouble about it, let me know, and I'll help however I can."

Blythe walked over to the single window in the room and stared out at the busy scene. Among the buildings on the medical campus, palm trees swayed in the breeze. This vacation had been the best, the worst of her life.

She turned back to face Donovan. Lines of worry marred his face, making him look older than he had just a few hours ago. It was obvious how he felt about Gran. Were the two of them so wrong to have a little fun in their lives? Blythe knew she'd have to defend them.

"Are you going to call your father?" Donovan asked.

"Yes, as soon as we see the surgeon following the operation."

Donovan shook his head. "I think you should call him now. It will give him more time to get a flight out of Hawaii. You can tell him she's under excellent medical care."

"I suppose you're right." Blythe let out a worried sigh, pulled her phone out of her pocket, and headed outside, dreading the call. In the warm air, she took a seat on a bench and clicked the button for his number. It was two o'clock in Tampa, which meant it would be eight A.M. in Hawaii. She hoped he wasn't still asleep.

"Hey, Blythe! How are you? Getting your work done at school?"

"Actually, I'm in Tampa with Gran. There's been an accident. She fell and fractured her femur. She's in surgery now at The Joint Center at Tampa General Hospital and is under excellent medical care."

"Whoa! Tampa? What in hell are the two of you doing there?"

"It's a long story, Dad. We had planned to leave tomorrow and drive back to Boston."

"You drove to Florida from Boston? Are the two of you crazy? My God! What surgeon is operating on Mom? What exactly happened?"

"Dr. Robert McDonald is the surgeon," Blythe said. She was grateful that the doctor's first name wasn't Ronald. That's how crazy this whole circus seemed. "Look, Dad, I've got to go. I want to be there when the surgeon comes to speak to us. Let me know what flight you're on, and I'll pick you up at the airport."

"But ... "

"' Bye, Dad," Blythe said firmly and clicked off the call. If she gave him much more information, he'd work himself into a rage by the time she was to pick him up at the airport.

# CHAPTER FIFTEEN
## AGGIE

Aggie heard voices and dragged herself out of the fog in her mind. *Where am I? What happened?* In time, an image of her laughing and dancing on the beach played out in front of her. Then, the fall. The horrible fall.

She tried to move her left leg and groaned—pain shot through her.

"Take it easy, sweetie," said a voice to her right.

Aggie turned her head.

A woman wearing scrubs and a cap covering her hair took hold of her hand. "Coming around, I see. The operation was a success. You're going to be good as new."

"Water," Aggie croaked.

"I'll give you some ice to suck on," the nurse said. "We don't want to put much of anything into your stomach right now. Later, you can have water or juice."

Aggie felt the coolness of the ice cube that had been slipped into her mouth, grateful for the wetness. Her eyes closed again.

What seemed like moments later, Aggie heard a voice saying, "Gran? It's Blythe. I'm here."

Aggie opened her eyes and gazed at the angelic face staring at her with concern. "I made it," Aggie said. "Where's Donovan?"

"He and Logan are in the waiting area. You can see them after you are in your hospital room. They both said to say hi."

"Good men," Aggie murmured. "Your father?"

"He's arriving tomorrow morning. I'll pick him up."

"Was he upset?" Aggie asked, knowing from the wary expression on Blythe's face that he must have been.

"Let's just say we've got a lot of explaining to do."

"Sorry, my darling. I'll say it's all my fault."

"No," Blythe said. "Though I'm sorry about what happened to you, I'm thrilled we made this trip. I won't let anyone take away the good things about it."

Aggie turned her head so Blythe wouldn't see her tears.

Aggie had just finished a session in the rehab area, walking and moving under the careful eye of a therapist, and was lying in bed resting when Brad burst into the room.

"Mom! I came as fast as I could. How are you?" He approached her bed, his face creased with worry. He gave her a gentle hug.

"I'm going to be just fine. The Joint Center here is among the best, and Dr. McDonald and his team did a wonderful job of repairing the bone."

"What kind of nonsense was it for you to come to Florida? You should be back home at New Life, where I know you'll be safe and well taken care of."

Aggie grabbed hold of Brad's hand and squeezed it. He'd always been a dutiful, caring son. "You make it sound as if I can't take care of myself."

Brad gave her a pointed look. "And you can? Really? I leave for a two-week vacation, and this is what happens."

"I can't stop living just because I'm getting older," Aggie said, trying to be calm and pleasant while inside her stomach was churning. This road trip was a crucial time for her, especially when she had plans of her own.

"Constance says you owe it to us to cooperate, that it's not fair to have us worrying about you."

Aggie felt unfamiliar anger rise within her. "I don't give a damn what Constance says. She's only cared about me because of the business. She wants you to take over for me. She wanted to move into my house in Dedham until you put a stop to it. And while we're talking like this, look at how she's treated Blythe all these years."

Brad's lips thinned. "I won't have you speaking about my wife that way."

"I applaud your protection of her, but it's the truth. And now it's time for me to take over my own life. With or without your approval."

Brad turned away from her, walked over to the window, and stared out. Aggie knew from the set of his shoulders how angry he was.

"Hi, Dad! Hi, Gran! Have I given you enough time to talk?" Blythe swept into the room like a breath of fresh air. "Feeling better today, Gran?"

"I've had my first session with rehab, and I'm doing very well," she replied with a note of triumph. Not everyone thought of her as an old lady who couldn't do anything right.

"Great. Do you know how much longer you'll be here?"

"I don't. But I've decided to go through the next few weeks of recovery here in Florida."

"Really? Where will you stay?" Blythe glanced at her father and sent Gran a warning look.

"I'll stay with Donovan," Aggie said, ignoring her. "It makes sense. He's got all kinds of equipment and facilities to help me. He's even offered to bring in a special aide—someone he's used before."

"Donovan?" Brad whipped around and glared at her. "Who is this guy? And why have I never heard of him before?"

"Because he was the man in my life before I married your father before you were born. Now, he and I are seeing each other." Aggie mentally waved away Blythe's white-faced concern. It was time to make a stand. "Donovan is ..."

"Right here," said Donovan coming into the room with Logan. Though he had a cane, he was standing tall and moving much better. He smiled at Brad. "You must be Aggie's son."

Brad held out his hand. "Bradley Robard."

"Donovan Bailey, an old friend of your mother's," he said, shaking Brad's hand.

"So I understand," Brad said, sizing him up. "Look, I appreciate that you and my mother are friends and all, but my mother belongs back in Boston, where I can step in to help her if she needs it."

"Why don't we let Aggie decide where she wants to be," Donovan said in a calm but steely voice that left no doubt in her mind that he would stand by her.

"Brad, I appreciate your concern as always, but I'm perfectly capable of making up my mind. I've already talked to the people here about continuing rehabilitation for a few days before I'm released. I'll continue with exercises and such here in Florida until I'm ready to return to New Life. In the meantime, I'll check in with Suzie daily. You know how excellent she is as my administrative assistant. We have only a few more weeks until Blythe graduates. Then I'll come back to Boston to help train her."

Brad's shoulders slumped. "You've got this all planned out. Is there anything I can say to make you change your mind?"

Aggie shook her head. "No, darling. There'll be some other changes too. But we can talk about those later. I love you and thank you for coming here. I'm sorry to ruin your vacation."

Brad gave her a sheepish look. "I was getting bored sitting on the beach all day. Constance and the boys are staying in

Hawaii for a couple more days, but I'll fly to Boston from here."

"I've called the rental office about the cottage. I'm to pick up our things this morning," said Blythe.

"Good. I know they have to prepare the house for their next guests. You can take my things to Donovan's house. And, sweet girl, I'll pay for an airline ticket to get you back to Ithaca. We'll keep my car here for the time being."

"Okay. You're right. I'd better get back. I have another paper to finish polishing before wrapping up my classes."

"Why don't I ride down to the cottage with you, Blythe? You and I need to talk," her father said.

Blythe grimaced. "I know."

"Remember, you two, all the blame is mine," Aggie said. "This road trip to remember was all my idea."

Brad's eyebrows rose. "Road trip to remember? Is that what you're calling this?"

"Yes, indeed," Aggie said with more than a little satisfaction in her voice. "Now, you two come give me a kiss before you go. Donovan's here, and I need my rest."

# CHAPTER SIXTEEN
## BLYTHE

As Blythe and her father were leaving the room, Logan came to the door.

"How's your Gran doing?" he asked Blythe quietly.

"Very well. She's making a nice recovery. Guess she's going to be staying with Donovan for a while."

"And you?"

"I'm flying to Ithaca as soon as I can. Right now, I'm taking Dad down to the cottage with me while I pack up." She turned to her father. "Dad, I'd like you to meet Logan Pierce, a friend of mine."

"A new friend?" Her father asked as he held out a hand to Logan.

Logan shook it. "Yes, we met through Donovan. I've been helping him out for a couple of weeks while his son, Curtis, is on a book tour."

"Curtis Bailey writes thrillers," said Blythe.

"Curtis Bailey? I just finished his latest book," said her father, sounding impressed.

"He's talented," said Logan. "When he gets back home, I'll make a final decision on a job and move on."

"One of his offers is from a company in Boston," Blythe said, giving Logan an encouraging smile.

"Tremont Associates," Logan clarified.

"Excellent." Blythe's father said. "Good luck."

"We'd better go," said Blythe.

"Will I see you again?" Logan asked.

"Probably not. As I said, I'm flying back to New York as soon as I can after I get the cottage cleared out and Gran's things taken to Donovan's house."

Logan frowned. "Let me check with Donovan. Maybe I can help you. What are you going to do about the car?"

"We'll leave it at Donovan's for the time being."

"Why don't I drop you off at the airport then?"

"That would be great," said Blythe. The thought of leaving without saying a private goodbye was unsettling. They might have agreed to be friends, but she wanted to have an opportunity to see him again.

"That would be helpful, Logan," her father said. "I plan on leaving sometime tomorrow, but if we can get Blythe on a flight today, she could get back to her studies."

A thread of resentment wove through her. He was treating her like a child. She was almost twenty-two and about to graduate from college, for God's sake! No wonder Gran was rebelling.

After getting Gran's car out of the parking garage, Blythe headed down the coast. She'd spent only a few days at Seashell Cottage, but she loved it there. As she'd told Gran, if the time ever came for her to get married, she hoped it could be on a beach similar to the one in front of the cottage. Between the beach at Seashell Cottage and the restaurants at the nearby Salty Key Inn, it was the perfect place for a wedding.

Her father's voice interrupted her musing. "I'm disappointed in you, Blythe. How could you be so ... so ... deceitful? You and Gran making some sort of secret road trip? If she'd wanted to go to Florida, she could've flown there without involving you. All she'd have to do is ask us."

"No, Dad," Blythe said, shaking her head back and forth. "She shouldn't have to ask anyone. Gran's a healthy, bright woman who has the right to choose for herself how she'll live. She moved into New Life to make you happy, but it isn't enough. There are things she wants to do, people she wants to see, and places she wants to visit."

"Constance is concerned about her mental health," her father continued.

"Gran's mental health is fine. She's as stable as you. I know you don't want to hear it, but Constance is concerned only about herself and her social appearance. She wants to keep it about being married to the head of the family corporation."

He sighed wearily and gazed out the window. "You and Constance have never gotten along."

"That's beside the point. Gran and I both know Constance will make a fuss when she learns about the new arrangement of my taking over for Gran. Is it going to bother you, too?"

Her father studied her and shook his head.

Blythe continued, "Gran hopes it will give you the chance to teach at one of the universities like you've always wanted. Not that you can just walk away from the business. She said if you had to take over her duties too, you'd never have the chance."

"You think you know someone, and then suddenly it's clear that you don't." He glanced at her. "Is this Donovan guy after Gran's money?"

Blythe couldn't help laughing. "No. He's got more than enough of his own. He manages a charitable foundation with only some of his family's resources."

"Then why does he seem overly protective of her? What's going on? I don't get it. Why are they both acting this way?"

"Because I believe they truly love one another," Blythe said. "It's a long story. I'll give you the basic details."

When Blythe finished talking, her father was quiet.

"It sounds like something out of a romance novel—a lost letter, a rich family who didn't want her," he finally said.

"Yes, but as Gran told me over and over, it worked out well for her because Papa was the love of her life. The two of them together were an inspiration to others. You know that."

"Yes. Many people told me so. It just seems odd that this new guy suddenly appears in her life again."

"He's not a new guy."

"Still, I don't like it. Did she make this crazy road trip because of him?"

"Gran didn't make this journey only to make amends with Donovan. We stopped to see others in her college gang. All nice people who were important to her. People she wanted to see for perhaps the last time. And when we started out, she wasn't sure Donovan would even allow her to make things right between them."

"Where does that leave us? She'll stay in Florida for a while. You'll go back to school, and then what?"

"I'll come to Boston, find a place to live, and began training with you and Gran. It'll all be okay. Maybe the changeover is a little faster than we'd planned. That's all."

"You can live with us until you find a place," her father said.

"Thanks, but no thanks," said Blythe. "You know that never works out. The only reason Constance wants me around is to babysit the boys. When I told her I had no intention of staying with the boys while the two of you went to dinner and did whatever she wanted in Hawaii, Constance got mad and disinvited me. My not going there wasn't about my need to stay in school. It was about our argument. And, as usual, you didn't say or do anything about her behavior."

"I didn't ... realize. I ... I'll find a time to talk to her about it. I hate for this friction between you two to go on and on." He worked on his phone for a while and then clicked off. "Got your flights home. You'll go from Tampa to New York and then catch a night flight to Ithaca, leaving New York at about 9:30. It's the best I could do."

"Thanks." Now that the road trip was over, she was anxious to get back so she could leave Cornell in excellent standing and begin her new life as a young executive—a job she'd been training for over a long time.

It wasn't until she was pulling into the driveway of the Seashell Cottage that Blythe remembered Donovan's clothes in Gran's bedroom. Her father would not be happy about that. But as she'd told him earlier, Gran didn't have to ask anyone's permission for Donovan to stay with her. Still … it would be awkward.

Her father got out of the car and looked around. "Very nice."

"You should see the beach. It's beautiful! Soft white sand that goes on for miles."

"Wonder where Gran heard about it."

Blythe grinned at the memory of the women giving Gran a send-off. "Two of her friends at New Life told her about it. They think it has magical powers. They sent one of their staff members here, and she ended up marrying some guy who owns hotels."

Her father scowled. "Is that why she came here?"

Blythe laughed. "No. She liked it because this area was as close to Hawaii as she could imagine. Come inside. It's nice."

They stepped into the house, which was tidy except for the kitchen, where Blythe had sorted through the cupboards for their departure.

"Why don't I put together some lunch, and then I'll finish

cleaning the kitchen. I'm all but packed."

"What about Gran's things? I can pack those up for you," her father suggested.

"Not to worry. I've got it. Why don't you sit on the porch and relax while I make salads for lunch? Want a soda? Water? Iced Tea?"

"A bottle of water would be great. I'll get it." He grabbed a bottle and headed out.

Blythe worked quickly. She put green lettuce leaves in a bowl and then slivered all the leftover sliced turkey, ham, and swiss cheese and added it to the salad before tossing it with a lemony dressing. She was just about to place the salad bowl on the kitchen table when her father entered the room, holding Gran's robe.

"After looking around, am I correct in thinking that a man, Donovan no doubt, shared my mother's bedroom?" His icy voice cut through the room like a sharp-pointed icicle.

Blythe set the bowl down and faced him. "It's not what you think. Besides, Gran is a grown woman. Until yesterday Donovan was using a walker, unable to get around much. A flareup of his MS."

"I don't give a good goddamn about his condition; he was sharing my mother's bedroom. And with you in the house."

"Me and Logan," said Blythe, purposely baiting him. She relented and added, "In separate suites. Logan is Donovan's physical assistant until Curtis gets back."

Her father clapped his hands to his head. "I can't believe this whole mess."

"Dad, you sound older than Gran."

He sank onto a kitchen chair. "I thought I knew her. She was always so strict with me."

"Not so strict that you didn't impregnate my mother," Blythe reminded him. "You're making this seem worse than it is. Gran, like everyone, simply wants to be loved."

Her father gave her a thoughtful look. "You're right. We all need that."

Blythe went over to him and wrapped her arms around him. "Love you, Dad."

His eyes filled. "I love you too, pumpkin."

While they were eating, Logan called her. "I'm on my way to help you. I'm to lead you to Donovan's house so you can leave your grandmother's car and her things there."

"That's great. I've got Donovan's things packed up too."

"See you shortly."

Her father gave her a questioning look.

Blythe filled him in. "After I take care of the dishes, I'll check the house once more to make sure nothing is left behind."

"If you'd like, I'll make sure everything is in order outside."

"Thanks, Dad." Blythe took a last bite of salad and rose. She was anxious to leave everything spotless, so if she ever wanted to make a reservation in the future, she'd be welcome. The more she thought about it, the more she liked the idea of a beach wedding. Her wayward thoughts flitted to Logan. She put the last dish in the dishwasher and moved on.

By the time Logan pulled into the driveway, Blythe was satisfied with the way things looked. She knew Gran would be pleased.

Logan got out of the car and shook hands with her father, who'd been waiting for him. Seeing them together, she thought how right it seemed that two of her favorite men seemed to like each other.

She rolled Gran's suitcase toward them.

"Here, let me get that," Logan said, taking the luggage and

loading it into Donovan's car.

While Blythe closed up and left the key in a lock box, her father helped with the other two bags as requested.

Her father rode in Gran's car with her as they followed Logan into downtown St. Petersburg and then northeast into Snell Isle, where signs indicated the Vinoy Golf Club was situated.

"Look at that gorgeous house," said Blythe, driving along Snell Isle Boulevard.

"Guess by the look of it, Donovan certainly doesn't need any of Gran's money."

Logan turned into the driveway and parked in the front circle of a stunning, two-story house whose beige-stucco exterior was softened by lush landscaping.

Blythe pulled up behind Logan, and she and her father got out.

Logan turned to Brad and said, "Sorry we don't have time for me to show you around, but I promise you that if Aggie stays here, she'll have every advantage for a smooth recovery. Donovan has an exercise room, a small spa pool in addition to a regular one, and every convenience you can think of."

"I see," said Blythe's father. "We can talk more about that tonight. We need to head right to Tampa airport so Blythe can catch her flight to New York."

Logan nodded and turned to her. Through the lenses of his sunglasses, she could read the regret in his eyes.

She longed to reach out to him, have him reach out to her, but the moment passed without either of them moving forward.

# CHAPTER SEVENTEEN

## AGGIE

Aggie lay in her hospital bed thinking of Brad. Poor guy! She'd done a number on him, surprising him the way she had. But it was long past time when she'd continue letting her concern for him dictate what she would or would not do with her life. Brad was a good man, a kind man who'd been shattered by his nasty divorce from Blythe's mother, who'd used every mental trick she could to make him feel unworthy of her or anyone else. It was one reason he chose to be as non-confrontational with Constance as he sometimes was. She knew from experience that each couple had to figure out their own path.

She turned her head and gazed at Donovan nodding off in the chair next to the window. He was a wonderful man whose willingness to take chances served as a reminder to her to enjoy living more. His life hadn't been as easy as hers. He'd loved and lost and had gained a son in the process. His optimism about his disease encouraged her to work hard to get back on her feet. As much as she wanted to play, she wanted to be able to pass on the business to Brad and Blythe in good shape.

After Donovan woke, he left to get her a cup of coffee.

Logan and Brad returned to the hospital room.

"Blythe's all set. She should get to Ithaca late tonight," said Brad. "She and I made sure the cottage was pristine when we left it."

"Thanks. I'm glad." Aggie smiled at him and turned to Logan. "And thanks for helping out with the car and all the other things."

"No problem," he said. "Do you know any more about a release date for you?"

"The doctor said it could be the day after tomorrow if I keep to the exercise schedule they gave me. Then after another four weeks or so, I plan on returning to Boston. By then, Blythe will be ready to graduate, and we can begin to work together."

"In that case," said Brad, "I'll stick around here until you're released, and then I'll return to work. Constance and the boys will be flying into Boston at that time. She sends her best."

Donovan came back into the room carrying a cup. "Got your coffee, Aggie." He gave a little wave to Brad. "Everything set?"

"Aggie's car is at your house," Logan told him. "All your things too. Are you ready to go home, Donovan? I'll bring you back tomorrow as we all discussed earlier."

"Sure thing. I know Aggie wants some time with Brad."

"Indeed, I do," Aggie said. "Even though we work at the same company, we often go days without being able to sit and visit with one another. Now's a good time to do it."

While Donovan gathered his jacket and phone, Aggie wondered what he'd do about saying goodbye. Would he try to kiss her?

He looked at her, winked, and gave her a quick peck on the cheek. "Keep up the good work. I'll see you tomorrow."

Her cheeks felt hot as he and Logan exited the room.

Brad watched them leave and took a seat in the chair near her bed. "It feels so odd to see you with another man, not Dad."

"I'm as surprised as you by how this reunion has gone. It feels so wonderful to see Donovan and pick up where we left off so many years ago."

"Are you hiding something from me? Are you sick or dying?"

She clasped his hand. "No, my darling. I just want to get a few things in order. It was delightful to see some of my old classmates. Blythe and I even stopped in Washington, D.C. to see the Vietnam Veterans Memorial in honor of your father."

"How did that go?"

"It's very emotional to see it, which is why your father never wanted to go there. But I think he would've been glad we did it for him."

"Ah, another loose end taken care of, huh?"

Aggie's heart filled with love for her son. Because of Arnold's drinking, their relationship had been unstable. For that reason, Brad had always been protective of her, which is why he'd pushed her toward living at New Life. "Yes, I guess you could say that."

"So where is this thing with you and Donovan going?" Brad asked, gazing into her eyes.

Aggie shrugged. "We've talked of doing some traveling together. He's getting over a flareup of his disease but will still need some assistance. Me? I realize I've had little opportunity to travel and like the idea of seeing new places, meeting new people."

"So that's why you're rushing to bring Blythe into the business?"

"Only in part," said Aggie. "I see how many hours you put in per week and didn't want to burden you with more. Just as I'm learning to have a bit more fun, I want you to have more time to do whatever you want. Being at New Life has made me realize that I have a lot more living to do."

"It's a wonderful place for you, Mom," Brad said earnestly.

"I agree. But I'm going to be leaving it from time to time to do my own thing. Several of my friends living there do that."

"I never wanted you to be unhappy. I hoped you'd have the relief of not worrying about the house and would be comfortable having help nearby whenever you might need it."

Aggie reached out for his hand and squeezed it. "I know that. You're one of the nicest people I know. I'm proud that you're my son. I love you."

"I love you too, Mom," Brad said, hugging her.

Aggie's eyes filled. It seemed like yesterday Brad was just a boy saying those very same words.

# CHAPTER EIGHTEEN
## BLYTHE

Even though she was working far into the night to catch up on classes and get a second paper done, Blythe was happy she'd made the trip with Gran. For the first time in her life, she was comfortable with who she was and where she was going. In the past, she and Gran had talked about her new position, and Blythe had spent some time training with her. Now, being this close to taking over was something Blythe was thinking about in a whole new way.

Her father drove over from Boston to see her, telling her it was something he'd always wanted to do but never felt he had the time for it. They talked about her upcoming position for a while and agreed that though they'd both work hard, each of them should follow Gran's steps and spend more time doing things that were fun.

One day, she bumped into Chad in the Arts Quad. He gleefully spoke about his new girlfriend, watching her reactions. Blythe listened politely, happy to let him go on because instead of hurting her as he might have wished, she thought of how fortunate she was they'd broken up. Now that she'd met Logan, Chad's total opposite, she knew what kind of man she wanted for the future.

In mid-May, after exams and before Commencement, Blythe flew to Boston to look for an apartment. When her father met her at the airport, he was driving a silver BMW X3.

"New car?" she asked.

"Yep." He handed her the key fob. "It's yours. A little gift from Constance and me."

"Really?" Blythe cried with surprise. "It's adorable."

Her father laughed. "Adorable? It's a great little car. Figured you wouldn't want anything big with the traffic and parking problems here."

She threw her arms around him. "It's perfect! Thank you so much!"

They loaded her suitcase in the back, and then her father sat in the passenger seat and spent a few minutes explaining all the features of the car with her.

As they left Logan International Airport, Blythe allowed herself another squeal of excitement. "I love her! She's so perfect."

"She?" her father said, grinning at her, pleased by her excitement.

"Of course," Blythe replied, laughing. "I'll have to think of a good name for her."

"Where are we going?" he asked when she headed downtown.

"There's a condo in the Leather District of Boston that I want to look at. A friend of mine lives there and thought I'd like it. I might even consider buying it with my savings as a down payment. Do you mind going with me?"

"No. I've got all the time you need. I've taken the afternoon off."

They drove through the Mass Turnpike Tunnel under Boston Harbor into Boston and made their way toward South Station until she found the location on Beach Street. She was able to find a parking spot down the street. "Here's the area she said was great for young professionals."

"Pretty pricey, I'm sure, but then everything has become that way in Boston," her father said. "Are you sure you don't want to be closer to our headquarters?"

Blythe gave him a thoughtful look. "I want time to enjoy being with others. If I'm too close to work, I'll find myself there for hours at a time when I should be through for the day."

"I see your grandmother's lessons have made you think about these things. You're right. You should be where the action is for young people."

"It doesn't mean I won't eventually move into the suburbs," Blythe said. "But not until I'm ready."

"Fair enough. Let's go look at this place. Shall we?"

They walked down the street to the red-brick building. A woman was waiting outside. "Are you Blythe Robard?" she asked with a distinct Boston accent.

"Yes," Blythe said.

"Glad to meet you. Joanne Davis. I got your message."

"Thanks for meeting me. This is my father, Brad Robard. My friend Liz Calloway spoke to me about the condo for sale in this building. From her description of it, I think it might be suitable for me."

"It's a lovely, 2-bedroom, 2-bath loft with exposed-brick walls in a professionally managed elevator building within easy walking distance of South Station, Chinatown, Downtown, and the different areas of Boston," Joanne rattled off. "A wonderful opportunity for you. The owner regrets having to sell it, but he's just transferred to the west coast. His condo has just come on the market, which is why it's still available. Believe me; it won't last long because the building has private parking on a lot in the back."

"I'd love a look at it," Blythe said, growing excited about the freedom to live in the city away from the rest of the family.

Joanne led them inside to the small reception area and the elevator. "The condo is on the top floor with a lovely view of the city, another plus for you."

They rode the elevator to the eighth floor and exited into a narrow hallway.

Joanne directed them to the end of the hallway and unlocked a door.

As she stepped back so they could enter, she proudly announced, "This city home features a granite and stainless kitchen, a wall of four oversized windows, large laundry and storage room, central a/c, and additional storage in the basement."

Blythe entered the space and sucked in a breath. She loved the light, the open space, the texture of the brick wall meeting the shiny wooden floor. Careful not to give herself away, she walked through all the rooms.

"Well? What do you think? It's in perfect condition," said Joanne with a gleam in her eye.

"How flexible is the owner in the price? I've just started to look," Blythe said, though she'd been raking through online listings for weeks.

"Let's sit in the kitchen and talk," Joanne said. "I'm sure we can work something out."

An hour later, Blythe had a verbal agreement for the first right of refusal while she worked out financial arrangements with her grandmother. Gran had been encouraging her to move carefully. But after seeing the condo and knowing Liz would be in the same building, Blythe already knew she'd never find something more suitable than this. Her father, bless his heart, had kept quiet for the most part, signaling her with a lift of his eyebrows each time he thought she could do better with the negotiations. All in all, when she was through, Blythe was pretty proud of herself.

As they drove to her father's house in Wellesley, Blythe and her father discussed compensation for the work she'd be doing and arrangements for making a down payment on the property. "It's pretty safe to say, you'll be able to carry this property quite comfortably. Gran has been setting aside money in your name for some time, for just this purpose."

Blythe let out a sigh of relief. "Thank you both so much. I know how lucky I am."

"You've worked hard for the past several years, and you're going to work even harder in the days and months to come," he said.

"I know. That's one reason I'm happy to get settled and begin the journey."

Her father laid a hand on her arm. "Gran and I have talked. We don't want you to give your entire time to the company. We want you to have fun too. She's always worked hard and long hours and regrets she didn't have more time for fun. I suppose that is what was behind this road trip of hers."

"Something like that, and a lot more," Blythe responded, recalling their meetings with Gran's old friends.

"She's a great role model for you, Blythe," he said.

"Yes, I know. Now I just have to get used to living here again."

"I'm glad you are, but I'd better warn you that Constance has been working hard on a charity event that will be held the first week of June, and she's wrapped up in it."

"How are the boys? I can't wait to see them."

He grinned. "They're doing well in both school and sports. Matt loves lacrosse, and Mike is starting to play baseball."

"They're so cute," Blythe gushed. As much as she might not get along with Constance, she adored her little brothers.

She pulled up to the house in Wellesley that her father had built for Constance ten years ago. Many of the homes in the area were older, Colonial-style houses, but Blythe liked this two-story, stone and beige stucco design better. A huge window above the wooden front door indicated the sense of space and brightness inside. She parked her car in the spot to the side of the three-car garage and climbed out.

Two chestnut-brown-haired boys ran out the front door to greet them. "Hi, Sissy! Hi, Dad!" they cried, hugging her with enthusiasm.

Laughing, Blythe wrapped her arms around one boy, then the other. "Wow! You guys are getting big."

"Soon, we'll be as tall as you," Matt announced proudly, his dark eyes shining.

"You just might be," Blythe said, surprised by how much they'd grown since Christmas. Standing at five-six, she was still ahead of them, but not for too long.

"Mom says you got a new car," said Mike. "She says she doesn't know why you couldn't have her old car."

"Enough, Mike," warned her father. "This is the car your sister should have."

"Can I take a ride in it?" Matt asked.

"Sure. Hop in the back and buckle up," Blythe said.

Her father stood by while the boys got in the car. He watched as she pulled out of the driveway to take a spin around the block. He was still standing there when they returned.

When they went inside, Constance was in the kitchen.

"Hi, Constance," Blythe said. "Thank you so much for my new car. I love it."

Constance's lip twisted before she glanced at Blythe's father and forced a smile. "I'm glad you like it. Your father insisted on it."

Blythe fought to find some connection between them, but Constance had already turned away. Mike tugged at her arm. "Can you play a game with me?"

"Maybe later. I need to go over some paperwork with Gran on the phone."

The boys followed her like galloping puppy dogs. "I've got your suitcase," said Matt.

"Okay, buddy, thanks." It had become a ritual for one or both of the boys to carry her suitcase up to her bedroom, which was also used as a guest room. It was a "welcome home" touch she enjoyed.

"How long are you staying this time?" Mike asked.

"I have to go back to school the day after tomorrow to take care of a few things. Then I'm graduating."

"Yeah, I know. We're coming to Ithaca to see you," said Matt. "Mom thinks I might want to go to Cornell someday."

"It's a great school," said Blythe.

"I'm smart." Mike grinned at her. "Mom says so."

"Both of you boys are smart. Keep up the good grades, and you'll be able to choose where you want to go to college." She knew that as smart as the boys were, they didn't like studying.

"I know. Mom says we have to be ready to take over all the Robard stores."

"Really? We'll have to see. Lots of things can happen."

"I might not want to do that," Mike said. "I already told Mom I want to be a veterinarian so I can have lots of pets."

"Still no puppy?" Blythe asked, feeling sorry for him.

He shook his head sadly. "Nope. Not until we get a little older."

Blythe kept her frustration inside. She'd always wanted a dog, but Constance said they were too messy and far too much trouble. She'd thought Constance might give in to the boys when they requested one, but that hadn't happened.

Her father stuck his head into the room. "Ready to make that call? We'll do it in my den."

"Thanks, I'll be right there." She turned to the boys. "C'mon, guys, let's go."

Mike looked up at her. "I'm glad you're my sister."

"You are? Why?" Blythe asked, wondering what had inspired that comment.

"Just because you're nice. My friend, Jake, has a big sister who's mean to him."

Blythe gave Mike a hug. "I'm glad I'm your sister too. Love you. Love you both."

Matt came over to share in the hug. Constance could be difficult, but she'd done a good job raising the boys.

They followed her downstairs and left her at the door to their father's den.

Blythe walked in and sat next to her father behind his desk. He had all the paperwork from the real estate agent laid out in front of him. "Ready?"

He punched in Gran's number, and they waited for her to pick up. It had been almost four weeks since her surgery, and she was still living with Donovan so she could complete the customized rehab program the doctors had given her.

After three rings, Blythe heard her grandmother's cheery hello. "Hi, Gran! Great news! I've found the perfect condo for me. I want to make sure you're okay with it because it's not near the office."

"Let's hear all about it," Gran said.

Blythe gave most of the details; her father filled in a few.

"Sounds like it all might work. You're sure this is what you want to do? Where you want to live?"

"Oh, yes. The condo is in a convenient area full of young professionals. I should be able to meet a lot of people. Living in the city will be fun."

"You're right. It's time for you to have some fun while you're working hard for us. Brad, what do you say?"

"I say it's a good investment and will be very doable financially."

"Then I say, do it!" Gran said. "I've got to go. Donovan is taking me out to meet some of his friends. I can't wait to watch you graduate, Blythe. I'll be there early enough in the afternoon that we can all go out to dinner together to celebrate. I hope no one will mind, but I've made dinner reservations at a lovely Italian restaurant for all of us."

"Sounds nice, Mom," said Brad. "Thanks. How are you feeling?"

"Great! I'm almost ready to dance again."

Blythe and her father exchanged looks of horror. "Don't!" they said together.

Gran laughed. "Don't worry! I need to learn some new steps before I try again. See you later. And remember ... have fun! Love you."

Blythe clicked off the call, laughing.

# CHAPTER NINETEEN
## AGGIE

Aggie was still chuckling when the call ended. She was having fun with the whole idea of having fun! When had she and her family become such stodges? Time to change up a few things.

Donovan knocked on her door. "Ready, Aggie?"

She glanced at herself in the mirror. To enhance the way her blond hair was bleaching out in the sun, she'd agreed with her new stylist to dye her hair an eye-catching white in a ruffled, short style that made the angles of her face and her blue eyes stand out. Her skin, darkened to a delicate tan, complemented her hairstyle and other features.

"I'm as ready as I ever will be," Aggie replied and opened the door.

"Wow! That new dress looks great on you," Donovan said. "When they meet you, my friends will know why I've been such a homebody lately."

Aggie smiled at him. She loved the attention he paid to her. He was full of surprises. Who knew he'd be willing to shop with her and would even help her choose clothes more suited to the tropical feel of Florida?

"Where are we going for dinner?"

"Gavin's at the Salty Key Inn. I've arranged a private dining area there for our group. Figured that would be the easiest way for you and my friends to meet."

"How many other couples?"

"Just ten. People I work with, people from a couple of charities, boating buddies, and Blake and Hilary Hutton, neighbors and best friends."

"It sounds just right."

They traveled from St. Petersburg to Gulf Boulevard, the road that followed the beach. When Donovan pulled into the driveway of the Seashell Cottage, she turned to him with confusion. "I thought we were going to the Salty Key Inn."

"We are. But there's something I need to do here. Better come with me."

She climbed out of the car and followed him to the front porch. *Was he going to go in?*

He helped her up the stairs and into one of the rocking chairs. "I'll be right back."

He returned carrying a small cooler. "Thought we'd have a moment to ourselves before meeting our friends."

"Okay," Aggie responded, still puzzled by his actions.

He set the cooler down beside her chair and, instead of sitting in the chair next to her, he knelt in front of her.

Aggie's heart pounded as she stared in surprise when he took a small, black-velvet box from his pocket and opened it. Inside, a large round diamond flanked on either side by a smaller one winked at her from its platinum setting.

Aggie clapped a hand to her heart. "Donovan Bailey, are you asking me to marry you?"

A happy smile crossed his face. "That's exactly what I'm doing. The last few weeks have been the happiest of my life. You got away once; I don't intend for that to happen again. Agatha Robard, will you marry me?"

She looked into the face that had become so dear, saw the raw emotion that filled it, and felt her eyes well with tears. She leaned forward, cupped his face in her hands, and kissed him.

His arms came around her, and he deepened the kiss.

When they finally pulled apart, they were both breathing hard.

"Well?" Donovan said, his eyes sparkling. "Was that a yes? You said you wanted to wait, but I can't wait any longer. We can easily iron out any legal issues. So is it a yes?"

Aggie giggled happily. "Yes. Donovan Bailey, yes, I will marry you!"

Beaming with happiness, he slid the ring onto her finger.

She stared at it with amazement. What had begun as a road trip was turning into the most magical journey she could ever have imagined.

He groaned softly as he got to his feet. "I swear I'll be ready for a dance with you by the time we marry."

"Let's take things nice and easy. Arnold and I were rushed into marriage by the death of his father. This time, I intend to strut a bit and enjoy every moment of being engaged before walking down the aisle."

Donovan laughed. "That's more like you. Take all the time you want, as long as I know you and I will end up together. I love you."

"Knowing how committed we are to one another means the world to me. I've loved you for a long time, Donovan."

"I know." He pulled her up into her arms.

She nestled against his chest, feeling as if she was in exactly the right place. "What's in the cooler?" she asked when her gaze settled on it.

"Champagne. I thought we should celebrate."

"Definitely. But how about doing that later? Maybe in your spa tonight, after dinner. It would give us more time."

"You just want to be naked with me," he teased.

"Maybe," she replied coyly. It had crossed her mind.

###

Sitting at one end of the private dining room where a small bar had been set up, Aggie observed Donovan with his friends. The respect and affection he showed them made Aggie more certain than ever she was doing the right thing by marrying him. He was a lovely man who filled her days with an easy, loving companionship she'd never known.

Their neighbor, Hilary, came and sat down beside her. "Again, my congratulations! I'm pleased for you. And I've never seen Donovan this happy."

"Thanks," said Aggie. She liked the outgoing younger woman and her laid-back husband. They'd already made plans to have dinner together before Aggie and Donovan left to go to Blythe's graduation.

Donovan came over to her after Hilary left. "The waiter is indicating it's time for us to take our seats." He held out his arm to Aggie. "Come, my darling."

He led her to a table where she was seated with two other couples associated with Donovan's charity work.

As they worked their way through a five-course meal, Aggie was sated by both the delicious food and the interesting conversation around her. Donovan's life was full with both work and play. She realized how much personal time he'd devoted to helping her get well. Now that the flareup with his MS had passed, he was without a walker or a cane. But Aggie knew there might be more problems in the future.

"The children's fund is the one I'm most interested in having your participation," Donovan was saying to her now. "I've done my best with it, but I think a woman like you with a child and grandchildren will add a dimension I don't have."

Aggie filled with pride. "I'd like that. Once Blythe gets her feet under her, I have every intention of sitting back and giving her a chance to bring a different perspective to the business in new, exciting ways."

"Wish I could convince Curtis to do a little more with me, but his success has grown so fast, it's all-encompassing for the moment."

Aggie was curious about his son. He was an excellent writer. She'd made a point of reading his latest book and found herself both terrified and amazed by the psychological thriller.

Donovan rose to his feet with dessert—a lemon tart in a puff-pastry crust topped with strawberries and crème fraiche.

"Thank you, everyone, for coming to meet Aggie. You are special friends who've been there for me in troubling times of the past. I'm thrilled to have you share a joyous occasion of mine. Here's to the woman who makes me whole. Here's to Aggie."

Aggie's vision blurred as she gazed up at him. He was such a dear man.

When the cheers had calmed down, she managed to get to her feet. "I'm so grateful to meet you and to know how much you mean to Donovan. I hope to get to know each of you better and earn the affection you show him. Thank you so much."

People in the room raised water glasses, wine glasses, and coffee cups to her in a salute that touched her heart.

Donovan leaned over and kissed her on the lips. "Well done, darling." He lowered his voice to a whisper. "Now, let's get home to that spa."

She laughed. She was going to enjoy every moment she could with him.


Aggie leaned back against the side of the large spa and gazed up into the night sky, totally relaxed. The warm water swishing around her felt good on her hip. The wound had healed nicely, and she was getting good use of her left leg due to the daily exercises she faithfully performed.

Across the spa from her, Donovan winked at her. "Nice, huh?"

"Oh, yes. I'm so relaxed. It was a lovely evening, Donovan. You have such nice friends."

"They were impressed with you. So am I. Especially when you have no clothes on. Like now."

He moved toward her.

She held out her arms, and he drew close to her.

Nestling up against him, she became aware of his arousal and felt satisfaction. The chemistry between them was still there. Her pulse sprinted ...

# CHAPTER TWENTY
## BLYTHE

Blythe returned to Ithaca more anxious than ever to get through graduation. Now that she had a place of her own, she was already envisioning her new life in Boston. She and her friend, Liz, had walked through her condo making a list of things she'd need to furnish the space. IKEA made one-stop shopping reasonably easy. And what they didn't have at fair prices, other low-cost furniture stores in the area did. When she returned to Boston, she'd be able to put together her choices quickly.

Though her brothers wanted her close by, Blythe knew she was wise to stay in the city away from her stepmother. Constance was already making the trip to Ithaca for Blythe's graduation all about her. She had declared the trip needed to be made in her brand-new Mercedes sedan so she could be comfortable napping, that without it, the trip would be agonizingly long.

"*Whatever*," thought Blythe, clicking off the call with her father informing her they would arrive tomorrow afternoon in plenty of time for the dinner Gran had planned for that evening.

Blythe might have been tempted to skip Commencement altogether, but she'd worked hard to graduate, and her father and Gran had seen to it that she had no student loans to pay off, which deserved her willingness to participate in the ceremony. As was tradition, Commencement would take place on Schoellkopf Field from 10 AM to Noon on Sunday. Thankfully, the weather was forecast to remain pleasant, giving her and everyone else a glimpse of a rare lovely day in Ithaca.

On this Friday night, Blythe gathered with friends in the off-campus house where she'd been living for the past two years. She and the six other girls in the house were compatible mostly because they were independent women, each with her own interests. Five of the seven were graduating. The other two were juniors who'd already recruited new girls to take the places of those leaving.

They sat in the living room of the house, drinking wine and nibbling on treats, talking about their futures. Blythe was impressed by the ambition of her friends. One had been accepted at Weill Cornell Medical College in New York City, another at the Cornell Law School in Ithaca. All were determined to live productive, busy lives. One girl, in particular, announced she had no intention of living like her mother, that the man she married would have to understand she was free to choose her own path.

Blythe listened, wondering what her life might have been if her mother hadn't gotten into drugs and heaven knew what else. Though she was still alive, her mother was frequently in and out of rehab programs. Whenever Blythe tried to see her mother, she was told that her presence would only upset her. Blythe stared into space, recalling the last time they'd spoken. Her mother had been on something then. The distance in her voice had squeezed Blythe's heart dry. No wonder her father stayed with Constance. Despite her shortcomings, she hadn't thrown his life into turmoil. She was a far better choice, at least for her father.

The friend sitting next to her nudged her. "Are you okay?"

Blythe realized tears were rolling down her cheeks. "I'll be fine. Just a bad memory." She got up from the couch and went into the bathroom. It was at weird times like this that she ached for a loving mother. Thank God she had Gran.

Saturday was as bright and beautiful as promised—day one of a two-day weather spectacular according to the news on television. After breakfast, Blythe checked her belongings once more. She'd shipped the majority of her things to her father's house and sold the furniture in her room to one of the girls who was coming to live in the house. Blythe had neatly packed a few things like framed pictures, posters, and some decorative items in a box to go home with her in her father's car.

Though she'd thought of bringing her new car to campus, she'd opted to leave it at the dealership to have some last-minute detailing done. But she couldn't wait to drive it again. It was the perfect car for her.

After spending a lazy morning drinking coffee, lying in the sun, and munching on left-over food everyone had set out on the kitchen table, Blythe took a shower and dressed for the day. Her father had called from the road. As usual, he'd made sure the family had gotten off to an early start so they would have plenty of time to spend with Gran before going out to dinner.

Blythe packed her suitcases with the remainder of her clothes with a mixture of sadness and excitement and put her bedding in large garbage bags to protect it. Except for her troubles with Chad, she'd enjoyed her college years. Like Gran, she'd made a circle of friends with whom she hoped to keep in touch.

When her father finally pulled up in front of the house, Blythe felt a wave of love and raced out to greet him.

Laughing at the way she launched herself into his arms, he hugged her close. "Seems like yesterday we dropped you off at school. Where have the years gone?"

"Hi, Sissy!" said Mike. He clung to her waist and then moved aside so Matt could join them.

Blythe looked up to see Constance smiling at them. "The boys love you, Blythe. It will be good to have you closer to home."

Caught off-guard, Blythe returned the smile. "Thanks, Constance. I'm looking forward to being in Boston and on my own."

"Shall we get your things?" said her father. "We *might* have a little space left in the trunk of the car." He grinned at Constance.

"Now, Brad, you know I had to make sure I had the right things to wear," Constance chided in reply.

Brad laughed and held up his hands in surrender. "I'm not even going to go there."

"Men!" said Constance. "They don't understand ..." She placed a hand on Brad's arm and kissed him on the cheek.

Blythe watched, pleased to see both of them relaxed and playful.

After some careful repacking of the trunk, Brad loaded Blythe's things into the car, and they took off for downtown.

Blythe was happily settled in her hotel room downtown when she got a call from Gran. "We've landed and are driving into the city. Is the rest of the family already at the hotel?"

"Yes! Can't wait to see you!"

"Me, too. I have a few surprises for everyone." She hung up before Blythe could pump her for more information.

She called her father. "Gran just called me to say they're on their way here. She said she had a few surprises for us."

"Oh, no! I wonder what she's up to now. We'd better go down and meet her. Constance is with the boys at the Fitness Center, hoping to get some of their excess energy under control."

Blythe and her father were sitting in the lobby when a commotion caught their eye. Blythe's eyes rounded as Gran entered the hotel. Walking with a cane, Donovan at her side, Gran stood a moment, gazing around her as others in the lobby stared. It took Blythe a moment to take in all the changes. Gran's blond curls were now white, tipped in pink, accenting her tanned face. Large sunglasses obscured her eyes and matched the deep-rose of the cap-sleeved, linen dress she wore, showing the tiniest bit of cleavage. The only things missing and keeping her from looking like a Hollywood star were her shoes. Instead of spike heels, she wore plain, black-leather flats on her feet.

"Mom?" Her father got to his feet and gawked at her.

Gran beamed at him and lifted her arms in the air. "We made it!"

Blythe rushed over and embraced her. "You look ... awesome!"

Gran laughed. "I hope so. It took me a while to get ready."

Just then, Constance and the boys entered the lobby.

"Gran!" the boys cried in chorus, running over to her.

"Careful," Blythe warned them. "Gran's still recovering from surgery."

"Hello, Aggie," said Constance walking up to her. "My! You look so ... so colorful."

"Good. It took long enough to get everything just right." Gran patted her hair.

"Oh, my God! What's that on your finger?" cried Constance grabbing hold of Gran's left hand.

Gran beamed and held up her left hand for everyone to see the enormous diamond that sparkled in the sun coming through the hotel's front windows. "Oh, Constance! You haven't met my fiancé, Donovan Bailey." She turned to him. "Darling, this is Constance, Brad's wife, and these are their two boys, Mike and Matt. You know Blythe and Brad, of course."

"My pleasure, Constance," said Donovan pleasantly, shaking hands with her. "Bet these boys would like a ride in my jet."

Blythe held in a chuckle at the startled look that crossed Constance's face. "Jet? You flew here in a private jet?"

"Yes. We thought that might make the trip easier. I've planned another surprise for tomorrow."

"Dad! Dad! Can we go for a ride in Donovan's jet?" Both boys were tugging on his arm.

"I don't see why not, but please call him Mr. Bailey," said Brad.

"Or Gramps," said Mike, displaying a devilish grin.

Gran's laughter rang out. "Perfect. You can call him Gramps." She elbowed Donovan. "How about it?"

His cheeks grew pink. "Sounds about right." His gruff voice couldn't hide the pleasure in it.

Blythe exchanged sweet smiles with Gran.

"Let's get you settled in your rooms and then meet back here to celebrate," said Brad.

"I believe we're in a hospitality suite," said Donovan. "If you like, we can celebrate there with room service."

"That way the boys can be more comfortable," said Gran.

"Thank you," said Constance. "That's a good idea."

"Before we go up," said Gran, "we need to wait for ... Oh!

Here he is." Gran turned to Constance. "Logan Pierce is a friend of Donovan's son and someone who's been a big help to us. "He's on his way to Boston for a job interview and hopped a ride on the jet with us."

"Hi, Logan," Blythe said, trying not to sound breathy. "Guess you're another of Gran's surprises."

Logan laughed. "Guess so." He shook her father's hand, talked with Constance, ruffled the boys' heads of hair, and finally turned to her. "So, this is your big weekend?"

She returned his smile. "Can't wait to get moving ahead on my own. I found a great condo in Boston."

"Really? I'm staying with a friend of mine. He lives somewhere near South Station."

"No way! My condo is very close to South Station."

"Maybe we can meet up," Logan said. "It'll be great to have another friend in town."

Blythe forced a smile. She'd been a fool to ever hope of becoming more than a friend to him.

"Are you in college too?" Mike asked Logan.

"No, I graduated a couple of years ago. Now, I need to start my career."

"I'm going to become a veterinarian when I grow up," Mike announced.

"Not me," said Matt. "I'm going to study space. Someday we may all travel in space ships. That's what we talked about at school."

Logan grinned. "Sounds pretty exciting to me."

"I might have studied along those lines if I didn't already know what I wanted," said Blythe.

"Exactly," said Gran overhearing them. "Someday, boys, your sister is going to run our company."

Blythe returned Gran's smile but noticed Constance's frown.

It would take time before everyone was on board, but Blythe didn't care. She'd made a promise to Gran, and she was going to keep it.

# CHAPTER TWENTY-ONE
## AGGIE

Sitting in the hospitality suite, sipping a glass of wine, and with her family all together, Aggie's heart filled with joy. Constance was making an effort to be pleasant, especially now that she knew Donovan was more than just a nice guy; he was an influential man in Florida social circles who did a lot of good for others. And if Aggie, herself, had posed a bit and had fun springing surprises on them, it was all part of the changes she was enjoying.

"Hey, Gran," said Mike coming up to her and standing by her chair. "Did you really fall dancing on the beach like Mom said?"

"Yes, unfortunately, it's true."

His blue eyes, so like her own, studied her with concern. "If I'd been there with you, I would've held your hand really tight."

"Thank you, Mikey. When you grow up and become a veterinarian, you're going to make a wonderful one." She kissed his cheek. "I love you, sweet boy."

"Love you too, Gran," he said and ran over to his brother, who was watching television in the bedroom.

Donovan caught her eye. "Great kids."

"Thanks." Brad and Constance had done a nice job with the boys.

Aggie glanced at Blythe and Logan talking on the couch. He seemed smitten. She knew Blythe well enough to know she was taken with Logan but wasn't about to let him know. No use pushing it. In time, they'd figure it out.

The next morning, the sun shone in a bright blue sky as they were driven to the Commencement ceremony at Schoellkopf Field. As she observed all the new construction on campus, Aggie's jaw dropped. The crowded campus bore little similarity to the university she'd attended a little over fifty years ago. She'd heard about the changes, but she was still amazed to see the end product of the continued growth.

"So, this is where some of my money went," grumbled Donovan. "All this new stuff."

"Progress is progress," Aggie reminded him, though she felt more than a little overwhelmed by all the changes.

The ceremony itself was well organized, allowing faculty to make a grand entrance, speakers to talk, and students to receive their diplomas in relatively smooth transitions. Afterward, Aggie gathered her family around.

"Now, for my next surprise. Instead of going to a restaurant for lunch, I've arranged a catered picnic aboard the jet. You're all invited to join Donovan and me."

"What about Constance's car?" Brad said.

"Logan is happy to drive it to Boston if you wish," Aggie said.

"No. You'd better do it, Brad." Constance turned to the others and beamed. "After we bought Blythe's car, we decided on a new car for me."

Aggie bit her lip to keep from saying anything, warning herself not to intervene. It didn't surprise her that Constance would compete with Blythe even in this way.

Brad shrugged. "That might be the easiest way to handle it."

"Do you want me to go with you?" Blythe asked him, giving him a concerned look.

He waved her concern away. "No, thanks. The trip will give me some time to think about how to handle the next few weeks with your coming aboard. You may be taking over for Gran, but you need to know how we interface with one another. And then I plan to take a couple of weeks off."

"All right, darling," said Aggie, disappointed. "If that's the way you want it. Stop by the airport, and I'll give you food to take with you."

"That I will gladly do," he said, giving her a big smile.

As they left the campus to return to the hotel for their things, Aggie realized this was the beginning of many changes for the family. For a moment, she felt a clutch of panic.

Aboard the jet, the excitement on the boys' faces at being given a tour of the cockpit made Aggie smile. Brad had been like that as a young boy too. As he grew older and became more aware of their family's responsibilities, he grew more serious. She hoped her wishes for him to have more free time would bring back some of that former carefree attitude.

The catering service had done an outstanding job of packing sandwiches, chips, cookies, and a few salads for those who wanted them. Constance chose the latter, making Aggie wish she could relax a little more and simply enjoy the moment without worrying about her status or appearance.

She glanced at Blythe laughing with her brothers. She, too, would need to be reminded to have fun. Why, Aggie wondered, did it take so long for some people, like her, to learn that life lesson?

###

The flight was smooth. It seemed to take no time at all for the jet to land at Hanscom Field outside Boston. The limousines she'd ordered were there, waiting for them.

"How are we going to divide everyone up?" asked Constance. "You can ride with the boys and me, Aggie. We'll drop you off at New Life." She gave Donovan an uncertain look.

Aggie hid her satisfaction at the surprise she hadn't announced yet. "Not necessary. Donovan and I will drop off Blythe and Logan downtown, and then we're meeting my lawyer to sign papers for the new house I've bought at the New Life Community.

"What? What on earth have you done now?" Constance exclaimed.

"Donovan and I wanted more privacy than in my apartment. I thought it might be better if we were living in our own house at New Life, even though we'll be sharing our time between Florida and Boston."

Constance's lips thinned. "Does Brad know about this?"

"Not yet. We'll tell him when he gets here. He and I will go over a lot of different issues."

"I see," said Constance, clearly annoyed. "Come, boys. We'd better get home." Before she climbed into the limousine, she turned to Aggie. "I'll discuss this with Brad privately."

*I bet you will!* "Nothing to talk about. It's a done deal." After Constance and the boys left in one of the limos, Aggie turned to Donovan. "It's a good thing we did as you suggested and quietly got that done."

"I think it's great, Gran," said Blythe. "Those houses are nice."

"Not big or fancy, but quite comfortable," Aggie agreed. "Okay, let's get going. I can't wait to introduce Donovan to my friends at New Life. They're going to be so excited for me."

Blythe grinned at her. "They gave you quite a send-off. They'll be thrilled at the outcome."

Aggie could hardly wait. Rose would be beside herself when she met Donovan.

As she left the offices of Lowell, Brown, and Dickson, Aggie let out a soft sigh of relief. Chester Lowell had ensured a quick, easy transition for her from an apartment at New Life to a private, furnished home there. She was glad they had taken care of the matter quietly and swiftly. She didn't want any disagreement from her family. The move to New Life had made her realize she couldn't make life choices based on keeping peace in the family. Besides, now that she and Donovan had decided to live together, she wanted to make their relationship appear as proper as possible and still have all the benefits of New Life care.

As the limo carried them back to New Life in Dedham, Aggie called Rose to tell her she and Donovan would arrive soon. When they pulled up in front of the main building, Aggie saw a small crowd had gathered. Rose and Edith stepped forward to greet them, their faces creased by broad smiles. At the sight of them, Aggie's heart leaped. They'd become dear friends. Without their encouragement, she might not have rented Seashell Cottage.

"Brace yourself," Aggie said to Donovan. "They're all going to love you."

He grinned. "I'll do my best to behave."

"Until later, when we're alone," she said, giving him a teasing smile.

He laughed and followed her out of the limo, where Aggie's friends soon surrounded them.

Rose threw herself into Aggie's open arms and whispered.

"I knew it! That place is magical! Look at you! He's a ... a ...dreamboat!"

Aggie couldn't help laughing. She hadn't heard that word in years. She hugged Rose and turned to Edith, who was glancing from her to Donovan with a silly grin.

"Guess it works," Edith said. "Welcome home, Aggie."

"Hey, everyone! I want you to meet Donovan Bailey, an old friend of mine and ..." she held out her left hand, "... and my fiancé."

As applause rang out around her, Aggie felt a surge of love for the people here at New Life. "We're going to be living in one of the private homes here, but you're welcome to visit anytime. I love you all."

More applause rang out, and a couple of staff members came outside to join in the mini-celebration.

Donovan handled both the handshakes and well wishes, leaning on his cane from time to time as everyone introduced themselves. Observing them, Aggie realized these people had become like family to her.

While Donovan remained outside chatting with them, Aggie went inside to take care of some paperwork and to arrange to move her things from her apartment to the house.

Louise Dreher, head of housing arrangements, greeted her with a smile and a hug. "I was so happy to hear your news, Aggie. When one of our own finds happiness in this way, it pleases all of us. Let's see how we can make this move as easy as possible. You know from your first tour here how the houses are laid out and furnished. So, it's just a matter of moving your few personal items into the house and making it your own."

They quickly drew up a list of things Aggie wanted to be moved, and then she introduced Louise to Donovan.

"Welcome to New Life," Louise said, holding out her hand.

"I've set up an appointment with our health services director for tomorrow morning. She'll take care of gathering all your medical information. After that, you'll meet with me to talk about things like your favorite foods."

"Thanks." Donovan shook her hand and turned to Aggie. "We want to make sure everything is the way we want it. We haven't set a wedding date yet, but we know the importance of ensuring all legal issues have been resolved. We met with Aggie's lawyer today."

"It's a wise thing to do," said Louise. "Now, let me take you down to the house, and we'll check that out together to make sure everything is suitable."

Outside, they climbed onto a golf cart, and Louise drove them away from the main building to a collection of private homes at the edge of the massive, beautifully landscaped property.

"Nice," murmured Donovan, taking hold of Aggie's hand and squeezing it. "Summers here and winters in Florida."

She was thrilled by the idea. She'd spent many winter months in Boston. Too many, it now seemed.

Louise pulled up in front of a small, Cape Cod-style house. Aggie had first chosen an apartment over a house so she could more easily make friends. Now, living here with Donovan was the perfect way to have both privacy and nearness to her new friends.

Louise led them inside. It was pretty much as Aggie remembered it. Open space, small, compact kitchen with dining nook, gas fireplace, two bedrooms, two and a half baths. The interior was laid out with wide doors and no steps to accommodate wheelchairs and other equipment easily, should it be required. Still, with her few pieces of furniture supplementing the minimum of what was provided, it would be a cozy place for Donovan and her. When they needed to have space of their own away from one another, the facilities for New Life had every convenience, every option available for woodworking, pottery, and other crafts, a music room, a beautiful dining room, a library, most anything someone would want.

"What do you think?" Aggie asked. Donovan had easily gone along with whatever she wanted, but she needed to be sure he'd be okay here. Should he have another relapse, he'd have every facility he'd ever need.

"It's nice. Small, but nice." He winked. "I like the bed they provided."

Aggie laughed. A dual-mattress, adjustable bed with multiple positions for each was part of the regular furnishings.

"We'll serve dinner at five-thirty as usual," said Louise. "I'll leave the golf cart here for you and walk back to the main building. Things will be better organized tomorrow."

"Thanks for everything," Aggie said, showing Louise out, anxious to be alone with Donovan.

When she turned away from the front door, Donovan pulled her into his arms. "I feel like I should carry you across the threshold or throw you over my shoulder or something."

Aggie smiled up at him. "That day will come. How about some wine to celebrate? The catering company packed that, some appetizers, and treats for us to bring home."

"Sounds good," said Donovan. "It's been a long day. After dinner, I don't promise anything exciting."

"Me either," said Aggie. "I figure I can use the desk area in the master bedroom for my computer, and you can set up an office in the second bedroom. You need the space more than I do. I can always travel to the company office."

"How?" Donovan said. "Your car is in Florida."

"Guess I'd better get another one. For here."

"How about I get one for us to share?"

"Thanks, but I want my own wheels. It's one of the things I fought with Constance about earlier. As I told her, 'I need wheels.' But I'd love it if you'd help me pick one out."

"Deal. And at some point, I'll have one of my cars brought up here," Donovan said. "Maybe Curtis can drive up after things quiet down for him."

"Good idea," said Aggie. "Now to the wine."

The temperature was pleasant enough for them to take their glasses of wine outside to the small patio in the back of the house. Aggie gratefully found a seat in one of the two patio chairs there. With a soft groan, Donovan lowered himself into the other chair.

"Thank you for being such a sport about meeting and being with my family. It means so much to me," Aggie said, observing lines of fatigue cross Donovan's face.

Though it might appear to others she'd made a spontaneous decision to marry him, she'd thought about the possibility of remarrying in the future. As independent as she was, she loved living with Donovan, provided he didn't present a barrier to what she was doing in both her business and her personal life. She knew before he asked her to marry him that they were a match.

She reached out and clasped his hand. "Are you too tired to go to the dining room for dinner? We could order in."

"No, I want to start off right, meeting people, being part of the activities." He held up his glass. "But I would like a little more wine."

She rose. "Okay, then. I'll be the designated driver."

He laughed. "I think I can handle a golf cart."


When they entered the dining room, Aggie saw that the staff had made a place for Donovan at the table at which Aggie usually sat. The ratio of men to women was around one to three, so Aggie was grateful that the staff had thought to make it comfortable for Donovan.

Aggie introduced him to the four other people at the table, happy that Edith and Rose were there. A gentleman named Samuel Grant had been moved to the table along with Carrie Dietz, a sweet woman Aggie didn't know that well.

Conversation at the table came easily to all six of them. Aggie overheard Donovan tell Sam he'd be glad to join him a men's discussion group and was pleased the conversation she'd had with him about the need to participate had taken hold. They might be engaged, but Aggie had no desire to spend every minute of every day with him.

After dinner, though, she was excited to be able to take the golf cart home for a quiet evening and an early bedtime.

# CHAPTER TWENTY-TWO
## BLYTHE

The limousine dropped Blythe and Logan off near South Station so Logan could find his friend's apartment, and Blythe could show him her new condo. They agreed to go to dinner and, afterward, Blythe intended to drive to her father's house to spend the night. She relished the thought it would be one of her last few nights there and that as soon as she had furnished her condo, she'd move to Boston.

She stood aside while Logan called his friend to tell him he was in town. Observing the frown that crossed his face, she studied him. In jeans and a light-blue golf shirt that caught the color of his arresting eyes, he was handsome in a wholesome way. More than that, he gave people a sense of honesty and trust. That would go a long way in joining a prestigious financial services company like Tremont Associates.

He clicked off the phone and shook his head. "Ben got the dates mixed up. He's out of town. He'll be back tomorrow night. Any chance I can bunk with you?"

"At my Dad's house? Sure. I don't see why not. In addition to my room, they have another room for guests. Let me call Constance and clear it with her."

As much as she hated asking Constance for a favor, she was eager to spend time with Logan. She enjoyed being with him. He already felt like part of the family.

Blythe spoke to Constance. After Blythe assured her it was

for one night only, Constance agreed to Logan's spending the night as long as he stayed in the guest room, and Blythe stayed in her room.

"We're just friends," Blythe said, "so, no problem. Thanks." They talked for a few more minutes, and then Blythe clicked off the call.

Logan gave her a questioning look. "What was that all about?"

"Constance thought we might want to share a room," Blythe explained, feeling her cheeks grow hot. "She said she didn't want the boys to get the wrong impression, that dealing with Gran was hard enough."

Logan's eyes widened with surprise. "Like you said, though, we're just friends."

Blythe wished she could take back her words. "I know."

"Okay then, friend, let's grab something to eat," Logan said. "How about Chinatown? We can walk there and then grab an Uber to get to your Dad's house."

"Works for me," she said, wishing she hadn't left her car with the dealership. "First, though, we'd better drop your suitcase off at my condo. We don't want to be walking around with it."

"Good idea."

"I have no idea what state my condo will be in. I know some deliveries have been made while I've been gone. My friend, Liz, has helped me with them."

The walk to her condo was only three blocks. Logan paused outside the red brick building and studied it. "Looks cool. Let's see the inside."

Blythe proudly pulled her key out of her purse, punched in the security code, and led Logan inside to the small vestibule outside the elevator. She punched the button for the eighth floor and turned to him. "I was lucky to find this place. My friend Liz lives in the building and is the one who told me about it."

He nodded thoughtfully, and when she opened the door to her condo, he let out a long, low whistle. "This is totally cool. I like all the open space and the windows."

"Even with boxes stacked everywhere?" Blythe said, thrilled that so many of her orders had been delivered, including a couch she'd bought as a floor sample from one of the contemporary furniture stores.

"Not bad. You've got a couch, and I think I see a bed in one of the rooms. All this other stuff won't be too hard to deal with."

Blythe emitted a sigh of happiness. She loved the idea of having her own place, with her own personal touches.

"Want help unpacking?" Logan said. "I see how anxious you are to get started."

"Really? You'd do that for me?"

He checked his watch. "It's too early for dinner. Why don't we work here for a while? Then we can go have drinks and dinner."

Blythe beamed at him. "That would be wonderful! Just wonderful!"

He returned her smile. "Okay, tell me what you want me to do."

"First of all, let's sort through the boxes and move some furniture around. I want the couch facing the fireplace. Then all the boxes from Ikea need to be placed in the kitchen. Most of the things I bought from them belong there."

Blythe set aside her purse, happy now that she'd changed into something casual for the flight back to Boston. One by one, she opened the boxes and peered inside. As she'd suspected, most went right into the kitchen. A couple contained things for the bathrooms and bedrooms. A few contained furniture that she would need to assemble. She'd need her father's tools for those.

Before she'd left to return to Ithaca for graduation, she and Liz had made sure to stock the condo with basic food and cleaning supplies. They'd even worked together to wipe down kitchen shelves and counters. Logan proved to be a godsend, unwrapping and stacking things like glasses, plates, and silverware on the counter where Blythe could check them and place them in the dishwasher.

The few pots and pans she'd purchased were already washed, dried, and tucked away in cabinets.

Excitement kept Blythe moving quickly. While she prepared her kitchen, Logan folded up empty boxes and stored packing materials in another. He was able to put together a lamp by just twisting the parts together.

Standing in the kitchen, looking at the living room, she observed how nice it would be. When Logan unrolled a rug and laid it out on the bare wooden floor, she exhaled a long, deep breath at how well the gray-fabric couch and patterned rug went together. It happened by pure chance because both were bargains that she'd picked up separately.

"It's looking good," said Logan as she approached for a closer look. "How about going out now? You ready?"

"Yes." She gave him a quick hug. "Thanks so much for your help. You made a huge difference."

He grinned. "Glad to do it. I figure if we're going to be neighbors, I might be seeing a lot of this condo in the future."

"I hope so," said Blythe. "It'll be fun to have you close by."

"I'll have to see how the job interview goes. It'll be my second one there."

"Anyone would be lucky to have you working for them," Blythe said. He was smart, personable, and, as she'd seen first-hand, willing to work.

"I'll drink to that. C'mon. I'm thirsty and hungry."

It was a quick walk from her condo into Chinatown. As she considered the various restaurants, Blythe's mouth watered. One of the advantages of city living was the abundance of restaurants, bars, and entertainment venues. She and Logan entered a cute restaurant and were greeted by the enticing aromas of ginger and other spices she didn't recognize.

They sat in a booth facing one another. When a waitress approached with menus, they ordered beers to sip while perusing their choices.

"Thanks once again for all your help," Blythe said. "I really appreciate it."

"No problem. After grad school, I traveled around a lot, and I get how important it is to feel settled."

The conversation was interesting and revealing to Blythe as Logan talked about the countries he'd visited and how he'd wanted to have that experience before deciding on a job. He was fortunate that companies were interested enough to tell him when he was ready to come to see them again.

"So, you think Boston is going to be the place where you want to live?"

He shrugged. "Sitting here with you about to have some of my favorite food, what's not to like?"

"Exactly. Living in town will give me a break from the family."

Later, after Blythe had finished her walnut and shrimp dish and Logan ate the last of his ginger-soy chicken, Blythe checked her watch. "Guess we'd better head out to Wellesley. We need to go to my condo to pick up your suitcase. We'll nab an Uber driver from there."

They paid and took a leisurely walk back to her condo.

Blythe couldn't remember when she'd had such a pleasant evening. Logan was easy to talk to, something that had grown more and more difficult with Chad. She turned to him with a feeling of gratitude. "I'm glad to have you in my life."

"Yeah, me too." He grabbed her hand and gave it a squeeze.

When they entered her condo, Blythe said, "Don't turn on the lights. Not yet. I want to see the view at night." She walked over to one of the large windows in the living area and stood a moment gazing out. The sparkling lights on the buildings and inside them made the city come to life under the darkening sky.

Logan came up behind her. "Beautiful," he said, smiling at her before looking out the window.

Blythe's heartbeat picked up pace. *Did he mean she was beautiful?*

He turned away from the window and walked into the kitchen.

She lifted her phone to call Uber and felt it vibrate as a call came through. *Constance.* She clicked on it.

"Blythe? Blythe? Are you there?" Constance said, her voice high with emotion.

"Constance, what's wrong?"

"It's your father! He's been in an accident outside the city on his way home from Ithaca." Her voice broke. "The police called to tell me. They've taken him to Beth Israel hospital. I'm on my way there in your father's car. I'm so scared. They said something about a head injury. Can you meet me at the hospital?"

Blythe held onto the edge of the kitchen counter as the room began to spin. *An accident? Her father in the hospital? Head injury?* Her breath left her. Gasping, she bent over to keep from fainting.

Logan put an arm around her. "What is it? Are you okay?"

"It's my father. He's been in an accident. I have to get to Beth Israel," she managed to choke out and realized she hadn't responded to Constance.

With shaking hands, she picked up her phone. "Constance, I'm leaving for the hospital now." She clicked off the call, blocking out her stepmother's sobs.

As she hurried to get ready to leave, Blythe felt as if heavy rocks weighed down her limbs. Sick with worry, her body seemed slow and awkward. *My purse,* she thought in a panic. *I have to get my keys and lock up the condo behind me.*

Logan had Uber on his phone and was explaining this was an emergency, and they needed a pick-up right away.

After ending the call, he helped her to the door and waited while she locked it. He held her elbow as they entered the elevator, exited on the first floor, and hurried out of the building.

Standing on the curb, Blythe said a prayer that her father would be all right. Because of her mother's illness, her relationship with him was stronger than many daughters had with their fathers. Tears blurred her vision.

"He's here," said Logan, taking her arm and leading her to a car marked as an Uber.

Later, Blythe wouldn't be able to recall the ride as more than a blur of sights and sounds as the driver wended through the streets of Boston to Brookline Avenue in the Longwood Medical Area and the Beth Israel Deaconess Medical Center.

At the hospital, Logan helped her find her way to the Emergency Room, where a nurse confirmed that a patient named Bradley Robard had been brought in and was undergoing treatment now.

"I need to see him now," Blythe said with as much determination as she could muster while still being reasonable.

"I'm sorry, but you're going to have to wait. A doctor will come to speak to you as soon as they've determined the extent of the injuries." The woman spoke calmly, kindly.

Blythe's hands fisted. *How dare she ask me to wait!! Didn't she understand it was my father who'd been hurt?*

Logan sensed her anger and led her to a chair in the waiting area. "Breathe. The doctors will let you know as soon as they can. Let's wait for Constance right here."

Blythe knew he was right. There was nothing she could do but wait. She sat back in the chair and tried to calm her racing thoughts. A head injury sounded ominous.

Constance arrived a short while later, her hair a mess, her face frozen into lines of anxiety.

Blythe rose and went to greet her. "They're working on Dad now. As soon as they can, they'll give us an update."

"Oh, thank God you're here!" Constance cried, giving her a hug. "I'm so worried. If only I hadn't asked Brad to drive my car home, he'd be all right." She stepped away to wipe her eyes and then twisted the damp handkerchief in her hands. "Thank you for coming, Blythe. You don't know how much I appreciate it."

Blythe was quiet, knowing how upset Constance was.

After a few more minutes of waiting, Blythe went up to the desk. "Any news of Mr. Robard?"

The woman behind the desk gave her a sympathetic look. "Soon."

As she returned to her seat, a nurse entered the waiting area. "The Robard family?"

Blythe stood with Constance. "We're here." She glanced at Logan, who indicated for her to go ahead without him.

The nurse led them to a room with several beds curtained off for privacy. "Dr. Goldsmith is here with your family member," the nurse said as a way of introduction.

Judith Keim

A young man with curly red hair and freckles splashed across his face smiled and held out his hand. "Mark Goldsmith."

Blythe introduced herself and Constance. "What can you tell me about his condition?"

Her father lay on his back in a hospital bed with his eyes closed. A heart monitor beeping with regularity was connected to his body with several wires, and an intravenous tube led from a bag of fluid suspended above his shoulder into a catheter inserted into his right arm. A blood-pressure cuff wrapped around his upper left arm with a tube leading to another monitor. His nose was swollen and both eyes were turning black. A white bandage wound around his head.

"What happened to him?" Constance whispered. "He looks awful."

"Surprisingly, aside from the injury to his head, he's suffered only bruising. The pictures from an MRI show a TBI. That's Traumatic Brain Injury. That occurs when the brain is shaken from one side to another. There is bruising on the brain, no blood clots that we could see. He's been unconscious since the accident, which is something of concern to us. We will monitor him closely to be sure there's no build-up of fluid on the brain, which can happen."

"What if he doesn't wake up?" Blythe asked, barely able to breathe.

"We'll take it one step at a time," Dr. Goldsmith assured her. "Chances are he'll come around within the next couple of hours. Sometimes, it's the brain's way of recovering from the trauma it suffered by shutting down. In his case, I'm suggesting that his isn't the most severe form of this type of injury. His eyes are responding to light, and there are other good signs."

Constance leaned over and kissed Brad's cheeks. "Wake

up, darling. It's me."

When her father's eyes remained closed, Blythe held back a sob. She exchanged a worried look with Constance, who released a shuddering sigh.

"We're going to be sending him up to the ICU. The woman at the reception desk should be able to let you know when you can join him," said Dr. Goldsmith. "I suggest you find a seat in the waiting area and give us time to get a room assigned and to make sure he's settled."

"Thank you, doctor," said Constance. Her eyes filled. "I appreciate all you're doing."

Blythe led Constance back to the waiting area, trying her best to remain optimistic. Her father was too young, too healthy, too needed, too loved to die.

Logan got to his feet when they entered the waiting room and walked over to Blythe. "How is he?"

"He looks awful. The doctor said he has a traumatic brain injury. He's still unconscious. They're going to take him to the ICU."

The seriousness on Logan's face caught Blythe's attention. Fear rolled through her. What would she do if her father died? Logan wrapped his arm around her and drew her to his side. She leaned against him, needing his warmth to chase the cold away.

Constance paced the room. Each time she passed in front of her, Blythe wanted to reassure her, but worry trapped those comforting words in her throat.

When they finally received news that her father was in the ICU, the three of them made their way there.

Blythe was sitting outside the ICU area waiting for Constance to exchange places with her when she thought of

Gran. She knew that if her father died, it would kill Gran. She stood as Constance walked back into the room.

"Constance, I've been thinking. Gran needs to know about the accident."

"It's going on eleven," said Constance. "Let's allow her to get some rest, and we'll call her first thing in the morning. The doctor didn't mention any concern about Brad dying. The graduation weekend and moving into a new place have, no doubt, been stressful for her. Aggie will need her strength for the days ahead."

Blythe thought about it. Constance was right. Gran couldn't do any good tonight. Her father wouldn't even know she was there, and they'd all need her in the coming days.

When it was Blythe's turn to be able to see her father for the short time allotted to family members, she tiptoed into the room. Her father lay still. Cautiously, she approached his bed.

She leaned over and kissed him on the cheek. "Hi, Dad! It's me, Blythe. Can you open your eyes and talk to me? I really need you to do this for me."

Blythe studied his face, hoping for a sign that though his brain might be traumatized, he was going to be all right.

He lay still, eyes closed.

"All right, Dad, I'm going to leave now. But before I go, I want you to promise me you'll try to open your eyes. Constance, the boys, Gran, and I need you to do that for us."

Her father's eyelids fluttered and then closed.

"I love you, Dad." Blythe kissed his cheeks once more and turned to go.

"No! Stop!"

Blythe whipped around to see her father moving restlessly on the bed. She hurried over and pushed the button for the nurse. A nurse appeared in seconds. "What's going on? I see some activity."

"I asked him to open his eyes. His eyelids fluttered, and then went I went to leave, he spoke, though his eyes are closed."

The nurse studied him. "Good. He's starting to come around. Where's his wife? Perhaps she can get a reaction out of him too."

Blythe went to get Constance. "Come with me. He's starting to wake up. The nurse wants to see if you can encourage him."

The two of them all but ran to her father's bedside.

"Hi, darling! It's me, Constance! Blythe is here too."

His eyes fluttered open. "Who are you?"

# CHAPTER TWENTY-THREE
## AGGIE

Aggie woke up feeling as if she'd been trying to swim a raging river upstream all night. Bleary-eyed, she climbed out of bed, careful not to disturb Donovan, who required a lot of sleep. After taking care of her morning routines, she tiptoed out of the room, closing the bedroom door behind her. Coffee might help, she decided, trying to shake off the gloom that had trapped her all night.

She got the coffee maker set up, and, acting on a whim, she picked up her phone, feeling an urgent need to talk to Blythe. Thank goodness, Blythe was an early riser. Something was going on. Something bad.

After punching her number on the phone, Aggie waited for Blythe to pick up.

"Gran? I was just about to call you," Blythe said, her voice shaking with emotion.

Aggie felt the blood drain from her face and sat in one of the kitchen chairs. "What's wrong?"

"It's Dad. He's been in an automobile accident. He has a head injury, a traumatic brain injury, to be exact. He was in a coma but was coming out of it last night when I finally left the hospital."

"Oh no! Why didn't you call me? I need to be there." Aggie couldn't hide the hurt in her voice.

"I'm going to pick you up as soon as I get Matt and Mike off to school."

"Where are you? At your father's house?"

"Yes. Constance is staying with Dad. She sent me here with Logan in Dad's car to be with the boys. The babysitter couldn't stay all night."

"I'll go get ready. Pick me up as soon as you can, Blythe. I need to see my son."

"Yes, I know. There was nothing any of us could do last night, which is why we let you get a good night's sleep." Blythe paused. "There's just one thing, Gran. He was awake, but he didn't know who we were."

"Oh, my God! It's that bad?" Aggie didn't bother to brush away the tears that flowed down her cheeks, forming a burning trail. "What did the doctor say about that?"

"It's not unusual for some patients to react this way. He's in ICU at Beth Israel so they can monitor his vital signs and fluid on the brain. They don't want any buildup of fluids on the brain to happen. I haven't talked to Constance this morning. The doctor isn't due to see him until later this morning, following surgery of other patients."

"Where did the accident happen?" Aggie asked Blythe. "I assume he was in Constance's car."

"Yes. Constance feels bad about asking him to drive her car home. Apparently, he almost made it to their house before the accident, which happened on Route 128. A truck ahead of him slammed on his brakes and stalled. There was nothing Dad could do except try to swerve out of the way. That's how he rolled the car."

"A Mercedes is considered a safe car to drive. Is damage to the car what caused the brain injury?" Aggie asked, her heart pounding with alarm.

"No. I asked the nurses who were there when the EMTs brought Dad in if they could tell me what happened. A full report will come later, but they did say the EMTs told them that the car didn't have much damage because it landed in the soft verge rather than the highway. It was the way Dad's head was jarred, more than once most likely, that shifted the brain inside his skull, causing the damage."

Aggie fought for a breath. "Blythe, promise me you'll get here as soon as you can. I need to see him, touch him, make sure he's all right."

"I'll call you when I'm on my way. Gotta go. The boys leave for school in fifteen minutes."

"I'll be ready," said Aggie. It was, she thought, against the laws of nature to have a child outlive a parent—a mother's worst nightmare.

Later, as Aggie climbed into Brad's vehicle, she couldn't remember feeling so shaken. She'd called the hospital and talked to one of the floor nurses and knew that Brad was alive and stable, but until she held him in her arms, those words meant little.

Aggie drew a breath and clutched her hands, trying not to rage against the cars that seemed to block or slow their every move through the streets of Brookline and Boston.

"Dad's strong," Blythe reminded her. "I wouldn't have left him last night if I wasn't assured that he was doing well."

"How is Constance holding up?" Aggie asked.

"Okay, I guess. I sometimes forget that beneath all those demands she makes of Dad, she does love him. She refused to come home and rest."

"I'm glad. I would hate to think of him lying there alone," Aggie said. "I'll do my share of spending time with him whenever I'm needed. Donovan was a good sport about staying at the house in New Life to help supervise the move. He understands how I'm needed here and at the office."

"Are you going to be happy in the house?" Blythe asked and cursed under her breath as a driver cut in front of her.

"It's a good situation for us." Aggie stopped talking when Blythe pulled into a parking garage, where after circling, she finally found an empty spot.

Taking a deep breath, Aggie stepped out of the car. She wished she could make a dash for it but told herself to calm down.

Blythe took hold of her arm. "Let's go."

Together they made their way into the hospital and to the ICU. Each step closer to her son filled Aggie with more and more tension. Brad, the darling boy she loved with all her heart, had grown into a fine man she couldn't bear to lose.

Constance was waiting for them in the waiting area. She hurried over to Aggie and hugged her. "I'm so glad you're here. Brad is the same. I'm hoping he'll respond to you." She turned to Blythe. "Thank you for taking care of the boys. I really appreciate it."

"You're welcome," Blythe said, surprised by the change in Constance. "I'm glad I could help. I dropped Logan off at the train station before I picked up Gran, but he might need to stay at your house for another night. There's a problem with his staying at his buddy's condo. He's away for the weekend."

"No problem. He's welcome at the house. I'll stay here for a little while," said Constance, "then I need to go home and change."

"And take a nap," said Blythe. "You look exhausted."

"That bad, huh?" Constance said with a new glimmer of humor that Aggie liked.

The nurse waved Aggie over to her. "You can go into Brad's room. He's awake and doing as well as can be expected, but he's confused. I suggest you speak naturally to him and let him know who you are and why you're here."

Aggie stepped into the room. Seeing Brad in bed hooked up to all kinds of equipment, she drew in a deep breath and forced a smile on her face. "Hi, Brad. It's Mom. How are you doing?"

He opened his eyes and squinted at her. "What are you doing here?"

She walked over to him and gathered the fingers of one hand into her grasp. "I'm here to see you. You've been in an automobile accident, but you're going to be fine."

"Huh. I wondered why I was in a place like this." He squinted at her. "Mom?"

"Yes, dear. I'm here. Constance is here outside your room, along with Blythe."

Brad closed his eyes. "Can't remember. Why am I here?"

"You were driving Constance's car home from Blythe's graduation and were in an automobile accident." She gazed into his face, willing him to remember. "You were in Ithaca at Cornell for the graduation."

He held his head in his hands. "I don't know if I remember that or if it was a dream."

"Just rest. It'll all come back to you in time." Aggie did her best to hug him without disturbing the tubes and monitors on his body. His body felt so good...so alive in her arms. Her vision blurred with tears of gratitude.

A nurse appeared. "Time for me to take some vitals."

"All right. I'll be in the waiting area," Aggie said.

"How is he?" Blythe asked her when she entered the waiting area.

"I think he knew me," Aggie said. "He still isn't clear about what happened, but he seems okay otherwise. The nurse is taking his vitals now."

"I'll wait to talk to her, and then if the two of you don't mind, I'll take the car and go home," said Constance, stifling a yawn.

"Logan said he'd help me get my car back from the dealership."

"I'll be back in a couple of hours. Maybe you and Logan could watch the boys this evening for a while," Constance said to Blythe.

"We'll work something out for sure," Blythe said. She took a seat and patted the chair next to her. "Better sit, Gran. It may be a while. Dad sleeps a lot."

Aggie lowered herself into the chair, still shocked by all that was happening. There was so much to think about.

"What are we going to do about the business?" Blythe asked.

Aggie let out a long breath. "It's clear your father isn't going to be able to work for a while. Earlier, he talked about taking a vacation. This accident will ensure that he takes quite a bit of time off. I'd planned to bring you aboard and begin your training right away. We'll still do that, of course, but at the same time, we need to fill in for your father."

"I'll do anything you need," said Blythe. "Dad's recovery is the most important thing."

Aggie got up and went over to the window. She'd hoped to give Brad more free time in the coming weeks, but only after being sure that Blythe had a good handle on the entire business. Now it was clear that they'd need extra help for some time. Maybe months. They'd need to find someone they could bring on board immediately, perhaps permanently in the future.

Blythe stood. "I'll be right back. I've got a message on my phone and have to return the call."

She went on her way, leaving Aggie to consider her choices among the staff she already had.

Moments later, Blythe returned to the area. "That was

Logan. He said his interview went well, but they won't bring him on board until after the new year, when their budget will allow them to hire him. Considering that he was even able to interview for a position there, he's okay with it."

"Too bad. What's he going to do?" Aggie asked with more enthusiasm than she thought polite. Her mind was already working on a deal.

Blythe's eyes widened. "Are you thinking what I'm thinking?"

Aggie gave her an impish grin. "If Logan would agree to work for us in the meantime, it would solve a lot of problems—his and ours."

"Would he be training with me?" Blythe asked, giving her a wary look.

Aggie shook her head. "Not really. You'll be taking over for me. He would be working on your father's end of the business."

"Okay," Blythe said, though there was a little hesitation about her reply that made Aggie curious. The two of them, she was sure, would be fine working together.

# CHAPTER TWENTY-FOUR
## BLYTHE

The thought of working with Logan every day both excited and scared Blythe. They'd agreed to be friends, but Blythe already knew she was more than interested in him. She had to stop fantasizing about Logan—wondering how it would feel to be with him, make love to him, live with him. The practical part of her suggested working together would be a good way to replace fantasy with reality, while the romantic part of her said a situation like this would eventually lead to heartbreak.

When it was her turn to visit with her father, Blythe walked into his room wishing some miracle would occur, and he would be alert, and things would go back to normal. But the sight of him stretched out in bed sound asleep made her realize that wasn't going to happen. It was confirmed when he opened his eyes and gazed at her with confusion. Hiding her tears, Blythe said brightly, "Hi, Dad. It's me, Blythe."

He studied her without speaking.

She took hold of his hand. "You're going to be all right. I don't want you to worry about the business. It will be fine until you're able to return. We want you to rest and get better." She leaned over and kissed him on the cheek. "I love you, Dad."

He squeezed her hand as if he understood, and this time Blythe couldn't stop the trail of tears down her face.

An alarm sounded. Blythe stood aside as a nurse rushed into the room. She checked him out and turned to Blythe. "He needs his rest. He'll be fine."

"Okay," Blythe said, hoping she hadn't upset him.

"Is he all right?" Gran asked, hurrying over to her with a worried look. "The nurse said he needs more rest."

"He's going to be all right," Blythe said with determination. "He just has to be."

Gran gave her a pat on the back. "I understand from the nurses that recovery from accidents like your father's take time. He's doing well, but he'll need to be away from work for quite a while."

"I think so too."

"Let's get ready to talk to Logan." Gran, efficient as always, took some blank paper and a pen out of her purse. "Let's make a list of things to discuss with him." She led Blythe to a couple of chairs in the corner of the room, and they each took a seat. "He'll need a better understanding of how we operate and the structure of the business. It would be good for you to review that too. We can negotiate pay, time of employment, and that kind of thing with him. Maybe our HR person can spend a couple of days with him going over some of the guidelines of working with The Robard Company."

Blythe looked up as Logan walked into the room. Her heart sped up at the sight of him, betraying her vow to treat him as any other potential employee.

"Hi! I'm here to help you with your car," Logan said to her.

Gran got to her feet and went over to him. "Hello, Logan. Come sit down with Blythe and me. We want to talk to you about a business proposition."

Logan gave Blythe a questioning look. She did her best to smile, although her nerves were making her feel cold all over. How could she work with him every day and not fall for him?

Logan sat in the chair Gran indicated. Smiling, he said, "What's up?"

Gran returned his smile. "I understand the company offered you a position but can't bring you onboard until after the new year. Correct?"

"Yes. There's an issue with the budget. It's a pain to have to wait to start, but I understand. It's a good company, fiscally conservative."

"Well, as much as it is a nuisance for you to be in that position, it's a blessing for us. We'd like to offer you a job to fill in for Brad for several weeks, maybe up to six months. It would involve financial monitoring, maintenance of records and that kind of thing. More oversight than getting into the nitty and gritty. Would you like to talk to us about it? I understand from what Donovan has told me about your work with him that you'd be a perfect fit."

Logan glanced at Blythe and back to Gran. "I'd definitely like to consider it."

"Good," said Gran. "Let's set up an appointment with you for tomorrow morning at the company headquarters. Let's say ten o'clock. This is no place to talk business."

"Okay," said Logan. "Thanks for your consideration."

Blythe got to her feet. "I need to get my car before the kids get out of school. I'm bringing them in to see Dad and will need my own 'wheels,' as you always say, Gran."

"That was the beginning of my idea for a road trip," said Gran, winking at her.

Blythe hugged Gran, so happy for her. "It was a trip to remember."

"As soon as Constance comes back, I'm going to leave for New Life," said Gran. "Donovan is covering for me there, but it's unfair for him to have to oversee the moving of my furniture."

Blythe gave her a little wave. "Okay, I'll see you later. Call me if there are any changes with Dad."

"I will, but I don't expect any," Gran said. "Go, you two, and have fun. It's a beautiful day out there. A 'high sparkler' as they might say 'down-east' in Maine."

As Blythe and Logan left the hospital, she filled him in on her father's condition. "It's sad to see him so unresponsive, so confused."

"How long do they expect that to last?" Logan asked her, looking concerned.

"I don't know. It's not unusual with this type of injury. The doctor told us his brain needs time to heal. It hasn't been that long."

Logan turned to her. "Then why does your grandmother want to talk to me about working for her for six months? I mean, it sounds perfect, but your Dad might not be happy about it."

"Gran has this plan to give my dad more time to himself. He's never really wanted to be in the business, but he stepped up when his father was ill. She wants to give him his freedom to teach and do other things."

"That sounds reasonable," Logan said. "What about when it's time for me to leave?"

"That's something we'll have to think about later," said Blythe. "Gran and I will be working together as much as possible. Come January, I know she and Donovan will want to head south. That's another problem that will have to be solved."

"Yeah, I thought they'd want to be where it's warm," said Logan.

"Yes. Who could blame them? By the way, have you talked to Curtis? What does he think about his father's engagement?"

"He wanted to know all about your grandmother. He was worried about her being after Donovan's money. I told him not to worry; she was the best thing to ever happen to him."

"My father wondered the same thing about Donovan."

They laughed together.

"Guess it's going to be all right," said Logan. "Who knew they'd get engaged in such a hurry?"

"Ever since Gran moved to New Life, she's decided to live her life to the fullest for as long as she can. That's why she made the plan for the road trip. She wanted to see old friends. Especially Donovan."

"I really like your grandmother," said Logan. "More people should be like her."

"I agree," said Blythe. When she saw the Uber car pull up and signal them, she grabbed hold of his arm and hurried to the curb.


Later, at the car dealership, Blythe inspected her car. Everything was in good shape.

"Cool car," Logan said.

"A total surprise, but I love it," Blythe admitted. "I'm glad it's fairly small because parking in Boston can be difficult. Thank goodness, my condo comes with a secure parking spot." She checked the time. "It's early. Do you want to head into town? I want to do more work at the condo. First, I need to make a couple of stops for groceries and supplies. I already bought some things, but I need a whole lot more."

He shrugged. "Sure. I've got the afternoon free. Tonight, I'm finally meeting up with my buddy. I'll be bunking in with him for a few days until I decide what I'm going to do on a more permanent basis. If his place is suitable, I might just stay there. We've talked about it."

As Blythe shopped for groceries, she was pleased to see once again that Logan was a real foodie. The thought of them occasionally cooking or eating together was exciting. She loved to try new things and wanted to do more creative cooking now that she lived on her own.

Later, as Logan helped her carry groceries inside, Blythe wondered if living with him would be this easy, then quickly told herself to stop thinking of it. With her current circumstances and problems lurking in the future, she couldn't afford to have such thoughts. What she needed to do was concentrate on learning all she could about the business, so her father could have more leisure, and Gran and Donovan could relax in Florida when winter arrived, as it surely would.

She set to work putting groceries away.

Constance called to make sure Blythe was picking up the boys from school.

"Yes. That's the plan. How's Dad? And are you feeling better?"

"Your father's the same, and I'm feeling more rested. But, Blythe, I'm concerned about the business."

Blythe tensed. "No worries there. Gran and I have things under control. It appears Dad might not be able to work for some time. Not if he's going to have a good recovery."

"That's what I'm afraid of," Constance said. "We can't let the business go."

Forcing a lightness to her voice she didn't feel, Blythe said, "It's being taken care of, Constance. We'll share the details with you later."

"Oh, well, I'm just checking. It's important to me, you know. The family has a reputation to uphold in the community. I'm expected to be involved with my work in society."

"Yes, I'm aware of it," Blythe said. Constance used income from the business for her social status. Blythe felt as if a spider was creeping across her shoulder. She couldn't hide her distaste. "Talk to you later."

Logan studied her as she clicked off the call. "That bad?"

Blythe made a face. "I try to like Constance for my father's sake, but we'll never be friends."

Later, as Blythe followed the boys into her Dad's hospital room, she found a reason to silently thank Constance. She'd done a wonderful job in helping to raise the boys. They each kissed him on the cheek and talked quietly to him. As she watched their reaction to her father, her vision blurred with tears.

Her father smiled at them, but Blythe wasn't sure he really knew them.

After they left the hospital, Blythe took the boys to her condo to show them where she'd be living.

"Take a look around and make yourself at home," she told the boys. "I'm going to unpack a few more boxes. But first, I've got some strawberries, apples, and cookies for snacks."

While they ate and played games on their iPads, Blythe sorted through boxes of things. She'd give the boys dinner and then deliver them home to their babysitter. She hoped to bring back the last of her clothes and finish getting things settled in her condo.

Tomorrow, the cable company would come in the afternoon, giving her time to be with Gran and Logan in the morning for his interview. Then she hoped to be able to see her father.

Thinking of him, Blythe glanced at the boys. They looked so much like him she wanted to cry. He'd be fine, wouldn't he?

# CHAPTER TWENTY-FIVE
## AGGIE

The moment Aggie walked into her house at New Life, she felt her spirits lift. The place might be a mess, but Donovan was there to greet her with a smile. She'd learned by living with Arnold that this feeling of being at home with someone made all the work on their relationship worthwhile.

"Sorry it's such a mess, but I wasn't sure where you wanted everything," said Donovan. "The movers took away the pieces of furniture you said you didn't want, and we placed the rest of your furniture where we thought best. What do you think?"

"I think I love you, Donovan Bailey," Aggie replied, settling against his chest as his arms wrapped around her.

"How's Brad? Any changes?"

"He's been sleeping quite a bit, which is good. He's still a bit confused but is making slow progress. By the time I left this afternoon, I'm pretty sure he knew who I was, but he doesn't remember anything beyond being on the road home. The doctor said some people never fully recover their memory, and if it's only the accident he doesn't remember, it's just as well."

"Yes, I would agree." He studied her. "How is this going to affect his work? Your work? Living arrangements?"

"There are a lot of things to figure out, but Blythe and I are interviewing Logan tomorrow to set up a plan for him to help us out for the next six months. He's been accepted for the position he wanted at the financial company, but he can't start there until after the first of the year. As it turns out, that's perfect for us."

"Ah, a great solution. As I told you, I've tried to get Logan to continue working with me on family foundation matters, but then I understood his need to be away and on his own and have encouraged him to leave. He's a great guy, super smart, and innovative. You're going to like having him around."

"I think so too. It's especially nice that he and Blythe get along so well."

Donovan held up a finger of warning. "This is going to sound old-fashioned, but remember, no fishing off the company pier and all that. They can work well together, but they shouldn't date."

Aggie glanced at him with surprise. "Arnold and I worked very well together."

"But you and he were already married. Blythe and Logan aren't even dating. Best to keep it that way."

"I don't know. I think Blythe is attracted to him."

"You do? If there was something romantic, shouldn't it have already blossomed by now?"

"I guess you're right. That's the smart thing to do. Establish that rule between them. I'll make that a condition of employment." She kissed him. "I'm glad we don't have to worry about things like that."

"Come see what I've done in the bedroom," he said.

Aggie shot him a teasing look. "Are you asking me to go to bed with you?"

He winked. "Not exactly. I had the movers put your workstation there where you wanted it."

Teasing him, Aggie pretended to be crestfallen. She knew that when they crawled into bed that night, there'd be plenty of time for fun.

### ###

The next morning, Aggie awoke with a sense of optimism. She'd had a sweet dream about Brad, and she was looking forward to getting Blythe and Logan started with training for their responsibilities. The more she'd thought about it, the more she thought Donovan was right. As long as they were working together, Blythe and Logan shouldn't date. A social or romantic relationship could compromise their independence when difficult decisions were necessary, which would not be in the best interests of either them or the company. Most companies had those rules in place for the owners and senior management of the business.

While Donovan slept in, Aggie went into the kitchen to make coffee. She loved the early morning hours, sitting and sipping coffee, anticipating the day. There was a little more to do in the kitchen from the move, but things had fallen into place with remarkable ease. She supposed that came from having pared her belongings down to a much more manageable size. It felt good.

She thought of Donovan's house in Florida. He'd told her she could make any changes to it that she wanted, but she loved it as it was. Living part-time there would be easy.

Donovan walked into the kitchen in pajama bottoms and slippers. Aside from his difficulty with balance and walking, he was in remarkable shape from all the exercises he did.

"Good morning," he said cheerfully. "Another beautiful day in a string of them. Is this how the weather normally is here?"

"Not really. Though summers can be lovely."

"I thought I'd try out the gym this morning," he said, "and then I've got to check in with work."

"Good. I'm going to do a little more straightening here. Later, I have a meeting at the office with Blythe and Logan.

But you and I are going to need to spend some time this afternoon finding a new car for me."

"My pleasure. I've already talked to the Mercedes dealer here. The manager remembered you and said he would help you get whatever you want."

She was relieved at hearing the good news. She'd made a terrific deal with the manager for the convertible she loved. This time, she'd choose something a little more sensible. Something more suitable for Donovan. "Great. We'll go together."

"Deal. Now, where's that coffee? It smells delicious."

He poured himself a cup and sat down at the table with her. "I've heard from Curtis. He's anxious to meet you."

"Why don't we invite him to Boston? It looks like I can't get away for a while. I could never leave with Brad in the hospital."

"Of course not. I'll invite him here. We'll put him up at one of the hotels in town. We can stay there with him. How does that sound? A mini-vacation of sorts."

"That sounds like fun. Blythe is downtown and Logan too. We can plan a dinner party." She paused. "How is he going to feel about me?"

"He's going to love you, Aggie, though I have to say he was shocked when he found out we were engaged. I told him not to worry; it was something I've wanted for a long time."

Aggie studied him. "Life doesn't always work out the way we want, but it's best when a circle is closed, and we're able to move on."

Donovan drew her close. "I'm so happy I have this chance of being with you."

"Me, too," she replied, snuggling in his arms.

###

Walking into the offices of The Robard Company, Aggie felt a sense of pride. The space was part of a collection of offices in a tasteful, six-story, beige stone building in Dedham near Route 128. The business had flourished under Arnold's and her guidance, but they'd kept things as simple, as low-key as possible throughout that growth. Retail in any form was a tough business and didn't need opulent office space draining profits.

Suzie Ridgeway, her long-time assistant, jumped to her feet from behind her desk and rushed forward to greet her.

"It's good to see you! You look fantastic! Spending time in Florida to recuperate must have been the answer. I'm delighted you're doing so well."

Aggie gave her a crooked grin. "I'm not about to run a marathon, but I've recovered well enough to please my doctor and my fiancé." She held out her left hand. "I met an old beau of mine and am now engaged to him. You'll meet him soon."

Suzie's jaw dropped. "Oh, my! How wonderful! I'm happy for you, Aggie. I know you've found the last few years difficult." Her face fell. "How is Brad? I've been praying for him."

"Thanks. He's recovering but having some memory issues. I'm worried about his ability to come back to work. I suspect it's going to be a long time before he'll be at 100 percent and return."

"I'm sorry. He's such a great guy. And so nice to work for."

Aggie's eyes filled. "It's hard to see him lying in bed, uncertain about who I am or why he is where he is. But he's under excellent care, and his doctors are optimistic."

Suzie hugged her. They'd worked together for almost twenty years and were friends as well. Aggie would trust Suzie with her life.

"Thanks for setting up the conference room," Aggie said,

drawing up straight. "Blythe is arriving soon with a young man named Logan Pierce, who I hope will choose to help us out while Brad is recovering. Buzz me when they get here. After today, Blythe will begin her work with me. As you and I have discussed, over time, she will assume more and more of my responsibilities."

Suzie gave her a woeful look. "It's going to be sad to see you go, but I understand why you're doing this, and I applaud you. I don't have too many years before I can retire. I'm looking forward to it already."

Aggie and Suzie laughed together softly. Suzie had already bought a little place on the Gulf Coast of Florida and spent as many winter days there as possible with Aggie's blessing.

After looking through the messages Suzie handed her, Aggie went into her corner office and stood a moment. She supposed Blythe might want to change things a bit, but Aggie liked the cozy way she'd set up her office. Her desk sat along an inside wall facing large windows that met in the corner of the room. An Oriental rug in light blues brightened the space in front of her desk and served as a nice accent piece to the two brown-leather chairs sitting by her desk and the off-white couch across the room positioned to give a view out the windows.

Aggie sat behind her desk and began to return calls and check on various reports. In between business calls, she phoned the hospital and received the news that Brad might be able to leave there in the next day or two if things continued to go well.

In what seemed no time, Suzie buzzed her phone, and Aggie stood, ready to greet Blythe and Logan.

Watching them walk in together, Aggie couldn't help the smile she felt lifting the corner of her lips. They were adorable—full of the energy and confidence that only the young can bring.

"Hi, Gran!" Blythe came over to her and hugged her. "We're here."

Logan shook Aggie's hand. "How are you?"

"I'm much better," Aggie said. "I called the hospital, and they think Brad will be able to go home in a day or two if he continues to improve."

"Great," said Blythe. "I stopped in last night for a few minutes, and I think he recognized me."

"Good to hear. I developed a list of things to discuss with both of you regarding Logan's stepping into a temporary position here at The Robard Company. Let's move into the conference room. We can talk there. Suzie has laid out some paperwork for us." She turned to Logan. "Suzie Ridgeway has been my assistant for almost twenty years. You can rely on her to follow through on any task she's given, to be prompt, and to be discreet. She's like one of the family."

"Understood," said Logan.

Blythe and Logan followed her into the conference room and found seats opposite her at one end of the long, mahogany table.

"One of the rules of employment here is no dating among the executives," said Aggie. She gave each of them a steady look. "I'm assuming that won't be a problem for the two of you."

"Not at all," said Logan smoothly.

Blythe glanced at him. "No problem, here."

# CHAPTER TWENTY-SIX
## BLYTHE

Blythe concentrated on the sheet of paper Gran handed her, working to hide the disappointment she felt over Logan's quick reply to Gran. He hadn't hesitated for one second about not dating her. He seemed almost relieved. She'd been such a fool to hope he was the least bit interested in her. Lesson learned.

One by one, they discussed each item on the list. By the time Suzie asked them what they wanted brought in for lunch, they had agreed that Blythe would start preparing an order for fall gift items, and Logan would familiarize himself with inventory figures for all the multi-purpose stores. He would then meet the managers of each location to review inventory and other operating procedures. Logan agreed to a salary a step above what he'd be making at the financial firm, hours from eight to five-thirty, and end-of-month extended hours for balancing the books.

As they sat eating the sandwiches they'd ordered, Blythe thought about her grandparents working together for so many years. "How did you and Papa manage being here day after day with one another and then going home together?"

"It wasn't always easy, especially if we'd had a disagreement earlier in the day. But we both agreed to keep work at the office as much as possible. It also helped that, like you and Logan, our areas of responsibility were kept separate."

"Good idea," Blythe said. "I can see the importance of that. Especially if we're going to be friends in the city."

"My friend Ben introduced me to Liz Calloway last night," said Logan. "She's offered to show me some of her favorite spots."

"Oh? I had no idea," said Blythe, hiding her dismay. "I was busy with the boys and missed her call."

"She seems really nice."

"She is. I wouldn't be in my condo if it weren't for her keeping an eye out for me. I owe her for that."

"Sounds like you two have already worked out the issue of 'no fishing off the company pier' as Donovan described it to me," said Gran. "Now, I'm going to leave you to Suzie. She'll help you get settled in your offices, and then you can get started reviewing paperwork from the previous month. Sometime this afternoon, our IT guy will come to get you hooked up to the network so you can get into our private files. If you have any questions, the two of them can help. I need to get a new car. You know how I am, Blythe. I want my own wheels."

Blythe laughed. She loved her grandmother's independence. "See you later, Gran. If you don't mind, I'm going to leave a little early. I have a few things to pick up at Dad's to take to my condo. That will make my move final. It'll also allow me to be there when the boys get home from school."

"No problem. One of the best things about working with family is the flexibility we have to help one another. Logan, that goes for you too. I gather from Donovan you'll fly to Florida this weekend to load up your things and bring them and your car to Boston."

"Yes, that's the plan."

"Just clear the dates with Suzie and Blythe."

Blythe realized with a start that, to a small extent, she'd be Logan's boss. She smiled at the thought.

That evening, loaded down with boxes, she was making her way from the parking lot to the entrance to the building when she heard a deep voice say, "Can I offer you some help?"

"If you can get the door for me, that would be a big help." From behind the pile of boxes in front of her face, she could only see the man's shoes and the bottoms of his khaki pants.

"No problem. Can you see the steps into the building?"

"Yes, barely," she replied, wishing she hadn't been so determined to make as few trips as possible.

Following his feet, she stepped into the vestibule of the building and onto the elevator.

"What floor?"

"Eight," she answered.

"I'm stopping at seven," he said. "But I'll push the button for eight."

"Thanks," she managed.

At the seventh floor, he said, "See you around sometime," and left.

Arms aching, she stepped off onto the eighth floor and realized she'd have to drop her boxes to unlock her door. She jumped when she heard a voice say, "I'd almost given up hope waiting for you here."

"Logan?"

"Yeah. Liz canceled on me tonight, and I thought maybe I could talk you into going out to dinner with my roomie Ben and his date."

"Do me a favor and reach into the left pocket of my coat for my house keys and open the door to my condo. I don't want to drop these boxes of clothes onto the floor."

She startled when she felt his hand groping inside her pocket so close to her hip and then reminded herself it was just Logan.

He unlocked the door and held it open while she stumbled inside and to her bedroom, where she dropped the boxes on her bed and let out a puff of air with relief. Maybe it was time to change out some of those clothes for more professional ones, she thought, gazing at her belongings. But not for a while. She was making good money but would still need to be careful. Living in and around Boston wasn't cheap.

"You've done a great job of getting the condo set up," Logan said.

"There are a few more things to get—lamps, small tables, and such. But most of the big things are here."

"I've decided to bunk in with Ben. He and his girlfriend recently broke up, and he needs someone to share the condo with."

"Works out perfectly," said Blythe. "Now about that dinner? I'm starving. Where are we going?"

"We're to meet at seven at Persnickety's, a fairly new nearby pub."

Blythe checked the time. "Give me a few minutes to freshen up, and then I'll be ready."

"No problem. I'll call Ben and tell him we're on our way."

Blythe loved the idea that she could find so many places to eat within walking distance of her condo. She and Logan strolled along the street in comfortable silence and found themselves at the door of a small neighborhood pub. When they entered, Blythe was pleasantly surprised by the assorted ages of the crowd inside, like a group of real neighbors.

Logan waved to someone and led her through the crowd

standing at and around the bar to the corner of the room. A man stood by a booth, waving them forward. A stunning blonde was seated near him.

"Hey, there, Ben! Glad you found us a table. This place is mobbed," said Logan. He turned to her with a grin and back to his friend. "This is Blythe Robard, one of my new bosses. Blythe, Ben Lowell."

Dark-green eyes gazed at her from a face with classical features. His easy smile showed off white, straight teeth. "I believe we've met before."

Surprised, Blythe said, "Oh! You're the guy who helped me with the door to my condo building. You're on the seventh floor."

"I'm not, but Elle lives there." He turned to his date. "Elle Monroe, this is my friend Logan Pierce and his ... date ... boss ... Blythe Robard."

Amused, Blythe grinned as she acknowledged Elle, who was even more striking up close. "Logan and I both work for my family's business." She slid onto the empty bench of the booth so that Ben could sit.

"I've already ordered us some of my favorite draft beer if that's okay with everyone."

Blythe nodded enthusiastically with the others. "Sounds great. It's been a busy day."

Ben gazed at her. "You're the friend Liz Calloway has been talking about, the one who just bought the condo on the eighth floor?"

"Yes. Liz and I went to prep school together. I just graduated from Cornell with a major in business."

"Logan and I went to Harvard together a few years ago." He grinned at Logan. "I'm glad he finally stopped traveling the world, came to his senses, and came back to Boston."

"How about you, Elle? What are you doing?" Blythe asked.

"I work in the personnel business," she said. "I manage the Boston office of Exec-o-Search."

"It sounds interesting," Blythe said.

"It's exciting and daunting at the same time as you help people make decisions for their future," Elle said. "If you ever need our services, I'd be glad to help you out."

Blythe glanced at Logan and back to her. "We're set for the moment, but thank you."

Their beers arrived, and they quickly placed an order for food.

As talk between them continued, Blythe found herself appreciating Ben's sense of humor. In a witty way, he was quick to move the conversation along. And when Logan started telling lawyer jokes, he laughed with the rest of them.

By the time they all walked back to their condos, Blythe felt as if she'd made new friends. She'd need them in the days ahead. She'd done a little research on brain injuries, and new things might not be easy with her father in the days ahead.


Before heading to work the next morning, Blythe called Constance to check with her on news of her father. They'd talked frequently because of Constance's need for her help not only with the boys but as someone to listen to her fears about her husband's recovery. It made Blythe realize how much Constance loved her father.

"All is going as well as can be expected. What swelling he had on the brain has all but disappeared, but other issues have come up. He's restless and angry about being in the hospital. I'm told that kind of abnormal behavior is not unusual. We all hope as he heals, his sweet temperament will return."

"Does he know who you are?" asked Blythe, fighting a sinking feeling in her stomach.

"Yes, but he doesn't understand or remember what happened to him. He's always had a sharp sense of humor. Now, it's like talking to a stranger."

Hearing the tremble in Constance's voice, Blythe's heart went out to her. "I'll spend some time with him this evening."

"That would be wonderful. Aggie is going to be there with him this morning. I'll go in this afternoon." She paused. "I really do appreciate you, Blythe."

Tears stung Blythe's eyes.

# CHAPTER TWENTY-SEVEN
## AGGIE

Aggie sat at her desk in her new house and quickly went through her calendar for the week. Interspersed among her business appointments were the times she scheduled for hospital visits with Brad. At week's end, he would, she thought, be able to go home to continue healing. The fluid on his brain was minimal though he was considered far from recovered. That would take time—time during which it would be best for him to be at home. How he would react to having Logan do some of the oversight he used to do at the company was a huge unknown. He'd always taken pride in his work.

She made additions to her calendar, marking times to set aside for Donovan. In a couple of weeks, he planned to return to Florida to take care of his own business needs. She hoped to go back with him but couldn't commit to it at this time.

Donovan appeared. "'Morning. What are you doing?"

"Just filling my calendar," she replied, hoping he wouldn't notice that he'd become one of her daily projects. With Blythe on board at the company, that shouldn't continue to be the case. Then she'd be able to spend most of her day with him.

He kissed her. "Remember, we planned to move into the hotel this afternoon. I've arranged for Curtis to take the boat from the airport to the hotel. His flight gets in at 4:30."

"I can't wait to meet him," Aggie said. "I want to make a good impression on him."

"Don't worry, Aggie. He's going to love you almost as much as I do. We're quite alike."

Aggie laughed softly. "No one is quite like you, Donovan Bailey. Even after all these years, you're still unique." She got to her feet. "Let's have breakfast together, and then I have to be on my way."

"You're sure you want to drive your new car into Boston?"

She placed her hands on her hips. "Any reason to think I shouldn't?"

Laughing, he held up his hands. "No, no. I just wanted to make sure you were comfortable doing it."

"From the hospital, I'll go to the office and check in with Blythe and Logan. I want them to be independent, but not until I feel comfortable with what they're doing."

Donovan saluted her. "Okay then. My assistant is emailing me some paperwork. I'll be busy right here for most of the day."

"Okay." She poured him a cup of coffee and added some to her own. She couldn't wait to be able to spend as much time with him as she wanted. Until then, she'd make every moment count.


Later, when Aggie entered Brad's hospital room, she was surprised to see him sitting up watching her.

"Hi, darling!" Aggie cooed, approaching his bed with her arms out and a smile crossing her face.

He frowned and turned away from her. "Are you one of them?"

Aggie's body turned cold. She stopped in her tracks. "Brad, darling, what are you talking about?"

He glared at her. "You know. One of the ones who want to hurt me."

"I'm your mother, Brad. I would never hurt you," Aggie said as calmly as she could while her heart was beating so fast she was lightheaded.

He studied her a moment and then leaned back against his pillow. "Mom?"

"Yes, Brad. It's me," Aggie said softly, cautiously moving toward him. "I'm here to help you."

He gave her a wary look but allowed her to take hold of his free hand. "There, there," she cooed. "Everything's all right."

He closed his eyes.

She waited until his breathing evened out and then pushed the button for the nurse.

"What's happening?" Aggie asked her, stepping over to the doorway to answer the nurse's inquisitive look. "Brad's talking about people wanting to hurt him."

"Sometimes brain-injury patients can't distinguish what's real and what isn't. They may see things or hear things that aren't there. Some patients become restless, nervous, and easily frustrated during this time. It can be disturbing to family members to see this happen, but it's part of the healing process. The brain is an incredible organ and recovers in different ways for each patient. I wouldn't be too alarmed. Perhaps it's part of a bad dream. He's sleeping peacefully now."

Aggie swallowed hard. It was so difficult to see Brad like this. Maybe she wouldn't be able to leave the day-to-day running of the firm to Blythe as soon as she'd hoped. They'd both been counting on her father's help through the transition. Now, more than ever, Logan would have to be able to step up to the job.

Though Brad didn't wake up but continued to sleep, Aggie stayed at the hospital as long as she could. She returned to the office discouraged.

Aggie walked into Blythe's office. "How are things going? Do you have any questions for me?"

Blythe looked up from working at her desk. "A lot of questions. I'd like to compare sales from last year to the year before. I have a few ideas about new items and want to get your opinion on those. And, Gran, I need to meet with the managers of the stores."

"Logan also has to meet with all the managers. The two of you can do that together. Most can be day trips. The stores in Hyannis and on Nantucket might take an overnight trip. We'll talk to him about that." Aggie sat in a chair in front of Blythe's desk. "Now, let's discuss the new items you want to introduce to the stores."

Aggie spent the next few hours going over facts, figures, and ideas with Blythe about how the inventory process worked, including the system of making items in one store available to the other stores when the need arose.

When they took a break for a late lunch, Logan joined them. They made plans for Blythe and Logan to travel to visit all the different stores. Satisfied that things were off to an excellent start, Aggie headed back to New Life, eager to get ready to meet Curtis. She'd done some investigation on her own and knew what a handsome and talented man he was. But she was anxious to get to know the real man, not the one she read about. She'd finished two of his books and was curious to know what parts of the main character, if any, he might be.

Donovan greeted her with a kiss and then performed a little twirl in front of her. "See how well I'm doing? The physical therapist here is great, and swimming has helped."

She reached up and cupped his cheek. "I'm ready to dance with you anytime."

He grinned and held out his hand.

She made a little curtsy and took it.

As they swayed back and forth, the years melted away. Aggie closed her eyes, storing this moment in her mind to savor over and over again.

The hotel, situated on the waterfront on Rowe's Wharf, was the perfect place to spend time with Curtis, Aggie thought, gazing out the window at the activity below. The late May weather was perfect for being on the water or strolling the streets of downtown Boston. Faneuil Hall Marketplace was a short walk away, something Blythe and Logan might elect to do with Curtis.

As she and Donovan awaited Curtis's arrival, Aggie wished she could stop the thrumming of her nerves. She hoped they'd have plenty of time to become acquainted before Blythe and Logan were to join them for dinner. It was important for Curtis to like her. Donovan adored his adopted son.

Donovan came up behind her and nuzzled her neck. "I can't understand why you're so nervous, Aggie. You've nothing to fear."

"I hope so. I gather from what you've told me Curtis is quite protective of you."

"Yes, in the past, he's wanted to protect me from the socialites in Palm Beach. Not someone like you."

She stepped back and gave him a steady stare. "And that makes me?"

"The most genuine, the kindest, the most wonderful woman I know," he said. "C'mon. Time to go downstairs. I told Curtis we'd meet him in the lobby."

Aggie and Donovan took the elevator to the lobby and stepped out onto an expanse of gleaming marble floors covered with colorful area rugs and surrounded by elegant appointments throughout the space.

They were headed to one of the couches when Aggie heard someone call out, "Dad! I'm here. I arrived a few minutes early."

A tall young man rose from a chair and hurried to Donovan. Aggie watched them embrace, touched by the show of affection between them. Though Donovan's marriage had been unhappy, he had, at least, gained a son.

After Curtis and Donovan broke apart, Donovan clapped him on the back and turned to her. "Curtis, here is the woman of my dreams, Aggie Robard, my fiancée. I want you to get to know her and come to love her as much as I do."

Deep brown eyes studied her from a craggy, handsome face that showed character. Thick, shiny, chocolate-brown hair met the collar of his blue-denim shirt. He looked, Aggie thought, like the hero in his books. His lips curved. "Hello, Aggie. Nice to meet you."

"I've been anxious to meet you," Aggie said. "Not only as Donovan's son but as a fan of yours. I've enjoyed your last two books."

"Thanks. That means a lot," he replied. "Especially after the day I've had."

Donovan gave him a look of concern. "C'mon, son. We'll have more privacy to talk and relax in the suite I've reserved."

The three of them walked through the lobby and stepped into the elevator. Aggie broke the silence. "I'm so glad we have this opportunity to meet, Curtis. My granddaughter, Blythe, and Logan will join us for dinner. We thought you'd enjoy being with them. I understand you and Logan are best friends."

Curtis' face lit. "Friends since we were kids getting into trouble. Dad has always made sure to include Logan as part of our small family."

"He's working for Aggie now," said Donovan, ushering them off the elevator and down the corridor to their suite.

"Really? I guess I missed out on all kinds of things while I was on the book tour from hell," said Curtis.

He followed them inside the room and walked over to the large windows overlooking the water. "What a view! I've always loved Boston."

"Me too," said Donovan, wrapping an arm around Aggie's shoulder. "Now, more than ever." He waved Curtis to one of the comfortable chairs. "Have a seat. I've ordered a bottle of pinot noir and a few appetizers. We have a lot of reasons to toast one another. Your book is a New York Times bestseller."

"Thanks, Dad. But I think we'd better toast you and Aggie. My career's a mess right now. My new editor doesn't get my main character at all. She's trying to change him, make him a swashbuckling fool."

"That doesn't sound good," said Donovan. "I've read every single book of yours, and your hero's appeal is because of his brains, not any phony brawn."

"Precisely. That's what I told my editor." Curtis held up a hand. "I don't want to talk about it anymore." He faced Aggie with a smile. "I want to learn more about this woman who stole your heart. My apologies, Aggie, but I looked you up online. I love the idea of your taking a small family business and building it."

"Thanks. It hasn't been easy, but it's fascinating work. To an ordinary person, hardware stores may sound boring, but our stores are multipurpose and mean much more than tools, nuts, and bolts. We like to think we've got something for every homeowner with home décor and gift items. Those parts of the business have carried us through some hard times."

"Interesting," said Curtis, accepting a glass of wine from Donovan.

"Yes, it certainly is," commented Donovan, handing Aggie her glass and taking a seat next to her on the couch. "A customer can count on Robard stores for quality, consistency, and service."

Aggie laughed with delight. "Well done. You must've been reading one of our ads."

"You started this business with your husband?" Curtis asked.

"Yes, Arnold and I had graduated from Cornell and started working at the store when his father died. We married and worked together to save the family store and grew it from there."

"I would think today it would be tough to compete with the big-box retailers and online businesses," said Curtis.

"The secrets of our success are the things Donovan mentioned that have been the core of our business philosophy since inception and have created strong loyalty from our customers. If an owner is fixing something, he can't wait for the proper screwdriver or wrench to be ordered and delivered; he needs that tool right away. We advise homeowners on how to do a certain project, demonstrate the tools required, and are a continued, convenient resource. It's real, knowledgeable people talking to real people. I must say, the camaraderie that comes from this kind of interaction is really satisfying. On Saturday mornings, you can often find a small group of men enjoying free coffee at one of our stores, talking to one another. We encourage it. Women, as well as men, enjoy our how-to classes."

"And Logan is working for you now?" Curtis asked.

"Yes. My son was in an automobile accident and is recovering from a brain injury. Logan has signed up to be with the company for six months while awaiting the start of his new job. I'll let him tell you about it at dinner."

"I'm sorry to hear about your son," Curtis said. "I know from doing research for one of my books that recovery from that kind of trauma can take some time."

"It's been scary seeing what the injury has done to him," admitted Aggie. The doctors are optimistic, though. And each day, there's a little improvement. I hope this time away from work will lead him into teaching, which has always been a dream of his."

"I hope so too." Curtis turned to Donovan. "So, tell me how all of this happened, old man. I go away, and you become engaged."

Donovan chuckled and looked at her. "As Aggie would say, it all began with a road trip to see old friends."

"A road trip to remember," Aggie said, feeling Donovan's fingers wrapped around her hand.

"This is the young girl I wanted to marry after college. It's taken years, but we're finally together." Donovan swiped at his eyes. "I'll always be grateful I had a chance to get things right."

Aggie's vision blurred. She gazed out the window, thankful for this time with him. It still hurt that his family had been so set against Donovan marrying her. They hadn't even known her well at all.

"Here's to both of you!" said Curtis, raising his glass.

"To *all* of us," said Aggie. "Health and happiness!"

'How about you, son? Any special woman in your life?" Donovan asked. "I know you've been pretty busy, but it's always nice to come home to someone."

Curtis made a face. "No. A lot of women think being married to a famous writer would be exciting, but it's a job like any other. When the time comes, I want to find someone down to earth. I'm pretty boring."

Aggie and Donovan glanced at one another. Curtis was anything but boring. Quiet, yes. Boring, no.

The more they talked together, the more Aggie liked Curtis. He was a very nice man. And the way Donovan and he interacted made her wish that Brad and Donovan would have the opportunity to get to know one another.

# CHAPTER TWENTY-EIGHT
## BLYTHE

After a grueling afternoon of going through the figures from all the stores' gift sales, Blythe could hardly wait for Logan to finish a call so they could drive together into Boston to meet Gran, Donovan, and Curtis. She knew all about Curtis and his books and was eager to see what kind of person he was. She knew from her earlier behavior that Gran was nervous about meeting him.

"Ready to go?" said Logan, coming into her office. "I'm looking forward to a nice dinner with everyone."

"I've heard the restaurant at the hotel is one of the best."

"Well, let's see for ourselves. I doubt I'll have too much opportunity to go there on my own."

On the way into Boston, Blythe and Logan easily talked business as she drove. They were more or less in the same boat, studying figures from the past so they could better judge what was happening in the business today.

"Suzie made reservations for us in Hyannis when we tour the stores," she said. "From there, we can fly into Nantucket to check out the store there. I'm anxious to see it because it's quite different from our other locations."

"It would have to be. Nantucket is an upscale market."

"I know all about it. One of the girls at the prep school Liz and I attended couldn't wait to tell everyone about her family's summer home there." Blythe shook her head at the memory. "She bragged about her family a lot."

"I like Florida beaches myself," said Logan. "But I'm going to try to spend some time on the Cape this summer. Ben's family has a summer home in Centerville. I used to go there with him when we were in college together. It's nice, not pretentious at all." He elbowed her. "Maybe Ben will invite you too."

"He seems like a good guy," Blythe said.

"With his looks and family connections, girls have always lined up to date him. He says he hasn't met the right girl yet, but I don't think he's ready to settle down with anyone. Just warning you."

"What is this? A big brother act?" Blythe said, giving him a teasing smile.

He grinned and shrugged. "Maybe. That's the kind of relationship we have."

She stared straight ahead, not wanting him to see how conflicted she was.


At the hotel, Blythe turned her car over to the valet and walked into the elegant lobby, pleased she'd dressed especially nice for work that day. Following Gran's directions, she and Logan took the elevator up to the suite Donovan had reserved.

"What's Curtis like?" Blythe asked Logan, straightening her linen jacket.

"You'll like him. Everyone does."

She drew a breath. She'd read about Curtis, seen pictures of him online, and had even taken the time to read his latest book. After all, he and she would soon be related.

Gran stood in the hallway by the door to the suite, beaming at them. "Hi! I'm so glad you're here. Blythe, you'll love meeting Curtis, and Logan, I'm sure he'll be glad to see you. Donovan's been grilling him about the possibility of coming into the family foundation work."

"Whoa! What about his writing career?"

"It's not a good time right now, apparently. He'll tell you all about it."

Blythe followed Gran inside and stood before Donovan and a young man even taller than Donovan. Looking up into his dark-brown eyes, Blythe felt it would be easy to fall into his gaze. Blinking rapidly to shake off the unexpected reaction to him, she stepped back.

"This is Curtis," Donovan said. "And, Curtis, this sweet young woman is Blythe, Aggie's granddaughter and a true treasure."

Curtis held out his hand. "Nice to meet you."

"Thanks. Nice to meet you too," she responded, wondering how he'd fit into Gran's life.

"Hey, Curt!" Logan exchanged man hugs with Curtis, drawing attention away from her.

They took seats in the living area of the suite. Sipping the wine Donovan had poured for her, Blythe listened as Logan and Curtis bantered about their lives these past few weeks.

She and Gran exchanged looks of satisfaction when Logan explained what he'd already learned about the business of handling multiple retail outlets. It was more complicated than a lot of people would imagine. Maintaining and managing inventory was just one aspect of the job.

Curtis opened up about his frustration with the publishing business. "No matter what I do, it's never enough for my editor, my agent, or a few of my readers. I'm getting ready to take a break, maybe work with Dad for a bit before starting a new series."

Surprised, Blythe said, "But you're doing so well; why step back now?"

He gave her a steady look. "It would be for only a short

break. My agent is working on a movie deal. I'm hoping to work with that. We'll see. Nothing is guaranteed in Hollywood."

"Sounds like you're getting close to burning out," said Logan. "I say relax. You still have lots of time to write."

"I agree. I couldn't ever give up writing; it's what I was born to do. I just need to slow down. Book tours are exhausting. Maybe I'm just tired."

"Florida will do you good, son," Donovan said. "Until I get things better organized, I'll be traveling back and forth from there to Boston. Both Aggie and I are trying to ease out of working so hard."

"We want to be able to relax and enjoy one another," Gran added, giving Donovan a smile that would melt anyone's heart.

Donovan winked at her, stood, and grabbed his cane. "Time to go down for dinner. I've made reservations at the best restaurant here. Figured that would make it easy for everyone."

Blythe followed the others out of the room, her mind spinning. Curtis had accomplished so much at his age. Logan, a year younger, had used his time after graduation to travel the world and learn the business of running a family charitable foundation. She, on the other hand, was just beginning to come into her own. Her thoughts flew to her father. What if he was never able to go back to work? What would happen then?

Blythe's morbid thoughts faded as she joined the others in enjoying the views out the window of the restaurant and, more importantly, eating delicious food. Her scallops, fresh from Georges Bank, were prepared with a browned-butter, lemon, and caper sauce and melted in her mouth.

She listened as the conversation swirled around her,

making her more determined than ever to balance her life, to travel, perhaps, and to have fun as Gran often told her.

When they rose from the table, Curtis turned to her with a smile. "I'd like to take you to dinner tomorrow if you're free. If we're going to be family, I want to know a whole lot more about you."

"That would be lovely," she said. "I live here in the Leather District. With you here at the hotel, it should be easy to find a convenient place to meet."

"Sounds like a good plan. Give me your number." He pulled out his cell, unlocked it, and handed it to her. "I'll call you tomorrow, and we can discuss place and time. I'm pretty much free all day."

"Thanks. It should be fun," she said and entered her info.

Blythe ignored the frown on Logan's face, kissed Gran goodbye, and gave Donovan a quick peck on the cheek before leaving the hotel with Logan. She found Logan attractive, would date him in a heartbeat, but he'd placed her firmly in the friend zone. Besides, she knew how important it was to follow Gran's simple rule. The one they'd both agreed to.


Before Blythe went into work the next day, she stopped at the hospital to check on her father. He seemed more relaxed as he lay in bed, staring out the window.

"Hi, Dad!" she called out cheerfully, coming to his side.

He looked at her as if she were a stranger. "Hello."

Blythe's heart plummeted. "It's me. Blythe, your daughter."

A shadow crossed his face, and then his eyes brightened. "Hi."

"I talked to Constance this morning. She'll be in to see you later today. And Gran said she'd stop by this afternoon."

Her father studied her. "Okay."

She kissed him. "I love you, Dad. I want you to get better. As soon as all the swelling is gone and you get the doctor's permission, you'll be able to come home to rest."

"Yes. I want to go home."

"I know. We all want you to be at home. I just stopped by to see you before going to work. I'll come by later."

"Blythe?"

She looked at him. "Yes?"

"Hi."

She inched closer to him. "Yes, it's me, Blythe. I love you, Dad."

He patted her back awkwardly. "'Bye."

Excited by his response to her, Blythe hurried to the nurse's station and told them what happened.

"Good," said one of the nurses. "This is progress."


That evening, when Blythe walked into J.P.'s Bar, she was exhausted both mentally and emotionally. Logan had uncovered irregularities in the financials at the store in Hyannis. After going over the situation with him, Blythe was convinced he was right. Someone was stealing from the company. A little bit here, a little bit there. It was recent enough for them to put a stop to it, but the thought of one of their employees doing this made her sick to her stomach. It also made her realize how overworked her father had been and how valuable Logan was to them.

Through the dim light inside the small, wood-paneled bar, Blythe noticed Curtis waving at her. She elbowed her way through the crowd and went over to him.

"Hi! Glad I came early," Curtis said. "This place is already crowded."

"Yes, one of the popular places in town."

He helped her into her chair at the high-top table and signaled the waitress. The redhead who hurried to their table grinned at Curtis. "What can I get you?"

Curtis turned to her. "What'll you have, Blythe?"

"A glass of pinot noir would be lovely. Something fairly light, with a smooth finish."

"And you?" the waitress asked Curtis, straightening and thrusting her breasts out.

"A vodka tonic," he said. "Thanks."

After the waitress left, he turned to Blythe. "How was your day?"

"Not the best," she said. "We've discovered some financial problems at one of the stores. It's disheartening."

"Oversight of any financials isn't easy," he said. "In the family's foundation, we get many requests for money from legitimate companies and others that aren't so honest. It involves a lot of investigation on our part. Even though we pay someone to do the day-to-day stuff, we need to make sure things are in order."

Their drinks came.

Curtis raised his glass. "Here's to better days!"

"Absolutely," Blythe said before taking a sip of the wine. "Thanks for inviting me out. It's a little weird that we might end up being related."

Curtis leaned forward. "What is this business with your grandmother and my dad? Do you think it's real? They certainly seem in love, but it's all so sudden."

"You're not a romantic guy?" Blythe said. "Your hero is."

Curtis gave her a shy grin. "My hero is a fictional character. Believe me, after living in the same house with Donovan and my mother fighting all the time, any idea of romance was destroyed."

"My parents divorced when I was young, and though my father remarried, I wouldn't say his relationship with my stepmother is very romantic. But Gran and Papa, her first husband, inspired all who knew them with the promise of romance. She loves Donovan too."

"A lot of women have wanted to entrap Donovan not only for his looks but for his money. I'm glad she's not like that."

"Wow," Blythe exclaimed. "You're a cynic about relationships. No girlfriends for you?"

"Not at the moment. I had a serious relationship that went kaput when she found out I wanted to be a writer. And then when I hit it big, she called and wanted to get back together."

Blythe swallowed a sip of wine before speaking. "I was fooled by a guy I thought I'd marry one day. But then I discovered the attention I enjoyed from him in the beginning was more about control than anything else. I have enough to worry about without juggling the demands of a relationship."

"What about Logan? I saw the way he looked at you."

"Logan? No, we're just friends. Besides, Gran has set a rule that as long as we're working together, we can't date."

"In that case, will you go to dinner with me again? I'm leaving for Florida in the morning to meet up with Logan to go over a few things with him for the foundation. I don't know how long I'll be gone. When I return, I'd like to take you out. I like you, Blythe, and like the fact that there's no pressure to do more than go out from time to time. Right?"

"Right." Her dating life was just starting, and already she was feeling like a total loser. Apparently, nothing but friends were in her future.

# CHAPTER TWENTY-NINE
## AGGIE

Aggie lay in bed next to Donovan feeling a sense of gratitude. The dinner she'd worried about the day before had turned out to be wonderful. Curtis was a kind man who obviously loved his adopted father. At evening's end, he hugged her warmly and wished them both the best. He'd seemed a bit lonely to her and liked Donovan's suggestion that he and Curtis spent much more time together while he regrouped.

Her thoughts went to the business. Blythe had told her that before he left for Florida to pack up his belongings to move to Boston, Logan had uncovered some issues they needed to talk about. As much as Brad sometimes chafed against the detailed work he was required to oversee, Aggie knew how important it was to the business. She hoped this discovery wasn't proof of Brad's growing disinterest.

"Hey, you," whispered Donovan. "Stop thinking and come cuddle with me." Smiling, she turned to him. She loved that he was so affectionate.

Soon all thoughts of business faded.


A couple of days later, after a short stint in the workout room to strengthen her hip and leg, Aggie and Donovan joined the other residents in the dining room for their morning meal. Donovan was already making friends with a group that used the health center in the morning and another group that played bridge in the afternoon. When he wasn't occupied with those activities, he was at his desk working on his family's foundation matters.

After breakfast, Aggie headed for Brad and Constance's house. With all signs of swelling gone and his memory slowly coming back, Brad was being released to go home. Physically he was good. His memory close to the time of the accident was fragmented, but the rest had come back.

She'd hired a nurse to help out the first week or so to make sure Brad received every bit of care he deserved. Constance was busy with a big social event she was committed to seeing through.

As she drove into the driveway of Brad's large home, Aggie admired the lines of it. Constance might not be the easiest person to get along with, but she had good taste. Aggie had learned early on a beautiful house didn't always mean a loving home. Her parents had spent their years together fighting. It wasn't until she and Arnold had moved into their first house that she'd discovered nothing mattered but the people inside sharing love.

She parked her car and went to the front door and stepped inside. The nurse was supposed to arrive any minute. Empty now with the boys at school, the house was quiet. She felt like walking on tiptoes as she entered the den. It was here, Constance hoped, that Brad would spend much of his time healing. She saw that Constance had placed a light blanket on Brad's favorite reclining chair.

The doorbell sounded. Aggie went to answer it and found a heavy-set, brown-skinned woman smiling at her.

"You must be Rita Gomez," Aggie said. "Please come in. The agency told me you were one of their best. I'm glad you're here. You can set your things down here in the front hall or in the kitchen, wherever you're comfortable. The patient, my son, will most likely be spending most of his time awake down here in the den."

"Thanks. Tell me about the patient. I understand he was in an automobile accident and had a brain injury that is healing nicely except for a bit of memory loss."

"That's right," Aggie said. "The doctors advised us there can be mood swings and other side effects as he struggles to remember everything and tries to get stronger. But each patient is a little different depending on their injury. Brad's isn't as severe as many."

"I see," said Rita. "Please show me the house, and I'll figure out the best way to handle things. Each family is different in how they want to work around my presence."

"Yes, I can understand. Besides my son and his wife, there are two boys, ten and twelve, who are in school most of every day. An older daughter works with me and may come and go but lives in downtown Boston."

Rita nodded with a look of calm. "Sounds easy enough."

They turned at the sound of a car pulling into the driveway.

"Here we go!" Aggie said, giving Rita an encouraging smile.

They went to the front entrance and watched through the screen door as Constance and Blythe walked slowly on each side of Brad, up the front walk to the steps.

"Welcome home, Dad!" Blythe said.

"Yes, darling, glad to have you home," said Constance.

He looked up at Aggie and Rita. "Who's that?" he asked, settling a gaze on Rita.

"A nurse your mother hired to help us out," said Constance.

Aggie opened the door and signaled Rita to join her. "This is Rita. I'm pleased she's able to be here. Say hello."

Brad frowned and then said a curt hello, which wasn't at all like him.

Aggie hid her disappointment. This wasn't the homecoming she'd envisioned but was one of a string of disappointments that were likely to come. The vibrant, active man Brad had always been was now a thinner, weaker, paler version of him, a sign, no doubt, of the other less tangible results of the accident.

"I'm sorry ..." Aggie began.

Rita held up a hand. "Not a problem. I've had many patients with similar injuries. He and I are going to be friends. You'll see."

Aggie studied the smile on her face and nodded. Rita was a true professional. She moved back out of the way as Constance led Brad inside.

"I thought you'd be comfortable in the den," Constance told him.

"Okay," Brad said. "I'm tired."

Aggie waited with Blythe while Constance led Brad to his chair and stood back as Rita helped him into it and then placed the blanket over him.

"Now, Mr. Brad, you call me if there's anything you need. Remember, I'm Rita and am here to help you. How about a glass of water or juice?"

"Water." He leaned back against the chair and closed his eyes.

Constance kissed him on the cheek and motioned Aggie and Blythe to follow her into the kitchen.

"Poor Dad. He's exhausted from the trip home," said Blythe. "I hadn't realized how weak he'd become."

"Aggie, thanks so much for hiring Rita," said Constance with a new note of gratitude. "With my commitment to the Summer Soiree Ball for the Newton-Wellesley Hospital, I can't give him the attention he needs."

"I understand. I made sure Rita's contract is for the whole

day, so she should be here for the boys when they get out of school."

"I can help out after five o'clock from time to time," offered Blythe.

"Or before if it's an emergency, Blythe," said Aggie. "You can have time off from work whenever you need it."

Blythe grinned. "A good thing I work for the family."

"That's something I want to discuss with both of you," said Constance, her features sharpening. "But not until after the ball."

"One thing at a time," Aggie said, suspicious of where that conversation would go.

Before she left, she went into the den and kissed Brad goodbye. "Have a wonderful day here at home," she whispered, observing the way his eyelids were drooping with sleep.

Blythe followed behind. "May I ride to the office with you? I left my car in Boston."

"Certainly. Check out my new 'wheels,'" said Aggie, pointing to the Mercedes SUV in shiny silver. "I figured this would be more comfortable for Donovan. He's doing so well now that I sometimes forget he might have another bad spell. My understanding is they come and go."

"Want me to drive? Test it out?" Blythe teased, grinning and her eyes sparkling.

Aggie tossed her the key fob. "Go ahead. It needs a workout."

Blythe laughed and climbed in behind the wheel.

As Blythe tested the car, she and Aggie were quiet, content to enjoy the time together until Blythe went too fast, then Aggie couldn't control herself. "Slow down, Missy. I don't want the police to stop you in my new car."

Chuckling, Blythe checked her speed. "Sorry."

When they pulled into the parking lot at the office building, Blythe said, "What do you think Constance wants to talk to us about?"

Aggie grimaced. "Can't be certain, but it won't be good."


After checking in with Suzie, Aggie and Blythe huddled in her office.

"Okay, let's talk about what Logan found," Aggie said.

Blythe drew a deep breath. "In comparing the numbers of certain items sold to inventory, purchasing, and requisitioning records, he discovered inconsistencies in the Hyannis store. Because of our suspicion, I checked personnel records. Most of the staff have worked there for years. We did hire two new people at Christmas. Only one stayed on."

"Okay, continue," said Aggie. Theft among her staff and customers was unusual, but it had happened. "Are we talking about one item, several items?"

"That's just it. The inventory counts are off by one or two on a variety of items. And because it was many items in such a short period of time, both Logan and I think it was an inside job. Without careful reconciliations, anyone could have missed it."

"I assume you made a list," Aggie said grimly. "Better show it to me."

Blythe handed her a printout.

Studying it, Aggie saw that most of the items were things someone could easily resell online—a tool kit, a coffeemaker, a crockpot, gardening tools, and other things that were stocked in the back of the store for ease of replenishing shelf displays.

"Let's look at the employee records. I believe that whoever is taking these things is not using them for themselves but is selling them online. A short while ago, I received a notice from the Better Business Bureau to owners of retail operations, warning about this kind of activity, especially during the holiday season."

In looking over the list of employees, Aggie mentally marked off each of the old-timers, including the manager, Paul Youngstrom. These people were loyal, settled in their lives, and didn't appear to be in financial trouble when she last met with them at Christmas time. The last name on the list was Anna Fields, a twenty-two-year-old divorced mother of two, whom they had hired just this past December.

"Instead of waiting until next week for you and Logan to visit the Hyannis store, I think Donovan and I will take a trip down to the Cape. I've wanted him to see some of the stores anyway. This will be a perfect time to do it."

"Who do you think is doing it?" Blythe said. "My bet is on Anna Fields."

"Mine too," said Aggie. "But we have to be very careful how we approach this. We don't want to judge too hastily. I'm not even going to tell Paul about my visit. I'll surprise him. My going there won't keep you and Logan from introducing yourselves to the staff. You'll do that as planned. It might end up being a good way of following up on our suspicions."

"What are you going to do if you find out who's been stealing from us?" Blythe asked.

"That depends on the circumstances. This hasn't been going on for very long, so we're not out a lot of money. Still, it's the whole idea of someone being willing to do this to us. Remember, we can't accuse anyone of doing such a thing without proof. Hopefully, we'll find a way to catch him or her without all that mess."

# CHAPTER THIRTY

## BLYTHE

With both Logan and Curtis out of town, Blythe was looking forward to an evening to do a little more work on her condo. She'd ordered some framed pictures. Bribed by the promise of wine and pizza, Liz had agreed to come to help her hang them. It felt good to spend time with Liz, who'd been one of her best friends in private school.

Though not beautiful, Liz, tall and lean, with long, deep auburn hair, was a striking woman whose intelligence shone through her hazel eyes. An assistant in a law office—Lowell, Brown, and Dixon, where she met Ben—she should've been a lawyer herself but had opted not to go to law school. Blythe knew she couldn't afford it, anyway. She'd attended their private school on a full scholarship.

Liz's roommate, Drew Spence, was a guy who sometimes shared his space with his partner Dave, something Liz was comfortable with as long as they both kept the place clean. One of six children, tidiness was essential to her. Blythe had found it easy to room with her.

Blythe unlocked the door to her condo and walked in, pausing a moment to sweep a critical gaze across the space. The gray couch looked perfect in front of the fireplace and went well with the subtle gray, green, and white pattern on the chair that sat on one side of it. She still needed a lamp, an end table, and a coffee table. Until she could afford another chair, she'd stacked a few floor pillows from college days on the other side of the fireplace below the wall-mounted television, a spot that allowed her to see the screen from the kitchen.

The abstract print she'd purchased would look stunning over the fireplace, she thought, adding a splash of color to brighten up what might otherwise be a fairly plain room. In the bedroom, she planned to hang a landscape over the bed and another on an inside wall outside the master bath.

As she surveyed the space, Blythe's heart welled with emotion. This was her first home, and she already loved it. She knew how lucky she was to have it, which made it even more special.

She'd just changed into jeans and a T-shirt when Liz knocked and called out to her. "I'm here!"

"Great!" Blythe replied, rushing to open the door. "Hi! I'm ready to share a glass of wine and, more importantly, ready to hang a few pictures,"

"The place looks great," Liz said, giving her a quick hug. "We've got a lot to talk about. Ben introduced me to Logan."

"And?"

"And he's a doll. I'm bummed I had to cancel a date with him the other night. A family emergency came up with one of my sisters."

"Is everything all right?" Blythe asked. As the youngest female sibling, Liz was often asked to help out with family issues.

"My sister Molly got called into work, and her husband is out of town. My mother usually helps out, but she had something special going on with friends. I was her last resort to stay with the baby." Liz emitted a sigh of frustration. "I couldn't say no. I'm little Mara's godmother."

"I filled in for you as Logan's date," said Blythe. "That's how I met Ben and Elle."

"They're great. We all got to know one another through work, and now we've become best friends. I'm glad you're going to be part of the group. Logan too."

"I love it," said Blythe. "Wait until you meet my new ... brother? Friend? In-law?"

Liz frowned. "Who are you talking about?"

"Curtis Bailey. My grandmother's fiancé's son."

"Wait a minute! You're not talking about the author, are you?"

Blythe grinned. "The one and only."

Liz's jaw dropped. "Girlfriend, you'd better start talking. You haven't been back two weeks, and all this has happened." Her expression grew serious. "But first, how's your father?"

"He was discharged this morning and is back home. Though he's healing, he's not quite the same. Depending on where the bruising takes place on the brain, different things can happen. He still can't remember the accident but now knows who we are. The doctors expect things will be all right after he's had a full recovery."

"Such a freak accident." Liz gave her a worried look. "Has the other driver been charged?"

"Haven't heard anything on that front yet. The driver of the truck came to a sudden stop for some reason, then his truck stalled. As you said, it was a freak accident."

"Thank God your father's alive. I've always liked him," said Liz, accepting the glass of wine Blythe offered her.

"Yeah, he's a good guy. It'll be interesting to see how everything plays out. There are certainly going to be lots of changes not only with work but with his outside life too." Blythe lifted her glass. "Here's to him and to us."

"Yes!" said Liz, clicking her glass against Blythe's. "Before we get started on the projects, tell me about Curtis Bailey. He's a friend of Logan's. Right?"

"Yes. They've been best friends since they were boys."

"What a pair they must have been. And I must say both are extremely handsome."

Blythe set down her wine glass. "There's something very appealing about each of them. Logan and I aren't allowed to date as long as he's working for the company. And it would seem odd for me to date Curtis, don't you think?"

"Hell no! Why would you think that?"

"Because of Gran and Donovan. They're so great together. I wouldn't want anything to interfere with their relationship if anything went wrong."

"Mmm, I think I see your point." But I can tell by the disappointment in your voice that you're attracted to him. Am I right?"

Blythe couldn't hold back a sigh. "I felt a powerful connection to him, but he just wants to be friends. I'm afraid that's the story of my life going forward. I sometimes feel as old as Gran with all the responsibilities I already have for the family business."

"Don't worry. You'll have plenty of chances to meet people. Our group is pretty social." Liz held out her glass for another refill. "Tell me about Logan. He seems like a nice guy who's a lot of fun and down-to-earth."

Blythe felt her lips curve. "Logan is smart and confident without any swagger or need to dictate. I think back to what Chad was like, and I wonder how I could've ever been attracted to him."

"It wasn't all your fault, Blythe. He turned out to be quite a chameleon. Who knew underneath all that charm, he was such a manipulator, such a control freak?"

Blythe frowned at the memory. "Maybe that's why I'm

clinging to the idea of someone like Logan or Curtis, someone the family already approves of and knows."

"Could be."

"No use pining for someone I've already agreed to keep as a friend."

"I'm sorry. Would it bother you if I want to get to know those guys better?" said Liz.

Blythe shook her head. "I'll introduce you to Curtis when he's in town. He's due to return soon."

Liz gave her a quick hug. "Thanks. I'll owe you big time if anything comes of it."

Blythe ordered pizza for a later time, and they set to work hanging the pictures. They worked well together as good friends do, but Blythe couldn't help wishing she at least had a chance of dating the man who'd had such a profound effect on her because Liz was pretty hard to beat.

# CHAPTER THIRTY-ONE
## AGGIE

Each time Aggie entered one of her stores, she filled with pride. One of her strict rules was that each operation had to be kept tidy and clean at all times. At the close of every day, the person in charge of the closing shift was responsible for dusting and vacuuming the entire display area. The people on the morning shift had to go through the store to make sure everything was in order, and they were also each to walk through and inspect the displays of merchandise so when customers asked about different products, they could walk customers to the items sought quickly and easily.

The Hyannis staff, without knowing of her unscheduled appearance, had kept to the task. As she glanced around, Aggie thought it was all but sparkling, especially in the gift and home décor departments.

"Hi, Aggie!" Paul Youngstrom, the manager, hurried toward her with a smile. "What brings you to Hyannis?" He let out a small laugh. "I should've said welcome first. Either way, it's a privilege to have you here. Would you like a cup of coffee? Some water?"

"No, thanks. Come and meet Donovan Bailey, my fiancé. I'm showing him around."

Paul and Donovan shook hands.

"Looks like a great 'toy' store," said Donovan. "I'm already tempted to go up and down the aisles looking at tools and gadgets."

Paul smiled and bobbed his head. "Whatever you want, we either have or will order for you for a quick delivery."

"I like that. I'll look around while you and Aggie take care of business."

After saying hello and introducing Donovan to a couple of other staff members, Aggie left him to browse and went into Paul's office.

"What's up?" Paul asked, offering her a seat in a chair by his desk.

"The beginning of a problem that could become concerning," she said. "Someone is stealing from our store."

"What? We do a careful inventory each month. How long has this been going on?"

"I believe it's only just started. Logan Pierce, who's stepping in for Brad for the next six months, has been working on a sales and inventory reconciliation. He's discovered around $600 of variances that make it appear as if someone is helping themselves to selected products. I've looked over the personnel records. Would you have any reason to suspect anyone of doing this? We're pretty sure it's an inside job because all the items in question are those that are in the back storeroom."

Paul gave her a thoughtful look. "You know my full-time staff members have been here for years. I can't believe they would suddenly do anything like this. I haven't heard of any financial or other motive for them to do this."

"And your part-time staff?"

"We currently have only one part-timer, though we'll be hiring more for the summer trade." He said, "Anna Fields is my part-timer. She does a wonderful job. As a special favor to her and the rest of the staff, I have her come in to clean the store after hours when she gets a neighbor to stay with her two young children. I can't believe she'd do anything like this."

"No financial troubles?" Aggie asked.

Paul let out a long breath and frowned. "Her husband took off on her. She's doing all she can to make it on her own, but one of the kids is constantly sick with asthma. She has no family support, leaving her completely on her own. I told her she could go to full-time so she could get our health insurance, but she's held off until the high school lets out for the summer, and she can hire a part-time babysitter cheap."

"Blythe and Logan are about to start visiting all the stores. Please see what you can find out about Anna. She has the motive and the opportunity, but we can't accuse her of anything without proof unless you can get her to talk."

"I agree. If it's her, would you be forced to fire her?" Paul's brow creased with concern. "Aside from this, she's a good kid. Hardworking."

"That will depend on Blythe and Logan. I have my own suggestion, but I'm waiting to see what they come up with. Please keep everything quiet until they come later this week."

"Will do," said Paul. "In the meantime, I'll talk to my other employees to see if anyone else would have the motive."

"Good idea. I'll go now. I'm going to drive around so Donovan can get a sense of the area and how Robard's fits into the retail community. I simply wanted to give you a heads up on Blythe and Logan's forthcoming visit and their concerns. Afterward, you and I can talk."

Paul got to his feet. "How's Brad doing? Suzie sent an update to all of us, but I need to hear from you that he's going to be fine. He's a great guy. I've enjoyed working with him through the years."

"Thanks for asking. The doctors and we are very optimistic about a full recovery for him. Secretly, though, I'm wondering whether his accident will lead to him wanting to step away from the day-to-day business of overseeing the stores, especially now that Blythe is taking on a bigger role. I, myself, want to be able to spend more time away from the business. It's time for me to have a little fun, and I've found the perfect man to do it with."

Paul's eyes lit with affection. "I've always said I want to be just like you when I grow up. After I retire, Lucy and I hope to be able to travel, but that won't be for several years."

"You're a great member of the management team, and we need you. We want you to be happy and able to have time for yourself. Having you happy keeps the entire store family happy."

"That's what makes us a better place to work than most," said Paul smiling.

"Indeed." Aggie gave him a quick hug. "Talk to you soon."


After Donovan and she got settled in their room overlooking Hyannis Harbor just steps from the wharf for the ferries to Nantucket and Martha's Vineyard, Aggie decided to sit out in the sun on their balcony. In addition to telling herself to have more fun, she needed to remind herself to slow down. Otherwise, when it came time for Blythe to take over, she wouldn't be able to walk away from her life's work.

Growing old was such a strange, awkward, and sometimes horrible phase of life, she thought as she gazed up into the sun. She still thought of herself as being in her forties, and yet, here she was, a woman in her seventies and newly in love. What was it the younger people in the office said? *"Just roll with it."*

The sliding glass door behind her opened, and Donovan stepped out onto the balcony.

"Pleasant," he said, sitting in the chair beside her. "Love the smell of the ocean air and everything that goes with it."

"Do you miss Florida?" she asked.

"Not yet. I will when the cold weather comes. But I'll put up with it to be here with you."

"By year's end, we should be able to spend as much time as we want in either place. That is if Brad is able and wants to continue to work for the company and Blythe is willing and able to take over for me as we'd planned."

"She's bright and capable. Is there any reason to doubt it?" Donovan asked.

"I worry that I'm being unfair to her. She's young and might want to do other things. Maybe travel, fall in love, have a big family."

"Working at the family company isn't going to prevent her from leading a normal life, is it?" Donovan said, gently chiding her.

Aggie thought about it. "No, I guess not. I just hope Blythe doesn't feel trapped by the expectations I've placed on her."

"I certainly don't sense any hesitancy on her part to take on the new role. She once told me how lucky she was to have it."

Aggie opened her eyes and smiled at him. "You always make me feel better. I love you for that, Donovan. It was always that way between us, which made our break-up so painful."

"If only we could go back and do things differently." He took hold of her hand and brought it to his lips. "This, being here with you, living with you, is the best outcome for our second chance. I love you, Aggie girl. I always have."

She arched an eyebrow. "I haven't, you know."

"What? Always loved me?" he asked, surprised.

"Right. For a long time, I despised you even as I loved Arnold." She gazed at him. "Sometimes our emotions place us on an endless, unhealthy journey. I didn't want that to happen to me, so I just stopped thinking of it and turned my attention to Arnold, who was a wonderful man. A lot like you, he made me happy except for those years of his drinking."

Donovan looked out at the scene beyond them. "In all honesty, neither of my marriages was great. There was an emptiness inside me that no one seemed able to fill. Some might think we're crazy to get engaged at our age, but those are people who've never had a love like ours, as broken as it once was."

Aggie thought about his words and knew he was right except for one thing. What they were sharing wasn't just a revival of old love but the creation of a newer, better love based on life's experiences. They were not the same. And neither was the love they shared.

# CHAPTER THIRTY-TWO
## BLYTHE

The planned trips to visit the stores began. Most were within easy driving distance. Hyannis and Nantucket were the farthest away. When at last it was time to travel there, Logan picked up Blythe at her condo, and they headed south.

As Logan drove down the South Shore on Route 3 toward the Cape and Hyannis, Blythe was content to look out the window and allow her thoughts to drift. She was excited to meet the store managers and as many of the staff as possible at each location. They would be important members of the team she was building. Loyal to Gran, they would, she hoped, be willing to help her as she took over. Like any business with different locations, The Robard Company relied on their staff to represent them well in the community, be honest and kind to their staff, and be loyal to the people who owned it.

Though Gran and Donovan had made a quick trip to Hyannis to investigate, Gran had informed them that she would wait for their recommendation of how best to handle the problem before taking any steps to remedy the situation. They now knew from Paul the young mother was the culprit.

"How'd your date with Liz go?" Blythe asked Logan.

"She's nice. I also have a date with Elle next week."

"Ben's date?" Blythe couldn't hide her surprise. Logan had been back in Boston for only a few days and seemed busy most nights.

"Yes. She and I hit it off the other night. Ben isn't serious about her. He asked for your number. You might be getting a call from him."

"It's beginning to sound a little bit like some television show with everyone dating everyone else," said Blythe laughing.

"Except that you and I can't date," Logan said.

At the sound of regret in his voice, she glanced over at him. He continued looking straight ahead.

Conversation ceased as Blythe took the time to look over some figures for Hyannis she intended to ask Paul about. Nothing was wrong; she just needed a clearer understanding of how things were categorized.

"What are we going to do about Anna?" she asked Logan. "She's admitted to Paul that she'd stolen several items."

Logan glanced at her. "What do you want to do about her?"

Blythe hesitated and then said, "I want to know her story. The one behind her doing that."

"Okay. That sounds reasonable to me. Paul had every intention of giving her more hours as part of the summer crew. That means something."

"I've got an idea on how to handle it, but it all depends on what we find out when we talk to her."

Logan grinned. "Holding back on me?"

She laughed. "Maybe so. If it doesn't work, I'll tell you about my idea anyway, so you know where I'm coming from."

"Any decision shouldn't be too hard. It's a straightforward business move."

Blythe nodded but didn't say anything. She was pretty sure she was right to sit back and think about the situation in a different way.

"We're almost there. Do you want to stop for lunch before we visit the store?" Logan asked her.

"Yes. I'm starving." Blythe knew some women either pretended they didn't eat much or ordered only small portions. She enjoyed food and wasn't ashamed to admit it. It was a philosophy she shared with her grandmother.

Instead of fast food, they decided to enjoy the warm air and bright blue skies and eat a leisurely lunch on the outdoor patio of a seafood restaurant.

Sitting in the shade of an umbrella, Blythe gazed out at the water watching seagulls circle in the sky above. Others swooped down to get crusts of bread tourists tossed out on the water. The squawking sounds they made were in direct proportion to the number of goodies available.

"I'd forgotten how lovely a day like this can be next to the water," said Blythe.

They each ordered fish and chips. They chatted about Logan's move to Boston throughout the meal and how he felt more at home here with friends both old and new than he had in Florida. Memories of unhappy times with his own family kept breaking into the protective shell he usually kept around him. His mother, who would never win a prize for parenting, tended to want more of his time as she was aging. It was something he wasn't prepared to give.

"I get it; I really do," said Blythe.

"You're lucky you had Gran. And I'm lucky I had Donovan to step in and help me deal with it. Funny how things have turned out. One big circle after another."

Blythe was pleased they could talk openly like this. Other people might not understand how deeply a mother could hurt a child.

After lunch, they drove to the store, climbed out of the car, and stood gazing at it. Gray clapboards covered the exterior of the building. White trim edged the large windows where attractive displays hinted at all kinds of treasures inside.

Inside, a few customers were wandering the aisles or standing at the checkout counter, waiting to pay.

Paul tapped on the window of the upstairs office and waved.

While they waited for him to join them, Blythe stood near the checkout counter so she could hear what was going on.

"I love the new line of garden décor," said one woman, placing two large, green-glazed pots and a frog figure made of cast iron on the counter.

"I love it, too," said the woman behind the cash register. "We always try to have unique things."

Blythe couldn't stop the smile she felt spreading across her face. She and Gran had ordered those items last winter.

A man plunked down a number of screws on the counter. "This ought to do it. If not, I'll bring these back and give it another try. You order something from China, and you're never sure what you're going to get."

"Not a problem," said the older gentleman behind the counter. "Keep your receipt, and we'll be glad to help out. As a matter of fact, if you bring in a sample of what you're working on, we can make sure you not only get the right screws but have all you need to make it right."

*"Oh, Gran,"* Blythe thought, *"You'd be so proud of everyone here."*

Paul joined her. "Good to see you again, Blythe. I understand you've finished school and are about to run the company."

She laughed. "Not quite yet. I want you to meet Logan Pierce. He's helping us out for a few months while Dad is recovering."

"Aggie said he was doing well," said Paul.

"He's been home for a few days now. He seems happier, but he's coping with some side effects—things like depression and anger that he can't remember details about things. Gran hired a great nurse's aide, and she's been a blessing."

"I'm glad to hear he's on the mend, though it sounds as if it's all a bit of a challenge." He turned to Logan. "Aggie's told me quite a bit about you. It sounds as if it's very fortuitous you'll be part of the team for a while."

"Yessir," Logan said, shaking Paul's hand. "In the short time I've been with The Robard Company, I've discovered I need to learn a whole lot more. I hope I can have you answer some questions."

"Sure thing. Let me introduce you to the staff before we sit down and talk."

A short while later, Blythe and Logan sat in Paul's office. Though there was a lot of paperwork on his desk, it appeared to be in neat piles, not scattered.

Paul cleared his throat. "Let's talk about all your questions before we address Anna Fields' situation. She's due to come in at three. I'd feel more comfortable if we waited for her."

"Fine with me," said Blythe, checking her watch. "That will give us time to take care of it before we fly over to Nantucket to check that store out."

Logan and Blythe went over their lists of questions and concerns about the store, discussing everything from inventory needs to new pricing on some of the standard items.

Blythe was relieved when she heard a knock at the door and turned to see a young woman looking at them warily as if she was about to meet the grammar school principal.

Small, thin, and dressed in jeans and a navy-blue golf shirt with The Robard Company logo in white and red, she looked more like a twelve-year-old than the mother of two young children. There was something so tentative about her demeanor that Blythe was more convinced than ever that her idea was the right direction to take.

"Come in, Anna," said Paul rising to his feet. "This is Blythe Robard, Aggie Robard's granddaughter and soon-to-be successor, and Logan Pierce, who's helping out in the financial department."

Anna's cheeks went white and then flushed pink. "Hello."

"It's good of you to set aside time to talk to us," said Blythe. "Logan and I are making trips to our various stores, and we wanted the opportunity to speak to you."

"Are you going to fire me?" she asked, her voice trembling. She remained standing by the door.

"Do you think we should?" asked Blythe, carefully waiting for an answer.

"Yes, I do," Anna said. "But I promise if you don't, you'll never have trouble from me again. I did what I did for my children. It was wrong, and I knew it, but at the time, it was my only option. I'd already worked out a plan to pay you back when you found out that I'd been taking a few things to sell on eBay and Craig's list. Here is a list of the things I took. It shows the date, the amount, and the value. You see, Mr. Youngstrom offered me summer hours and overtime. That's how I was going to pay for everything." Her whole body sagged, and her eyes filled with tears. "My son, Darin, has asthma. My ex hasn't paid child support for a year. I don't think he ever will. Without insurance, I can't afford the medicine that Darin needs."

"What do you do here?" Blythe asked quietly.

She shuffled her sneakered feet. "I help out wherever I can—cash register, gift sales, working in the stock room. Mr. Youngstrom allows me to stay after hours to clean the store. As soon as I can get a babysitter from the high school to help me, I'll be able to put in more hours here."

"And then you'd qualify for health insurance for your family?" Blythe said.

"I hope so. This is the best job I can imagine. I don't have any other skills. I got pregnant in high school."

"And you went ahead and had your baby and then another?"

Anna gave Blythe a steady stare. "I love my children. They're the best thing I've ever done."

Her words hit Blythe hard. Anna's children were lucky to have her in their lives. They had something Blythe had never known—a mother's unconditional love. Blythe indicated a chair. "Please, sit down, Anna. I'd like to offer you a deal."

Anna took a seat beside her and clutched her hands together.

"First of all, we'll bring no charges against you. As you pointed out, you already have a plan to pay us back. Second, I would like to arrange with you to do some work from home, if you're willing and able. That should help with babysitting worries. And third, we will give you a special position and title that will allow you to have health insurance coverage."

Blythe turned to Logan, who looked surprised. "Do you agree?"

"Sounds like a solid plan," he said.

"I'll work with Blythe and you, Anna, to come up with that new position," said Paul.

Anna gazed at them wide-eyed and burst into tears. "Thank you! Thank you for giving me another chance!"

Blythe went to her and gave her a good, long hug. Gran, she was sure, would be proud of the way she'd handled the case.

# CHAPTER THIRTY-THREE
## BLYTHE

At five o'clock as scheduled, Blythe and Logan flew from Hyannis to Nantucket. The short, twenty-five-minute flight gave Blythe the chance to gaze out the window at the water shimmering in the sunlight below. She needed this time to reflect on Anna's story. They were almost the same age, yet their lives were so different.

The trip from the airport to downtown always filled Blythe with excitement. Nantucket was charm itself with its gray or tan clapboard houses accented with bright white trim, boutique shops, and a marina filled with high-end sailboats and power cruisers.

"Looks like we hit it at the right time. It's not too crowded yet," said Logan.

"School's out next week. Then it will be different," said Blythe. "That's why Suzie booked us now."

They got settled in their rooms at a small hotel downtown, not too far from the store. Within walking distance of restaurants and bars, it was the perfect location.

The store, near the marina, was a compact space filled with every imaginable thing a homeowner, boat owner, or workman might need to maintain a property.

Ignoring the closed sign, Blythe rapped on the door and peered through the front window.

Margo Nolan, the manager, strode toward them with a smile on her face. She'd grown up on the island with a houseful of brothers and knew everyone in the contractor and boat business. She, as Gran emphasized, was a great find and someone to keep happy.

Margo opened the door and motioned for them to come inside. "We're trying to get geared up for the onslaught of the summer people. They always need a thing or two. Just finishing up my monthly inventory."

"Good," said Blythe. "I'd like you to meet Logan Pierce. He's helping us out for the next six months while my father is recovering."

Logan and Margo shook hands. She was as tall as Logan and almost as broad and muscular as he. "Glad to meet you, Logan," she said. "Brad and I worked well together. I hope we can do the same." She turned to Blythe. "How is your father? Suzie gives us information from time to time, but it isn't the same as talking to you."

"Dad is home resting and recuperating, but I think it's going to take all of the six months for him to return to work. He might choose to come back on a part-time basis if he accepts Gran's offer to slow down. He's always wanted to teach school. I don't know any more than that."

"Each day is a gift. He might better use it doing what he really wants to do. That's what I tell my girlfriend. She's thinking of opening a clothing store. It's a tough business, but she's talented at that kind of thing."

"How is Lindsay?" Blythe asked, pleased she'd reviewed the notes Gran kept on her managers so she could keep personal information straight.

Margo beamed at her. "She's great. We've been together for five years now. I went ahead and made dinner reservations for the four of us."

"Wonderful. Tomorrow, we'll dig into figures and facts, but tonight I'm hoping we can just enjoy being here."

"Come on into the back. I've got a couple of beers chilling in the refrigerator. It's always a big occasion when we get a visit from headquarters."

Blythe and Logan exchanged glances and followed her into the back of the building and into the small storage/office area Margo used.

As they sat and sipped their beers, Margo filled them in on all the island gossip—what new stores had opened up, what big names were expected on the island this summer, and what had happened during the slow winter months and busier spring months of prepping for summer.

Lindsay joined them, and the four of them walked over to a seafood restaurant Margo thought they'd like. A pretty woman with gray hair and sparkling dark eyes, Lindsay was in her early fifties and had an endearing sense of humor, making even the most somber moments seem funny.

The restaurant was busy when they walked inside. Blythe took a moment to look around. Off-white walls were accented by dark wooden floors and shaker-style pine chairs and tables in warm-brown tones. Vases and tins of wildflowers in a variety of colors softened the clean lines of the furniture and starkness of the décor. Blythe's attention was drawn to the delicious aromas filling the room. She could hardly wait to taste the food.

Later, finishing the last of her broiled scrod with herb-lemon butter, Blythe let out a soft groan of pleasure. "That was so good!"

Logan grinned with evident satisfaction. "Nothing like fresh lobster." He patted his mouth with his napkin to capture a drizzle of butter.

"My brother will be happy to hear this," said Lindsay. "He's one of the cooks here."

"Thanks so much for suggesting this restaurant," said

Blythe. "I'll tell Gran about it."

"Thank you for making the trip. With the video conferencing we're doing, visits aren't as necessary as they once were." Margo turned to Logan. "You and I will, I hope, set up a system of communication much like Brad and I have. It works well."

"Sure. We can go over that tomorrow," said Logan. "Now, let's get to that dessert you mentioned. The one you said we'd need to share."

"It's so fun to be with foodies." Lindsay signaled their waitress. "Bring on the Butter Cake."

"One or two?" asked the waitress glancing around the table.

"Ah, what the heck, two," said Margo. "Okay with everybody? We skipped the wine."

Blythe agreed with the rest of them. In the morning, she'd have to walk an extra mile to make up for it, but it sounded delicious.

When the dessert arrived at their table, Blythe gazed at it. Her mouth watered with anticipation. A small, round, buttery cake was topped by a scoop of vanilla ice cream drizzled with both a chocolate fudge sauce and caramel.

After tasting it, she decided it was worth not one but two extra miles in the morning.

Sated by excellent food and good company, Blythe and Logan bid goodnight to Margo and Lindsay. It was still too early to go to bed, especially with full stomachs.

"I'm going to walk around for a bit. I love looking at all the houses and shops," she said.

Logan shrugged. "I'll join you for a while, and then later, I might stop in at one of the bars before calling it a night."

Glad she'd worn comfortable shoes, Blythe headed out.

Glancing at him walking beside her, she knew Logan was attracted to her, just as she knew he wouldn't act on it.

She stepped up her pace.

He caught up to her. "Hey! What's the hurry?"

"Just trying to work off my dinner," she said, trying to act as if she hadn't been thinking about him. It was driving her crazy, knowing there couldn't be a "them."

He checked his watch. "You go ahead. Meet me at the bar next to the hotel."

She took off, needing some distance from him. She enjoyed the cool air, the smell of saltwater, the sounds and sights of people busy with their lives.

Blythe lost track of time as she meandered down one cobblestoned street and up another. When she realized how late it was, she hurried to the bar where she was to meet Logan.

Inside, people were leaving. Logan was sitting and talking in earnest to an older gentleman.

"Hello," she said, joining them. Logan's pink-cheeked face lit up at the sight of her.

"I wondered where you'd gone," he said. "It's getting late."

"Apparently so," Blythe said, realizing from the slowness of Logan's speech that he was drunk or close to it. "We'd better go."

"Goodbye," Logan said to the gentleman. "My woman is here."

Blythe blinked with surprise. *My woman?*

Logan stood and took hold of her arm. "I'm fine, but I'd better help you get back to your room."

His gallantry didn't fool her.

They walked into the hotel side by side and climbed the stairs to the second story, where they each had a room.

Logan stumbled once, but Blythe caught him. He looked at her and grinned. "Guess they added a step while we were gone."

"You've had way too much to drink. You're going to regret it tomorrow morning when I

call to wake you up," she said, standing outside his door.

He gazed at her with those amazing eyes of his and cupped her cheeks in his hands. "What I regret is that agreement we made with your grandmother." He studied her. "Do you have any idea how beautiful you are? I've wanted to kiss you all night. Way before that even."

She melted into a sea of light-blue as he continued to stare at her with such tenderness her breath caught. He lowered his lips to hers. She paused for the briefest moment, and though she knew it might lead to trouble, she kissed him back, allowing herself to give in to the urge she too had fought for so long.

He deepened the kiss, sending desire in shocking waves through her.

She forced herself to pull away. "We can't ..."

Logan stared at her in confusion and then shook himself as if coming out of a dream. "Don't be mad. I know that was against the stupid rules, but I'm not sorry." He turned his back to her and, fumbling a bit, unlocked the door to his room, stepped inside, and closed the door behind him.

Standing alone in the hallway, Blythe wanted to cry. The connection between Logan and her felt so strong, so right. His kiss held a promise of things she'd dreamed of. Why, oh why, had she made an agreement she never really wanted?

The next morning, Blythe waited to see if Logan would say anything to her about the kiss that she'd dreamed about all night long. Would he even remember it?

Logan, sitting opposite her at one of the breakfast tables in the hospitality room at the hotel, seemed oblivious to the quiet between them. "Sorry about last night," he finally said, shaking his head. "I don't remember getting back to my room. Guess you helped me."

Disappointment, sharp as a knife, cut through her. "Yes, I walked you to your room. You usually don't get drunk."

He put a hand to his forehand. "The old man at the bar kept buying me shots of what he called 'Sailor's Delight'—some kind of whiskey which we drank with our beers. God, I feel sick even thinking about it."

"We have our meeting with Margo in a half-hour. Are you going to be ready?" Blythe asked.

"Oh, yeah. I'm not doing anything to jeopardize this job." Logan said. "I'm enjoying being an active part of the business."

As she heard his words, disappointment reared its ugly head once more. Blythe knew she was being silly, but she'd never felt the sensations Logan had aroused in her with just one kiss. With an effort to put on a cheery smile, she rose and said, "I'll go pack and meet you down here in time for the meeting."

Logan saluted her and remained seated, holding his head in his hands.

Later, Blythe admired the way Logan rose to the occasion. Dressed appropriately in pressed khaki pants and a golf shirt that brought out the blue in his eyes, he remained alert and active in the discussion they had with Margo about seasonal business.

Instead of flying back to the mainland, they took a boat. The trip on the high-speed catamaran took only an hour and gave Blythe a chance to make some notes while Logan napped.

In Hyannis, they picked up Logan's car and headed back to Boston.

The trip seemed to take forever, but maybe, Blythe thought, it was because she was anxious to get home to her own space where she'd have time to put the business trip and Logan's drunken admission in perspective.

# CHAPTER THIRTY-FOUR
## AGGIE

Aggie sat in her office listening to Blythe replay her conversation with Anna. Satisfied, she said, "And what about you, Logan? Did you agree with how Blythe handled the situation?"

Looking surprised at the question, he nodded. "I think she did the right thing. I'm not sure I would've thought of it, but Blythe was understanding about Anna Fields, and her actions demonstrated the company's compassion. I've learned The Robard Company always takes care of its people, and that's a big reason it's so successful. I admire that."

"Well done, you two," Aggie said, thrilled they both understood one of the underlying principles of the company. She and Arnold hadn't always agreed on things, but they both believed in treating both staff members and customers well.

"The managers have filled out their monthly reports," Aggie continued. "I think it would be helpful for you both to go through them to garner information about the stores, the managers, and their staff. Another round of visits, if you will, but done in the office this time. Now, I'm off to spend some time with Brad. He's doing better and has become more active. He's asked to see me."

### ###

On her way to Brad's house, Aggie reviewed what the managers had privately reported to her about Blythe and Logan. Though relatively young for their positions, both had presented a thorough knowledge of the business and seemed eager to learn more—two great things. Aggie thought they made a terrific team.

She pulled into the driveway and was surprised when Constance came out to greet her.

"Aggie. Just the person I need to see. Can we talk? Privately."

"Sure. Is everything all right with Brad?"

Constance placed her hands on her hips and shook her head. "He's got this foolish idea about leaving the company. I'm against it, of course, but then I thought I should take over his position. It seems fair. I'm as capable of learning what I need to know as that young friend of Donovan's."

"That young friend of Donovan's has a Master's in Business," said Aggie, telling herself to remain calm though her pulse had begun to pound. She couldn't, wouldn't work with Constance, and she wouldn't ask Blythe to either.

"And Blythe? She's just barely a college graduate," said Constance.

"With a degree in business and is someone who's trained for years in the company." Aggie refused to be baited by her.

"If Brad leaves the company, how are we going to afford all this?" Constance said, indicating the house with a sweep of her hand.

"Let's take one step at a time," Aggie counseled. "I'm interested to hear what Brad has to say."

"I think the accident has done permanent brain damage." Constance glanced away. "He's ... changed, critical of me, telling me he wants to do something different with his life, that life is too short not to."

"And you would stop him?" Aggie asked, frowning. She'd tried very hard to get along with Constance, but sometimes she found it close to impossible.

"He owes me," Constance said. "Me and the boys."

Aggie could feel the heat in her cheeks. "He owes you to be a good husband and father, which he has been. Like you said, you're capable of working. If it comes to your getting a job, I'll give you a reference." Aggie knew she was being snappish, but she couldn't help it. Constance had always felt entitled to the best of everything.

"Don't you dare talk to me that way," Constance said. "That sweet, old man you're engaged to will discover just how difficult you are."

Aggie closed her eyes and walked on into the house. She would not get into a fight with Constance about Donovan. He knew every bit about her, good and bad, and loved her all the same.

When she walked into the den, Brad was sitting on the couch. At the sight of her, his face lit up. "Hi, Mom! Thanks for coming."

She hurried over to him, wrapped her arms around him and held on tight. "You're so much better!"

"Yeah, I feel a lot better. I still can't remember much beyond Blythe's graduation and the beginning of the trip home, but the doctor said not to worry about it."

"Not the best of times anyway," Aggie said, trying to bring a little humor into the situation.

He gave her a weak smile. "Right. It wouldn't be a good memory." He indicated the chair near him. "Have a seat. There's something I've been mulling over as I've tried to regain my memory."

"Yes?"

"I've been doing a lot of thinking. I realize I've been doing my best not to make waves, to try to keep everyone happy. But I've made some big mistakes. I love Constance, but ... she can be difficult."

Surprised, Aggie covered her mouth to hold in a laugh. "I'm sorry, but I agree with you on that."

"The thing that's been bothering me most is that by trying to keep the peace in my home, I've disappointed both you and Blythe. I've influenced you to live at New Life because I didn't want to lose you, and I knew at New Life you'd always have someone around to help you if you needed it. We could've hired staff so you could stay in your house, but Constance finally persuaded me the move to New Life was the better option for everyone."

Aggie smoothed her hand over his head, the way she'd done a thousand times when he was growing up. "I understand. You've always been protective of me. And look how things have turned out. Better than either of us anticipated."

They shared a warm smile.

Brad's disappeared. "And Blythe? I should've been more forceful in trying to intercede between her and Constance. After all, Constance is the adult."

"That's something you can tell Blythe yourself," said Aggie, pleased with his acknowledgment.

"I'm still taking medication for the pain, but I'm thinking clearly, maybe more clearly than I have in a long time. I don't want to stay in the business full-time. I want to teach somewhere nearby, do something I've always wanted to do."

"I'm not surprised," Aggie said. "Would you remain on the Board of Directors?"

"Oh yes. I can't just walk away from the company you and Dad built. I'd want to do my part as long as it's on a much smaller scale."

Aggie took a deep breath. Who would have thought that terrible accident would help Brad rethink his life, that something positive could come from the crash? "What about Constance? Will she support you?" Though she knew the answer, Aggie had to ask the question.

He released a long sigh. "We'll work it out. We're making some changes around here. I'm not ready to go to work anywhere until I'm stronger, but I wanted you to know my thoughts."

Aggie reached out and hugged her son. "I've been doing a lot of thinking too. We've talked for months about Blythe's eventually stepping into my role at the company, but we now have Logan taking on some of your responsibilities. I don't want to go any further with that idea until you're even better and have worked things out. Truthfully, I've begun to see how your father and I took away choices for you by having you take over for him when he was having problems. I don't want to do that to Blythe. She and I will talk about it after Donovan and I return from Florida."

"I'm happy for you, Mom. I like Donovan."

Aggie's face lit with pleasure. "He likes you too and can't wait to get to know you better. Why don't you come to Florida for a week or so? The sun and relaxation might do you good."

"Thanks. I'll think about it." Brad yawned. "Sorry. Naptime."

"Sweet dreams, sweet boy," Aggie said softly, rising and kissing him on the cheek as his eyes closed.

###

When she related the incident with Constance to Donovan, he gave her a steady look. "I think you did the right thing by not getting into a protracted argument with her. She and Brad are going to have to work things out for themselves. It was good of Brad to tell you what he's thinking of doing. It will give you a chance to work out a new plan."

"I think so too. I've invited him to come to Florida."

"He's welcome at my house anytime, Aggie. I'll be glad to get back there and check in with Curtis. We have solid people running the foundation, but it would be foolish not to oversee them. I hope Curtis will take on more responsibility there."

"I'm comfortable enough to leave Blythe and Logan in charge of the company while we make a short visit to Florida."

Donovan's eyes sparkled as he wrapped his arms around her. "I was hoping you'd say that. I've got a special plan in mind."

"Are you going to tell me what it is?"

"Nope. I'm going to surprise you. You know how we like surprises."

Aggie laughed. Her life had become one surprise after another.

Two days later, Donovan walked into the kitchen as she was sipping her morning coffee and announced that he'd reserved a hotel room for them at the Don Cesar in St. Pete Beach, Florida.

"What's the occasion?"

"Nothing special unless we're talking about a honeymoon," he replied, giving her a roguish grin. "It's a perfect time for us to elope."

"What? Elope? Why would we want to do that?" Aggie said, even as she became enthralled by the idea.

He sat down at the table beside her. "We need to be able to protect one another in making health care decisions, end-of-life decisions. I've been talking to some people at New Life and my lawyer. They all suggest that marrying will provide those opportunities. Otherwise, the decisions will be made by family members, and you have already experienced some of that. You weren't happy with the way that was handled."

"No. I was treated as if I couldn't make any decisions on my own, that I should just hand the entire business over to Brad and Constance." She'd been herded into New Life to try to appease Brad's concern.

She gave Donovan a coy smile and fluttered her eyelids at him playfully. "So, Mr. Fiancé, you can't wait to marry me. Is that it?"

"You got it, lady. I say we get married at the courthouse and then have a luxurious night at the hotel to celebrate. Unless you want to go somewhere else, maybe take a trip to Europe?"

"No, this will be perfect," said Aggie. "Just spending time with you, enjoying each day right here means everything to me."

"I love you, Aggie, for so many reasons." Donovan crooked his finger to her, and, giggling softly, Aggie rose and hurried over to him and settled in his lap. Nestled against him, she let out a sigh of happiness. She didn't need a fancy wedding or honeymoon. She much preferred to keep things simple and joyful. Getting married in a quiet ceremony sounded perfect. And if it was another surprise for her family, it was a good one.

# CHAPTER THIRTY-FIVE
## BLYTHE

On a hot, late-August Saturday afternoon, Blythe sat in the crowd at Fenway Park with Ben, Logan, and Liz cheering on the Red Sox. Blythe had been a fan since she was a child. It was something she and her father had liked to do together. She couldn't help thinking of him now. It had been three months since his accident, and he'd changed. He usually was easy-going, amenable to do as others wanted, content to keep Constance happy. But now, he was quietly determined to live a different life—one without the stress of keeping a business doing well. As he'd told her privately, the fire inside him had become a steady, soft glow from the embers that still burned within him. He'd continue to help the company however he could, but he needed more than that. More importantly, he'd apologized to her for not defending her against the friction between Constance and her, and he'd informed Constance that she must treat her better, more fairly.

Blythe barely heard the noise around them as she recalled how, when Constance heard about Blythe's new role in the company, she'd had the nerve to accost her, to try to insist that she should be brought into the business—a decision only Gran could make. Blythe knew very well that Constance's real concern was money, an issue that Blythe wouldn't or couldn't address. Her father had always provided well for their family. She was sure he'd invested wisely and knew he had a good savings program through the company.

Ben nudged her. "Stand for the seventh-inning stretch."

Jerked out of her thoughts, Blythe grinned at him. "Sorry. I was thinking of something else."

She got to her feet and stretched along with everyone around them. The Red Sox were doing their usual thing, toying with fans' emotions, winning some games, losing others. Still, she'd always root for them.

It didn't take long for the game to end. The opposing team was just too good.

"Let's go to the North End for dinner," Liz suggested. "I could go for some good Italian food."

"Sounds good to me," said Logan. "What do you say, Blythe?"

Blythe glanced at him. "I'm game. Ben?"

"As long as everyone wants to do it, I'm in."

They took the Green Line from Kenmore Square to the Haymarket station and walked into the North End. Blythe liked living in the city, being with her friends, and keeping busy.

As they walked, Ben took hold of her hand. "Hey, beautiful. I'm glad you were free to come to the game. You've been doing a lot of babysitting for your brothers lately."

"Too much," said Blythe, "but things are tense between my father and stepmother. They've been trying to spend some time alone to work things out."

"It's nice though that you have family," said Ben. "I have only one sister and always wished I'd had a brother. Especially being raised by my grandparents."

"What happened?" Blythe asked.

"Motorbike accident in Bermuda while they were on vacation. Even though I was only six when it happened, I remember how awful it was for my grandparents suddenly to have us come live with them. I owe them a lot."

"Is that why you're a lawyer working at your grandfather's law firm?"

"I like it. Working with fraud cases is challenging." He winked at her. "I like challenges."

Blythe couldn't help laughing. Ben was a nice guy who took good care of her. They hadn't had sex, though she knew he wanted more from her. As much as she liked him, she didn't want to start something with him until she knew where it would lead.

Ahead of them, Logan and Liz were laughing at something Logan said. Blythe held in a sigh. To Logan, she was a business associate, a friend.

Dinner was low-key in a restaurant known for good, home-style food. Blythe ordered pasta with a delicious white clam sauce. That, the glass of wine and excellent company filled her with a sense of well-being. When Ben invited her to his place, she said yes.


Ben's condo was similar to hers with brick walls and a contemporary feel but lacked the finishing touches she'd added. Still, it was comfortable. She took a seat on the couch and put her feet on the stool facing it. The summer was almost over. School would soon start for the boys, and her father would begin taking a few online courses to get ready for a career in teaching. A couple of colleges nearby had expressed interest in his qualifications due to his business experience and reputation. Constance was unhappy about it, but her father had remained firm.

"What'cha thinking about?" asked Ben bringing two cans of cold beer over to her.

She took one. "Things are so different from what I thought

they'd be. My dad is planning to leave the company, and my grandmother surprised us by eloping and is now a happily married woman. All this happened so quickly."

He rested his hand on her shoulder. "We've only known each other for a couple of months, but I'm falling for you, Blythe."

He took the beer out of her hands and set the can down on a nearby table. Cupping her face in his hands, he pressed his lips against hers.

Heat ran through her body. It felt good to be desired. She told herself to relax into the kiss, to let go and enjoy it. She felt his arms go around her and draw her closer.

He rubbed her back, soothing the muscles that had tightened with anticipation or dread; she was unsure which it was. He unsnapped her bra and cupped her exposed breasts.

"Do you have any idea how beautiful you are?" he murmured.

The echo of Logan's words made her gasp. She pulled away and hid her face in her hands. "Damn! I'm sorry, Ben. I can't do this right now. It's nothing to do with you and everything to do with me."

As she scrambled to her feet, Ben stood. Obviously aroused, he stared at her with shock.

"What's going on?"

"I'm sorry. I really am, but I'm not ready for this. This isn't going to work. I wish like hell it would."

"That's it?" He watched as she re-hooked her bra and straightened her shirt.

"There's so much going on for me right now; I just can't do this. Ben, I'm so, so sorry." The tears that had blurred her vision escaped, rolling down her cheeks in a trail of despair. Her whole life was totally messed up.

"Forgive me." She gave him a quick kiss on the cheek and

quickly made her way to the front entry, leaving Ben standing in the middle of the room staring at her as she exited. She closed the door behind her, trying to stem her tears.

Outside, as she made her way into her building, she met Logan coming out of it.

"Hey! What's wrong?" he asked, looking at her with concern. "What happened?"

She raised a hand to keep him away from her. "Can't talk about it." She hurried past him and to the elevator.

Left outdoors without a key to come into the vestibule, Logan watched her through the glass door.

Doing her best to ignore him, she waited for the elevator and stepped inside when it finally arrived.

Her cell phone rang with his unique chime, but she let the call go. He was the last person she wanted to talk to tonight. He'd ruined everything for her.


Blythe arose the next morning with a headache. Blaming it on the beer and wine she'd had, she knew she was lying to herself. The headache came from the heartache that had kept her tossing and turning all night. As she placed laundry into her washing machine, she told herself she had to get past this crush on Logan. She couldn't afford to fail in taking over for her grandmother because she'd fallen for him. She'd have to ignore her feelings. Not only was her grandmother counting on her doing that, but her father was also. Besides, she was lucky to have the chance to run the family business. Some of her classmates hadn't even found a job yet.

Her cell rang.

"Hi, it's Curtis. I'm back in town for a quick visit and wonder if I can hang out for a bit and then take you to lunch."

"That would be great," she said.

"You sound a little down. Is everything all right?" he asked.

"Just life. It'll be nice to see you." She gave him directions to her condo and clicked off the call, feeling better.

When she opened the door to Curtis, Blythe had forgotten how handsome, how easy-going he was. The day that had started so badly might be pleasant after all.

"Come on in."

"Thanks. I'm in town to see Dad about the foundation but wanted to have some time away from him and Aggie. It's a little depressing. They're lovebirds."

"Ah. And you haven't found anyone yet."

He shook his head. "It's hard to find someone who gets me and what I do for a living. Some see my life as all glamour. Others see it as unsteady, unreliable." He shrugged. "The best thing for me is just to keep doing my thing. And right now, this is a bad time. I'm between books and working with an agent who now wants me to move in a different direction with my next book to accommodate the editor."

"Well, sit down and relax. I promise not to keep asking you about your books. It's a nice day out. I thought we could drive up to the North Shore for the afternoon, maybe have lunch or dinner at a seafood place in Ipswich.

Curtis's face lit up. "Are we talking clams?"

Blythe laughed. "Sure, if that's what you want."

A knock at the door interrupted them.

Blythe went to the door and opened it.

"Do you have a minute?" Liz asked.

"Sure. What's up?" Blythe said, noting the look of distress on Liz's face.

Liz stepped into the room. "Oh! I didn't know you had company. I can leave."

"No, don't. Liz Calloway, this is Curtis Bailey."

Liz's eyes widened. "Oh, you're Blythe's new brother." She held out her hand, and Curtis shook it.

He turned to Blythe. "Brother or step-brother or whatever. Right?"

She smiled and nodded. She saw how Liz's face had lit and the grin that had spread across Curtis's face when they'd greeted one another. Maybe, she could help them out.

"We're thinking of driving up to Ipswich. Want to join us?"

Liz glanced at her. "Are you sure I wouldn't be horning in?"

"Don't be silly," Blythe said.

"In that case, Logan and I have split up, and I need to have a little fun," Liz said, beaming at her.

"What happened?" Blythe asked.

"The truth." Shaking her head, Liz sighed. "We both agreed it wasn't happening between us. I think Logan tried, but his heart wasn't in the relationship. You know?"

Blythe knew exactly how that went. It had happened to her because of him.

The day trip turned out to be fun—her gift to Curtis and Liz, who talked and laughed together as they discussed their families and various places Liz wanted to see and Curtis had already visited. Liz talked easily of her large family and asked about his.

They sat at a picnic table outside the Clam Box eating fried clams in comfortable companionship.

"So, you're not dating Logan anymore?" Curtis said to Liz, stealing one of her fried clams. The smile between them lingered, and Blythe knew the idea of having dinner with Curtis was over. It was just as well. She needed time to regroup.

"Like I said," Liz replied to him. "We both decided to move on. He's a great guy, just not for me. He wants to date a lot of different girls. I don't blame him. He recently moved to Boston, and many women are interested." She glanced at Blythe. "Good thing you two decided only to be friends. That avoids a lot of problems with you working together."

Blythe forced herself to nod in agreement but remained quiet.

By the time she drove back into Boston, Curtis had already made arrangements to take Liz out to dinner. He invited her, but Blythe declined. Three was an uncomfortable crowd.

# CHAPTER THIRTY-SIX
## AGGIE

Aggie sat in her office, thinking about her family. Constance, thank goodness, had backed away from any idea of working at the company once it became clear that her style of living wouldn't change that much. Brad had invested well and was very conservative financially, paying off the house early and establishing a healthy savings program for the boys' college educations.

They'd been shocked by her elopement, but then it was just another surprise in a string of them. She figured she'd just about worn out any idea for a new one.

Suzie came in to see her. "Can we talk?"

"Sure. Have a seat," said Aggie, waving her into a chair in front of her desk. "What's up?"

"I've been thinking that with your retirement coming up, I should consider retiring too, leaving it to younger people to run the company."

"Suzie, you know I never could have handled things alone through the years without your devoted help," said Aggie, feeling a lump form in her throat. Suzie was more than an assistant, friend, and confidant. She was the one who'd held her afloat when Aggie had needed that extra bit of strength to get through troubled times, both personal and in business.

"I do know, Aggie. Heaven knows you've been generous beyond belief as a way of thanking me. I've loved being part of the company, and I'm thrilled for you that you've found

Donovan. Blythe is the perfect choice to take your position and carry on, but I truly believe it's best if she begins training an assistant of her own, someone who will grow with her."

Aggie blinked back tears. "It's all so crazy, this getting old. But I agree with you. It's time for you to have some fun in your life. You've worked so hard all these years." She lifted the phone on her desk. "Let me call her in here, and we'll break the news together. She'll be devastated."

Blythe came into her office and took a seat.

As Aggie explained the situation, Blythe's cheeks flushed with emotion. "I can't convince you to stay, Suzie? How will I be able to handle things without you? Who would I get to replace you?"

"I have the perfect person for you. A niece of mine. She's in her mid-forties and is looking for something to keep her busy while her son is away at school. She's extremely capable. Without your knowledge or Aggie's, I've been talking to her about it, making sure she'd give you the same attention I've given the company."

"Okay. Some of the younger people don't understand the time commitment required to become an integral part of any business. Give me her number, and Blythe and I'll set up a time to interview her."

Blythe rose and hugged Suzie. "You have no idea how sorry I am. But I get it. Maybe you won't take a road trip like Gran, but you should have time to do some fun things."


Blythe sat with Aggie in the office to interview Mara Gilbert. After reviewing the resumé they'd requested, they both agreed she was an excellent candidate.

Now, talking to her, Aggie was convinced of it. Anyone could type well, handle phones, work with numbers—all the things listed in a want ad—but it was the chemistry between people that mattered most. In this case, Mara's quick sense of humor connected Aggie to her. She saw by the smile on Blythe's face that Mara had had the same effect on her.

"I like what you're saying about your past experiences," said Blythe. "Is there any way you can start working part-time with Suzie? Let's say a trial period of one month. At the end of that time, we'll reassess the situation, and if either of us is uncomfortable or dissatisfied, we go our separate ways, no questions asked."

"I'd be delighted to do that," said Mara. "You won't be disappointed." She rose and shook hands with Blythe and turned to her. "I know how special The Robard Company is, Aggie. I promise to make you proud."

Aggie glanced at the happy expression on Blythe's face and turned to Mara. "I'm sure you will. As I mentioned, you will be working directly for Blythe and Logan as well."

Blythe walked Mara out and then returned to the office. "I think we have a winner."

"Me too," said Aggie, feeling a pang of sorrow to know that things were moving ahead without her.

# CHAPTER THIRTY-SEVEN
## BLYTHE

When Logan came into work, Blythe told him about Mara, describing her and her skill set. "I think she'll be a good replacement for Suzie."

"No young secretary that I wouldn't be able to date?" he teased.

"No, sir. Not at this company." Blythe was surprised by the tinge of bitterness in her voice and told herself to stop being foolish.

As if he'd heard her thought, Logan said, "I've got a date tonight. She's someone new. We've agreed to meet at Dunwoody's. Will you come too? I need some advice. Apparently, I'm not very good at the dating game. I go out with a woman and immediately lose interest in her."

Blythe's jaw dropped. "You're asking me to help you choose a woman in your life?"

"Sure. Why not?"

"Because ... I don't know ..." Blythe fought off the hurt she felt. "Better tell me what she's like."

Her name is Daphne Neville. She's an assistant to Ben's boss at the law firm. According to Ben, she has a lot of men interested in her. She's hot, really hot."

*Didn't he know how hot he was?*

"Well? C'mon. You know I can trust you to tell me. You've got nothing to lose."

Blythe let out a sigh that spoke of many things she couldn't say. "All right. But I'm not staying long. I'll meet her and then go on my way."

"Deal. I just want you to get a first impression. Thanks, Blythe."

"We'll see. Now I'd better get to work. I have a lot on my plate with new holiday inventory coming up."

That night, Blythe walked into Dunwoody's, a typical downtown bar and grille in the Financial District. The pine-paneled walls, the buzz of the crowd, the loud music all made it seem exciting after a rather dull day at work.

She'd done a little research of her own, googling Daphne online. She came from a well-known family in the area and was an active member of the Junior League and a graduate of Boston University, all excellent "credentials."

Blythe recognized her immediately.

"Hi, Blythe!" Logan said, coming over to her and leading her back to his blonde date. "This is Daphne Neville, the woman I was telling you about. Daphne, this is my best friend, Blythe Robard."

Blythe responded to Daphne's smile. Up close, she was even more attractive with toffee-colored brown eyes, perfect white teeth, and sculptured features.

"Josie, Daphne's friend, got tied up at work," Logan said, checking his watch. "But no need to wait for her. We can go ahead and order drinks. Your usual, Blythe?"

"Thanks," she said, ready for one.

"What would you like, Daphne?" Logan asked her.

"I'll have what Blythe is having. You get it, and we'll grab a table," said Daphne. "Josie should be here any minute."

Blythe followed her to a table and sat down, already anxious to leave.

Daphne leaned forward. "How do you know Logan so well?"

"It's a long story. We met in Florida when my grandmother and I took a trip to see her now-husband."

"Have you dated?" Daphne asked.

"No, it's complicated, but we can't date as long as we're working for the same company."

"That's archaic!" Daphne said. "In this day and age, we should be allowed to do anything we want, including dating a cute guy in the office."

Rather than try to explain the situation to her, Blythe said, "I agree."

Logan returned to the table with two glasses of red wine. "I'll be right back," he said to Blythe. "I've got to grab the beer."

Daphne frowned. "He was speaking to you."

"What?" Blythe didn't know how to respond. Was Daphne jealous?

"Ah, here he is." Daphne smiled up at Logan. "I was getting worried about your being gone for so long."

He grinned. "You know I'm here for you." He set down his mug of beer and took a seat next to Daphne.

After exchanging small talk, including the weather, Blythe got to her feet. "Thanks for inviting me to meet Daphne, Logan. I'm sorry, but I have to leave. I'm helping Liz hang some pictures in her condo. Payback for her help."

Logan got to his feet. "See you tomorrow."

Blythe gave a little wave and left, glad to be out of the awkward situation. It was clear Daphne didn't like her presence.

###

The next day, Blythe drove to Plymouth to work with the manager of the store. They were trying to arrange a separate space for gifts that were more than standard souvenirs. When she finally was ready to leave the store, it was too late to return to the office, so she drove home.

She was in the middle of typing up notes from her meeting when she heard a knock at the door of her condo. Pretty sure she knew who it was, and wondering how he'd made it inside, she let out a soft groan and went to answer it.

"Well?" said Logan as she opened the door. "What did you think?"

He walked inside and stood before her, smiling.

"Are you talking about Daphne?"

"Yeah, a looker, huh?" He grew serious. "But that's not what I'm really interested in. I need to know if you think this is something that can last. I already have my doubts."

"Better come in," said Blythe. "We need to talk."

He held up a bottle of wine. "I brought you a treat. As a thank you."

She was going to need it because she would be truthful with him, and he might not like it.

She opened the bottle and poured out two glasses. She handed him one and took a seat at the kitchen bar next to him.

"What is it you're looking for, Logan?"

He stared into her eyes, shifted, and looked away. "I think you know damn well what I want." He stood and drew her into his arms. "You. Is that plain enough? You want what I want too. I know it."

"I do," she said, her eyes filling. "But there's so much going on for me right now. I don't want a fling. I'm looking for more than a one-night stand."

He gazed into her eyes. "I don't want a single night with you. It wouldn't ever be enough. And I don't want to be like Donovan and your grandmother and lose all those years by not being clear about my feelings." He brushed his thumb across her cheek. "Ah, Blythe. I love you."

His lips came down on hers.

She trembled as desire swept through her. God help her, she didn't think she could ever love anyone else.

He kissed her again, filling her with a need she'd never known.

Logan brushed gentle kisses against her lips and gave her a questioning look before leading her to the couch. She didn't object. She wanted more too.

Slowly, carefully, step by loving step, she succumbed to his touches, loving the lemony smell of his aftershave, the smooth, hard feel of him, the tenderness he showed her while holding back his own needs.

It was dark when they finally left the living room to rummage for food in the refrigerator.

"What are we going to do about us?" she asked.

He stood in front of her with a grim look of determination. "I'm going to figure out a way to fight for us. I don't care what it takes."

The next morning, Blythe was in the middle of balancing the cost of gift inventories for all the various stores when her desk phone rang.

"Blythe Robard," she automatically answered.

"Please come to my office right away," Gran said in an unusually crisp tone.

Blythe's mind whirled as she hurried to her. She'd sounded so upset Blythe couldn't imagine what was wrong.

Blythe knocked and entered the office.

Gran looked up at her with an expression that could only be called stricken. She held up a sheet of paper.

"What's wrong?"

"You'd better read this." Gran thrust the paper at her.

As her gaze swept over the information, Blythe sank into one of the chairs in front of Gran's desk. "What? I don't believe it. Why would he do this?" She lowered her gaze to the printed words in front of her.

**Dear Mrs. Bailey,**

**Thank you so much for offering me the temporary position with The Robard Company. I've learned a lot about the retail business and respect you for what you've done with the growth of the company. In order to meet that level of respect, I feel I must hereby resign.**

**Again, thank you for the opportunity.**

**Sincerely,**

**Logan Pierce**

"What the hell? How can he just walk away from us!" sputtered Blythe. "I don't know what's going on with him, but this is ... bullshit."

"Is it, Blythe?" Gran said, giving her a penetrating look. "I asked Suzie to get in touch with him, but she's been unable to reach him. Donovan called me to tell me that Logan asked for permission to stay at his house in Florida while he sorts out a few things. Something happened to make him feel this way. I suggest you go and see if you can talk him out of this. We can't lose him. Not now with the holidays coming up."

Suspicion heated Blythe's cheeks. "Okay, I'll go. But I'm not sure I can get him to change his mind." She turned on her heel. As she opened the door to leave, she heard Gran say, "Good luck!" and knew she'd need it.

# CHAPTER THIRTY-EIGHT
## BLYTHE

On the flight to Florida, Blythe mentally went over and over the entire evening with Logan. Looking down at the fall colors dotting the landscape, she wondered if she'd been foolish to let her feelings run wild. They both wanted a relationship, but Blythe wasn't about to sneak around, even when it might cost her the one man that she knew would enrich her life, the one man she wanted more than any other.

After the plane landed, Blythe made her way through the airport to where the driver of the car she ordered would meet her.

When she walked into the baggage claim area, several uniformed drivers were holding up cards with the names of the parties they were to meet. Blythe looked around for her name and stopped in surprise when she saw Curtis smiling and holding up a card for her. Gran and Donovan must have been busy.

"Dad and I canceled the car service," he said, approaching her. "I'll drive you home and then leave. You and Logan need to figure a few things out."

Blythe simply nodded.

Less than an hour later, Curtis pulled up in front of Donovan's house. She and Curtis had made small talk but kept away from discussing the circumstances that had brought her to Florida.

"Logan doesn't know you're here. I'll drop you off, and as I told you earlier, I'm taking off for Miami for a few days. Good luck with everything."

Even as she stepped out of the car, she wanted to climb back in, to ride away from the situation she faced. But she couldn't do that to Logan. Curtis was right. They needed to resolve their issues. She loved him. That she knew for sure.

When Blythe entered the house, a somber quiet met her. She left her suitcase by the front door.

She walked into the living room, checked the kitchen, and then walked out to the back of the house. Logan was lying in a lounge chair by the pool. Seeing him in his swim trunks, Blythe was reminded of the night she'd spent with him, the marvelous things he'd done with that body of his. Unexpected tears filled her eyes. She couldn't lose him.

Sensing her presence, he sat up and turned to where she was standing by the sliding glass door.

His gaze was steady as he got up and walked toward her.

She slid open the door to meet him. "Hi," she said quietly.

"What are you doing here?" he asked.

"Gran ordered me to come," she answered, knowing immediately how lame that sounded.

"So that's it?" His look of disappointment was telling.

"Not exactly. I needed to come here—for myself and for you. We have to resolve things between us. I'm not sure what you want."

"Really?" he said. "I couldn't be clearer. I want us to be together, Blythe. I meant it. If it means quitting my job, so be it."

"But that's it," Blythe said. "My family needs you."

"I understand. But I need *you*. And unless you tell me I have a future with you, I'll be right here." He stared at her, his body stiff.

Blythe swallowed hard. He was stating his intentions. Was she willing to do the same?

She stepped forward. "I want you in my life, Logan. We can work it out. I promise."

His shoulders relaxed, and a smile crossed his face. With one giant step, he reached her and tugged her into his arms. "I'll do anything for you, Blythe. I've been crazy about you since the moment we met you at Seashell Cottage. But you shut me down, said you weren't ready for a relationship. A crazy road trip brought you into my life. I'll be forever grateful to your grandmother for that."

Blythe laughed with relief and hugged him hard. "No matter what happens with the business, we belong together. I've known I loved you from the beginning, even when you were dating all those other women."

"Just biding my time, making sure you realized I was the one," he murmured before his lips met hers.

Blythe melted into his kiss, aware the heat she felt had nothing to do with the sun shining down on them.

When they pulled apart, Logan said to her, "What are we going to do?"

Blythe gave him a reassuring smile. "I'm going to resign too."

Logan laughed. "Perfect."

# CHAPTER THIRTY-NINE
## AGGIE

Aggie looked at the message from Blythe on her computer. Imagine that! Blythe was resigning. A chuckle escaped her. Blythe had her spunk all right. Aggie knew why she'd resigned, of course. Everyone in the family and in the office knew those two loved one another. *"Well played, sweet granddaughter,"* Aggie thought as she began writing up new, amended offers of employment.

# CHAPTER FORTY
## BLYTHE

With the decision to resign behind her, Blythe embraced the time she and Logan had together. Lying next to him in bed the next morning, Blythe gazed at him with wonder. Making love with him was as much a spiritual celebration as anything else. She fit her body next to his and matched his breathing pattern, feeling as one with him.

Later, after making love once more, they rose and went outside for a morning swim. She loved the privacy of Donovan's pool and, like Logan, didn't bother with a swimsuit, finding a new sense of ease with him. It felt good to be so natural, so unafraid to simply be here, with only the necklace of the green flash to remind her of how far they'd come.

"What shall we do today?" she asked him, floating on her back.

"After making love?" Logan said, giving her a playful leering grin.

She laughed. "How about driving over to the beach near the Seashell Cottage? We can have lunch at Gracie's at the Salty Key Inn," she said. "Curtis told me their grouper sandwich is the best."

"Sounds like a plan," said Logan. "I've got something in mind for later."

"Oh?"

He laughed. "I'm not going to tell you. Not yet. Come here. Did I ever tell you how beautiful you are?"

Blythe recalled the night in Nantucket and decided not to say anything about it. That was in the past. Though he hadn't remembered saying it to her then, she'd make sure he would never forget it now and in the future.

Later, they lay in the sun to dry and then went inside to dress. The promise of a good lunch at Gracie's was too tempting.

Gracie's was crowded, but after waiting ten minutes, they were seated at a table outdoors.

Blythe loved sitting in the sun, especially when she knew that Boston had experienced its first frost.

Their sandwiches and drinks arrived.

"Should we respond to Gran's new employment offer together?" Blythe asked him. "Maybe you should go first since I was sent here to make sure the company didn't lose you."

He raised an eyebrow at her. "So, this was a matter of seduce and conquer?"

She laughed. "I think it happened the other way around. Seriously, are you happy with the new contract? I see Gran's giving you a raise with the promise of better things." She tensed. Though she'd asked the question in a casual way, his answer meant everything to her.

"If you're asking me if I'm willing to stay with the company for many years to come, the answer is yes. I'm hooked on the business, the people, and especially you." He gave her a steady look, his beautiful eyes showing concern. "The question is, are you going to be able to work with me every day and eventually run the company together?"

She hesitated. Not because she didn't know the answer but

because of what he really might mean.

He reached across the table and took hold of her hand. "I guess I'm asking you to marry me. Good God! This isn't how I wanted it to happen, but here goes." He got down on one knee and looked up at her. "Blythe Robard, I know what I want. And you're it. Will you marry me?"

Her face felt on fire when she realized everyone in the restaurant had stopped what they were doing and were staring at them.

"Well?" Logan gave her a hopeful look.

Her heart pounded with happiness. "Yes! Oh, yes, Logan, I will marry you."

The sound of clapping filled her ears.

She watched Logan get to his feet, take a bow, and sweep her into his arms. Not caring who observed them, she wrapped her arms around his neck and kissed him long and deep.

When they finally sat down, Logan lifted his glass of lemonade. "This isn't how I planned to ask you, but I meant every word. I love you, and I don't care who knows it. Here's to us!"

"Yes! To us!" Blythe clicked her glass to his. It hadn't been an ordinary proposal, but she was still glowing with love from the offer he'd made her. She gazed at him, certain she'd never find a man as wonderful as he.


"Ready to go to the beach?" Logan asked when they'd finished their food.

"Sure. I want to see the cottage. I hope when the time comes to marry, we can have the ceremony on the beach at Seashell Cottage and the reception here at the Salty Key Inn."

"Sounds like a plan to me," said Logan, grinning at her. He

rose and took her hand.

As they prepared to leave, their waitress came over to them. "You're the first couple to get engaged here at the restaurant. Gracie, the owner, and Bertha, the baker, are offering you a free wedding cake."

"How sweet!" said Blythe. "I've already decided I want the reception here at the hotel."

The waitress beamed at them. "When the time comes to talk to them about it, be sure and tell them about the offer."

"I will," said Blythe, thinking how unexpected the day had turned out to be.

They left the restaurant and drove to the beach close to Seashell Cottage.

"Come with me. There's something I want to show you," said Logan, taking her hand and tugging her onto the sand.

"What?" said Blythe. "There's nobody around."

"Exactly." He knelt on the sand. "I want to do this right." He pulled a small, black velvet box out of his pocket and opened it. A sparkling round diamond surrounded by smaller diamonds winked in the sunlight at her. "I know this is sort of backward, but I left the ring locked in the car, which is why I couldn't give this to you at the restaurant."

Blythe studied him. "How long have you had this planned?"

"Since I decided I couldn't live without you several weeks ago. You've already said yes, but will you say it again?"

Her laughter rang out. "I'll say it again and again. Yes, Logan, I'll marry you. I'll marry you."

He slid the ring on her finger, rose, and drew her into his arms. "You make me happy. I want to do the same for you."

She held out her hand. The ring was beautiful, but it was the commitment behind it that signified so much to her.

"What are your parents and Gran going to say about it?"

Logan said. "It's pretty sudden."

"If Gran can rush an engagement, so can I. But we'd better not elope."

"Deal," said Logan, smiling. "Now come here, almost Mrs. Pierce. I want to kiss you properly."

Sighing with happiness, Blythe leaned into him and lifted her face.

# SIX MONTHS LATER
## AGGIE

Spring weddings are so lovely, Aggie thought. The season was one of promises, with plants and flowers coming to life. Even the birds scuttling along the beach outside the Seashell Cottage seemed to have extra energy as they raced across the sand searching for food. She looked up at the blue sky and let out a sigh. This place was so special to her. She turned to Donovan, sitting in one of the rocking chairs on the porch. He'd come through another episode with his disease and was finding it a little more challenging to move around. But each day with him remained a gift for which she'd always be thankful.

Blythe emerged from the cottage and lifted her hands to the sky. "This is great—being here again at the cottage, everything. I'm going to take a walk on the beach."

"Go ahead, sweetheart. It's a beautiful day for an afternoon wedding."

Blythe hugged herself. "I can't believe it's really happening."

"It is," said Logan, coming out on the porch and putting an arm around her. "Mind if I join you?"

Blythe gave him a loving look Aggie recognized as her own when she gazed at Donovan.

"Curtis and Liz should be here soon," Gran reminded them. "Then it will be time to get ready for the wedding. Your father, Constance, and the boys will be here shortly."

### 

Later, as white puffy clouds danced in the blue sky above her, Aggie stood on the broad sandy beach with others in the family. Curtis stood beside Logan, waiting for the wedding procession to begin.

The soft sound of guitar music intensified.

Aggie watched Liz walk toward them, wearing a long, sleeveless dress in the palest of pinks. The light-green hydrangeas she carried were edged in pink, a perfect match to her dress.

Then it was Blythe's turn.

Aggie dabbed at her eyes.

Blythe seemed to float toward them, her gaze on Logan. Her silky, white, ankle-length dress billowed in the sudden breeze as Blythe, barefoot, all but danced on her toes joyfully. The green necklace she wore complemented the green flash from the setting sun. Brad, holding onto her arm, beamed with a deep-felt happiness that came in part, she knew, from his newfound happiness. How she loved him!

The minister, someone recommended by the Salty Key Inn, whose staff had helped plan the wedding, observed them all with a benevolent smile.

Aggie took hold of Donovan's hand. Seated in a chair next to her, he looked at her and winked, aware of her emotions.

As words of love and promises were spoken and exchanged, Aggie took them in, finding new meaning in them. She'd had such a wonderful life, loved by two exceptional men. She hoped that Blythe and Logan would have many years together, loving each other, helping one another as they carried on the family business.

Her drifting thoughts were interrupted by Blythe's words. "We owe everything to my outrageous, wonderful Gran. This all started with her road trip to remember."

"And how," said Logan and Donovan together.

Even as she laughed, Aggie cried tears of joy. It was such a perfect moment.

Thank you for reading *A Road Trip to Remember.* If you enjoyed this book, please help other readers discover it by leaving a review on Amazon, Goodreads, or your favorite site. It's such a nice thing to do.

Enjoy an excerpt from my book, *Margaritas at The Beach House Hotel,* Book 5 in the Beach House Hotel Series, which will be out in June 2021.

# CHAPTER ONE

Ready?" asked my business partner, Rhonda DelMonte Grayson, on this early April morning on the Gulf Coast of Florida.

I stopped typing on the computer and turned to her with a grin. "As ready as I ever will be."

Wearing a yellow caftan that went with her hair, Rhonda waved me up and out of my chair with a grin that lit her face and had her dark eyes sparkling. "Then let's get this show on the road! It's not every day a vice president visits The Beach House Hotel."

I rose and looped my arm through Rhonda's, and we headed out to the front lobby to greet the latest VIP to come to our upscale hotel.

As we stepped outside to wait for our guest, the spring day greeted us with a kiss of sunny warmth. A soft breeze bobbed the colorful blossoms on the hibiscus bushes that lined the front of the hotel, softening the edges of the pink-stucco, two-story building that stood like royalty at the water's sandy edge.

"Seems like old times, huh?" said Rhonda, grinning at me as we approached the entrance.

"I'll say." Five years ago, when we'd first opened the hotel,

Rhonda and I had greeted our guests like this at the front steps of the hotel, welcoming them personally as much as possible. Hospitality, discretion, and service were the three things we still relied upon to maintain the hotel's fine reputation. A warm welcome to the property was a must.

I studied her. When I'd first met Rhonda, I'd thought the large, colorful, bossy woman, who said exactly what was on her mind and had no sense of private space, was completely overwhelming. I'd thought I'd never make it through my first visit to her seaside estate—a visit made to please my daughter, Liz, who roomed at college with Rhonda's daughter, Angela.

Now, even though my strict upbringing with my grandmother in Boston sometimes made me shudder at what came out of Rhonda's mouth, I loved her like the sister I never had. And I'd learned her heart was as big as her irrepressible spirit. Rhonda nudged me. "Here she comes!"

I ran a hand through my shoulder-length dark hair, flicked a speck of dust off my bright-blue suit jacket that matched my eyes, and drew a deep breath.

We headed down the front stairs of the hotel as a black limousine followed a large, black SUV through the gates of the hotel and drew up to the front circle. As soon as the limousine came to a stop, three different people, two men and a woman, Secret Service agents, I presumed, jumped out of the SUV and assessed their surroundings before the woman went over to the limousine and stood outside the back door. One of the men faced out to the road while the other climbed the stairs to the hotel and stood guard there. Then a somber-looking man stepped out of the front of the limo and stood a moment, scanning the area. Satisfied, he stood by as the female agent outside the limo opened the back door, and Vice President Amelia Swanson prepared to climb out of the car.

A tall, striking woman in her late 40s with chestnut brown

hair and blue eyes noted for missing nothing, Amelia Swanson stepped out of the limousine and smiled as she walked forward to meet us.

"Welcome to The Beach House Hotel, Madame Vice President," I said, holding out my hand. "I'm Ann Sanders, one of the hotel's owners."

Strong fingers gripped my hand. "Very glad to meet you and to be here." She turned to Rhonda. "And you must be Ms. Grayson."

"Yes. We're honored to have you stay with us," said Rhonda, looking as if she didn't know whether to curtsey or not.

"Let's go inside where we can talk privately," Amelia said.

"Please, come in." I took her elbow and led her up the steps. The security agent who'd stood by the door headed indoors while another followed at our heels.

Behind me, I noticed the female guard pacing outside the limousine and wondered who or what she was protecting.

We entered the hotel.

"Come this way," said Rhonda.

She led us to the small, private dining room we used for confidential gatherings. Sound-proofed, it had housed many private discussions that never left the room.

The vice president waited for one of the agents to finish his visual sweep of the interior, and then she motioned both men to stay back before closing the door, leaving the three of us alone in the room.

"Would you like a seat?" I asked, a little confused by all that was happening.

"No, thank you," she said, smiling. "I've been sitting for a while and need to stretch my legs." She studied Rhonda and turned to me. "What I'm about to tell you can go no further. Understand?"

Rhonda and I glanced at each other and spoke together. "Yes. We do."

"I won't be staying here but will instead be secretly traveling to Central America to try and rescue a woman from a revolutionary group that's been holding her prisoner. I made the reservation here at the hotel because you're known for being discreet. Tina Marks, that fabulous actress, credits the two of you with saving her life. So, if newspaper reporters ask about my staying here, it won't seem out of the ordinary for you to decline to give out any information. A woman running from domestic abuse will be using my reservation in my place."

"I see ..." I began, but she held up her hand to stop me.

"This woman is my sister and the wife of the president's brother."

I felt my breath leave me in a rush and gripped Rhonda's arm.

"Oh my God! I read about her in the newspaper," gasped Rhonda. "It's a terrible story of abuse."

"You understand how important it is that no one, not even other members of the family, know where she is or what I'm about to do on a secret mission for the government."

"Not even the president?" Rhonda asked, wide-eyed.

"Definitely not him, though he knows, of course, that I'm pretending to be here and where I'm going," Amelia explained. "The president thinks my sister's recuperating in total privacy at their home in Vermont while her husband is in a rehab program in California. See why this is so important?"

I nodded silently, wondering what would happen if we failed. Lives were being placed in our hands. I recalled that Amelia's sister had met her husband on the campaign trail a couple of years ago. Their wedding had been the romantic story of the year. What on earth had happened?

"We're gonna take good care of your sister. What happened to her shouldn't happen to any woman. Right, Annie?" said Rhonda, elbowing me.

"Absolutely. I understand what a difficult situation this must be for everyone, but we'll do everything you ask. We've seen many people come and go at the hotel, heard many stories, and helped many people in various positions. We routinely have VIPs here at the hotel who need discretion," I assured the vice president. "Our staff is trained to protect privacy."

Amelia let out a long breath. "Okay, then. I've announced I'm taking a private vacation. My sister, Lindsay Thaxton, and I look enough alike to be twins, which is why people might not question my 'supposed' presence here. You have her placed in the private home here, correct?" she asked, looking at me.

"Yes. She'll be staying in the guesthouse on the property as you requested."

"My trip shouldn't last more than a week. During that time, Lindsay will decide if she wants to continue staying here or find another place to hide until things calm down. The president isn't happy about the situation, but there's no way I could let Lindsay remain vulnerable to that brute of a husband of hers. Now that she's filed for divorce, she still needs protection."

Amelia Swanson's history was much like her sister's. Married to a wealthy man who'd mistreated her, Amelia made her escape and began a foundation for abused women. A reputation for speaking out and holding steady helped her build a political career. Nearing fifty and single, she was known as a formidable woman who didn't take bullshit from anyone, not even Edward Thaxton, the president of the United States.

"Is there anything special we should do for your sister ... you ... while she's here?" I asked.

"A young woman I trust from past Secret Service experience will be staying with Lindsay in the house. She can be a confidential source of communication for you. Both of you come with me, and I'll introduce you to them."

"Would it be better if we met them at the house to avoid drawing attention to your sister or her companion?" I asked.

The vice president settled her blue-eyed gaze on me. "Good idea. As you can imagine, Lindsay's a little skittish anyway."

"Don't worry, we'll see that she's well taken care of," said Rhonda. "I've read the stories about it all, and I promise no frickin' rat bastard will ever treat her like that again."

Amelia's eyes widened, and then she laughed. "I like you two as much as everyone said I would."

Rhonda and I accompanied Amelia back to the limousine. She and the agents smoothly disappeared inside, leaving us with two other guards—the man and woman we'd seen now walked beside the limo as it began to roll along the front circle and over to the guesthouse.

Originally a caretaker's cottage that I'd transformed into a small but comfortable home, the house had served as a private retreat for my husband, Vaughn, and me for a time before we moved off the hotel property. Then it was turned over to the hotel as a unique, private accommodation for VIP guests. Nestled and nearly hidden among the greenery in a corner of the property, it was the perfect place for Lindsay Thaxton to hide.

We met the limousine in the guesthouse driveway and waited while the Secret Service did a quick check around the area before signaling me to open the door to the house.

I unlocked the door and stood aside as one of the bodyguards checked the interior. At a thumbs-up sign from him, the vice president stepped out of the car and turned to help her sister.

Lindsay Thaxton emerged and stared at her surroundings. So thin that she seemed a fragile china doll, she looked like a much more vulnerable version of her older sister. They shared brown hair, blue eyes, and facial features, but there the similarity ended. Lindsay's hunched shoulders, the way she glanced around nervously, and the trembling of her lips presented a much different woman from her take-charge, confident sister. After they'd entered the house and surveyed each room, Lindsay gave a slight nod of approval. "This is lovely. I'll be comfortable here."

As Lindsay stepped out to the lanai with Rhonda, I caught hold of the vice president's arm. "We'll have to tell a few others on the hotel staff and in our families about Lindsay. Rhonda and I are slowly introducing our daughters, Liz Bowen and Angela Smythe, to our business in the hopes they will someday assume duties here. We want them to know what's going on, along with Bernhard Bruner, our general manager. And, both our husbands are trustworthy. It would be awkward if they didn't know. Especially because of the time we'll commit to keeping Lindsay safe."

The vice president's smile was a little sheepish. "Oh, yes. I should have told you. We've done background checks on your families and all the staff here. It will, however, be up to you and Rhonda to control the information and help keep my sister secure. Failure is unacceptable." Her steady gaze unnerved me, but I dutifully bobbed my head. Rhonda and I had had to deal with a lot of challenges. Indeed, we could meet this one. Couldn't we?

# # #

# About the Author

Judith Keim enjoyed her childhood and young-adult years in Elmira, New York, and now makes her home in Boise, Idaho, with her husband and their two dachshunds, Winston and Wally, and other members of her family.

While growing up, she was drawn to the idea of writing stories from a young age. Books were always present, being read, ready to go back to the library, or about to be discovered. All in her family shared information from the books in general conversation, giving them a wealth of knowledge and vivid imaginations.

A hybrid author who both has a publisher and self-publishes, Ms. Keim writes heart-warming novels about women who face unexpected challenges, meet them with strength, and find love and happiness along the way. Her best-selling books are based, in part, on many of the places she's lived or visited, and on the interesting people she's met, creating believable characters and realistic settings her many loyal readers love. Ms. Keim loves to hear from her readers and appreciates their enthusiasm for her stories.